CLOSE TO HOME

Michael Magee

PENGUIN BOOKS

PENGUIN BOOKS

UK | USA | Canada | Ireland | Australia
India | New Zealand | South Africa

Penguin Books is part of the Penguin Random House group of companies
whose addresses can be found at global.penguinrandomhouse.com.

First published by Hamish Hamilton 2023
Published in Penguin Books 2024
002

Line on p. 4 from *The Shawshank Redemption*, written by Stephen King/Frank Darabont (1995)
Line on p. 93 from 'Joe McDonnell', written and composed by Brian Warfield, Skin Music
Line on p. 103 from 'Question Time' by Ciaran Carson, reproduced by kind permission of the author's estate
and The Gallery Press (Loughcrew, Oldcastle, County Meath, Ireland). From *Belfast Confetti* (1989)
Lines on p. 201 from *War and War* by László Krasznahorkai, trans. George Szirtes (Profile, 2016)
Line on p. 278 from *The Joke* by Milan Kundera, trans. Michael Henry Heim (Faber, 1992)

This novel is a work of fiction. The story is inspired by the author's real-life experiences
but the characters and events in it are fictionalized and are not real people or events

The moral right of the author has been asserted

Typeset by Jouve (UK), Milton Keynes
Printed and bound in Great Britain by Clays Ltd, Elcograf S.p.A.

The authorized representative in the EEA is Penguin Random House Ireland,
Morrison Chambers, 32 Nassau Street, Dublin D02 YH68

A CIP catalogue record for this book is available from the British Library

ISBN: 978-0-241-99640-9

www.greenpenguin.co.uk

CLOSE TO HOME

'A vision of a post-conflict Belfast that didn't deliver what it promised, blighted by poverty, pain and memory. But far from being bleak, I laughed out loud many times. And it is full of love. Each character is so vividly drawn that I felt like I had met them somewhere before; even the most flawed of them is treated with dignity and respect, and an absence of judgement that reminded me of Annie Ernaux. And the writing! Supple, rich and demotic – Kneecap meets Chekhov – no one else is doing this. I had great hopes for this novel and Michael Magee has booted it out of the park. Absolutely glorious' Louise Kennedy

'Michael Magee is a born storyteller. By the end of the novel I wanted to book a flight to Ireland just to walk around and imagine who was where . . . I read this in two or three sittings only because I wanted to slow down and spend more time with Magee's considered and companionate writing' Derek Owusu, *Guardian*

'An exceptional debut . . . Every detail rings true, every character is fleshy and real and heartbreaking. Magee captures the stark beauty and distinctive humour of Belfast' *Sunday Times*

'Unflinching, direct, disarmingly sensitive . . . Suffusing his narrative with honesty and grace, Magee succeeds in bringing his neighbourhood to life for readers and suggests that, amid what seems like a never-ending struggle, there is always room for hope' *Washington Post*

'Michael Magee's *Close to Home*, amazingly a first novel, is about what it's like to be young and working class right now in Northern Ireland, and is a tremendous read, tensed and immersive, punching the air between hope and despair, deeply decent, unputdownable' Ali Smith, *Guardian*

'A genuinely necessary book . . . Magee writes tenderness with serious skill . . . a staggeringly humane and tender evocation of class, violence and the challenge of belonging in a world that seems designed to keep you watching from the sidelines' *Guardian*

'Wonderful. A debut overflowing with years of experience and carefully worked craft. By turns hard-edged and soft-hearted, this novel is a gift from Michael Magee to us all' Jon McGregor

'*Close to Home* does for Belfast what *Shuggie Bain* did for Glasgow. Its portrayal of a particular kind of masculinity – self-destructive and romantic by turns – is unsparing, funny and desperately sad. Keep an eye on Michael Magee; he's the real deal' Patrick Gale

'How beautifully Magee has brought his characters to life, and how intricately he has created their world' Kevin Power, *Irish Independent*

'Magee is his own man in his restrained approach . . . I took Sean to my heart and the last line of the book left me with a satisfying shiver' *The Times*

'The best debut I've read in years – a tender examination of class, masculinity and place' Nicole Flattery

'An amazingly assured first novel. Magee is too good a writer . . . Gentle as well as brutal' *The Tablet*

'As beautiful as it is brilliant. Reading *Close to Home* is like crossing a frontier into a new and thrilling territory' Glenn Patterson

'A shard of authenticity, originality and brilliance' *The Times*

'*Close To Home* announces an exciting new voice – at once open and wary, tender and unyielding – and sharply alive to the pains and discoveries and mysteries of youth' Colin Barrett

'Ringing out clear and true as a bell, it gleams with tenderness and perception. There are few narrators so unassuming and unaffected, yet so full of sharp intelligence' Wendy Erskine

'Precise, compulsive, companionable and genuinely moving. Michael Magee writes a world we see far too little of in contemporary literature. We need books like this' Seán Hewitt

'A beautiful and devastating debut novel about political memory, violence, masculinity and the impossibility of escaping your origins' *Jacobin*

'A sharp and humane novel about a young man, and a city, caught in the painful throes of reimagining themselves. It rings with authenticity, and the wisdom of hard-won observation and experience – a hymn to the ways in which art can be a lifeline and an escape. Michael Magee's debut is an important addition to the burgeoning new canon of Belfast literature' Lucy Caldwell

'Sharp, immediate, beautiful writing. A vivid portrait of modern Belfast and of how our circumstances shape our lives. Every character is drawn with nuance and complexity, with great precision and attention to detail. I really loved this book' Rachel Connolly

'Compulsively readable – you will need to know how this ends!' Emilie Pine

'Artfully crafted, compassionate, precise and unafraid. I loved this book' Susannah Dickey

'It's hard to find fault with a debut novel that unfold its storylines and characters with such care, handling themes of class, masculinity, addiction and trauma with both tenderness and a matter-of-factness' RTÉ

'*Close to Home* tracks brilliantly written characters across a vividly drawn Belfast' *Business Post*

ABOUT THE AUTHOR

Michael Magee is the fiction editor of the *Tangerine* and a graduate of the creative writing PhD programme at Queen's University, Belfast. His writing has appeared in *Winter Papers*, *The Stinging Fly*, *The Lifeboat* and *The 32: The Anthology of Irish Working-Class Voices*. *Close to Home* is his first novel. It was shortlisted for the Waterstones Debut Fiction Prize 2023 and won the Rooney Prize for Irish Literature 2023.

For my mother and my brothers

PART ONE

In thee, O Lord, do I put my trust:
let me never be put to confusion.

Psalm 71: 1

I

There was nothing to it. I swung and hit him and he dropped. A girl came flying forward and pushed me: What'd you do that for? The lad was lying there and I was standing over him and there were people all around me making noise. By the time I got away from the tussle, two Land Rovers had pulled up. A jaded-looking peeler with a receding hairline came towards me.

Is that blood? he said, pointing to a stain on my shirt that could've been anything. He took my name and number and told me he would be in touch.

I held my hands up and said that was no problem.

The lad came at me, I said. I didn't know what to do.

At the top of the street, the lad was put on a stretcher, and the stretcher was heaved into the back of an ambulance.

I think it's best you make your way home, the peeler said.

I decided he was a good peeler, a helpful peeler. We'll be in touch, he said, and I thanked him.

Thanks very much, I said.

Back at the flat, Ryan had his phone in his face and was pacing up and down the living room, looking for a party. But it was five o'clock in the morning and the birds were out. He pulled the blinds closed as if that would help and nearly took the window with him. The brightness. I grabbed the purple throw my ma had given us as a moving in present

3

and pulled it over my head. I lay with my head on the pillow and stared through the space between the empty bottles. Ryan checked the fridge, the cupboard next to the fridge. He lifted a can from the counter and gave it a shake.

I give up, I said.

Give up? You haven't done fuck all.

I'm going to bed.

Fuck sake, Sean. Don't be leaving me hanging here.

I'm not leaving you anywhere, I'm in the next room.

Bounce into my bed sure. We'll watch a film.

We need to stop doing this.

Doing what? Come on.

The window above the bed was open and the breeze wafted through cold. I stripped down to my boxers and climbed under the covers but stayed on the outside so I could creep into my own bed as soon as Ryan passed out. The wall was black with mould and it made the room smell damp. There were clothes all over the place, takeaway cartons. Cups and glasses and empty cans. Ryan smoked too much weed, that's what it was. It made him lazy. It made him not give a ballicks. I said to him, You smoke too much of that shit, and took the spliff off him. He didn't care. He was sinking into it nicely, and he had his favourite film on: *The Shawshank Redemption*. He made me watch it every time we ended up like this. It gave him hope.

Watch this, he said.

It was that scene he loved, the one where Andy Dufresne arrives at the penitentiary and all the inmates are going mad, screaming at him. Calling him and the rest of the newcomers fresh fish.

I didn't think much of Andy the first time I laid eyes on him . . .

That was Ryan's favourite line, he thought it was brilliant. I did too. Never judge a book by its cover, that's what that means. Never judge anybody, because you never know.

*

The next morning, or later that morning, whatever way you want to put it, somebody was at the door. I rolled on to my side and tried to go back to sleep, but Ryan was up, he was shaking me, and he was like, That doesn't sound good. I sat up on the edge of the bed, it was better to do these things in stages, and watched Ryan lean with his ear against the door.

Sounds like there's a few of them, he said.

Men?

Aye. Men.

I looked out the window and saw a car parked up out the front of the block. The driver's side door was open. I heard a radio. Not the kind that played music, the other one.

It's not the peelers, Ryan said.

How do you know?

Because they would've shouted. They always shout.

The knocking stopped. Footsteps echoed out the hall and were gone.

The living room was a state. There were feg butts everywhere, spilled drink. Some dirty bastard had been flicking ash into bottle caps and the bottle caps had fallen on the floor. I brushed and mopped and got rid of the empties, then I sat for a minute and looked out the window. We had a good view, the flat was on the fourth floor so we could see right over the rooftops to Casement Park. And the mountain, you can't miss the mountain. It's everywhere you go, every street and road in West Belfast, you can't get away from it. Whoever's writing those messages up there knows fine rightly as well, they couldn't have picked a better spot. Today it was a massive tricolour, and underneath it they had written the words:

END INTERNMENT

Who do you think it was? Ryan said.

Dunno. Dissidents?

Why would dissidents be calling here?

I thought you meant the mountain.

Ryan looked out the window. That's not dissidents, ya rocket.

Who is it then?

Fuck knows. Could be anyone, he said, then he clapped his hands.

It's the Illuminati. The Illuminati have infiltrated the Ra.

He opened the fridge and stared at the empty shelves. The acne on his back was getting worse. The pimples had gone purple and bubbled under the skin. Six months in the gym will do that, and the steroids he made me inject into his arsecheek every other day. You could see it in his face, the puffiness. The jacked-up redness around his neck and shoulders.

We need food, he said.

Have you cash?

Do I fuck. Spunked everything last night.

Me too.

I boiled the kettle and brought it with me into the bathroom, filled the sink with hot water and topped it up with cold. The boiler was broke. There was no heat in the radiators, no hot water, and it wasn't like we could phone the landlord and ask him to sort it out; he went bankrupt and did a runner to Spain, leaving a load of properties to be repossessed. That's why we didn't answer the door that morning – it could've been someone looking to turf us out.

I started on my hair, giving it a good go with shampoo. I used a cup to rinse the suds and got to splashing my balls and torso. Then I sat on the edge of the bath and looked at my hand. The knuckles weren't swollen and my fingers were all intact. I made a fist and stared at it, then at my arm right up to the shoulder where the thin lines of my tribal tattoo were so black they looked blue.

I need to get out of this, I thought.

I didn't know what this was.

The quickest way to get to work was by train. There was a station at the top of the road. I sat on a bench in the middle of the platform and counted how much cash I had: nine quid to do me until the end of next week, and it was only Saturday. The train pulled up. I got on, but instead of taking a seat, I hid in the toilet from the ticket man then spoofed the cheapest fare when I got to the barrier in Central Station. El Divino was across the road. It was one of those places that used to be hard to get into. Now it was all students. That's how you know a nightclub is going downhill. It starts doing promotions five nights a week. The more exclusive clientele moves on somewhere else, the club starts tanking money, and within a few months, the shutters come down for good. We'd all be out of a job. We knew this, but we kept working there anyway; there was nowhere else that would take us.

There was a delivery waiting for me round the side of the building: five pallets. I lifted the Stanley blade that had been left on the windowsill and got to work cutting the plastic wrap and wheeling the crates one after another into the stockroom. Then I went up to the club, wrote everything I needed in my notebook, went back to the stockroom, and loaded the spirits and mixers into the hoist. It took three runs to empty the hoist and half an hour to stock the bar, which I stretched to forty-five minutes. I had arranged the bottles neatly, labels facing outwards, when a group of PR lads stepped out from behind the stage. They wore black body warmers with the club's logo stitched on the back, and they thought they were great strolling about the place in their beige chinos and Ralph Lauren T-shirts. One of them pressed the button for the smoke machine and smoke billowed across the dance floor. Our manager was with them. His name was Dee. He was young, only a few years older than me, and there was talk that his da, a millionaire property developer from Holywood, Co. Down, had given him the nightclub for his birthday. He had never worked a bar in his life. He hadn't a clue about anything, but he carried on like this was his show, he called the shots, even though we were the ones keeping the place going. He leaned with his elbow on the bar and watched as I filled the sink with hot water and cleaned the speed pours.

What do you reckon? he said to me, nodding at the ground.

I leaned over the counter to see what he was on about: there was a wee black pug sitting at his feet.

Isn't he class?

Aye, brilliant.

He took a picture on his phone, showed me the picture, and then looked at me like I should be doing something. I got down on my knees and worked my way along the bar, cleaning out the shelves under the counter. There was a lot of dust down there and the bottoms of the bottles had got all gunky. I got the brush and scoop and cleared the bottle caps, and when I turned to get started on the fridges, the music stopped. I could hear the PR lads playing with the wee dog and the wee dog running across the floor.

Here, grab us a plastic bag there, Dee said.

I pulled one from the pile that was squeezed between the wall and the dishwasher and tried to give it to him, but he backed off with his hands held up and shook his head from side to side.

Sort it out for me, will you? he said.

Sort what out?

The shit. The wee bastard's only after taking a shit.

He patted the dog on the side and the wee dog fell over.

Seriously. Look.

I could see it, the little mound of coffee-coloured crap piled like stones in the middle of the dance floor.

I'm not cleaning that up, I said.

Are you not?

No chance, it's your dog.

Right, well. Get the fuck out of this club.

I stared. You serious?

I'm not joking, get your coat. You're sacked.

Fuck sake, Dee. Don't be at it.

Don't be at what? I told you to clean the shit, so clean the fucking shit.

The PR lads had their T-shirts pulled up over their noses. I could tell by their eyes that they were laughing.

Hurry up, it's starting to smell.

I pulled the bag over my hand the way I had seen people do and scooped the shit up quickly, without looking at it, and was surprised by how warm it was, and heavy. Dee lifted the dog up into his arms as if to protect it from the sorry sight of me walking all the way downstairs and out the back of the club, with the bag held like a dirty sock, where I threw it without thinking as far as I could into the river. The bag popped up further downstream, towards the bridge. Starlings made shapes in the sky.

I looked at my phone. I still had half an hour to go.

I was supposed to work again that night, at ten. The only way I could think to fill the time between now and then was to find a table in the corner of the cordoned-off area outside Kelly's Cellars and sit for as long as I could over a pint of Guinness I could just about afford. There was a group of tourists sitting at the table across from me. Americans, by the looks of it. They were having a great time watching the long-haired lads playing fiddly-dee music out the front of the bar, but no matter how much they tapped their feet and muttered along to the words of every tune they thought they knew, their hearts weren't in it. They slung their bags over their shoulders and headed towards Castle Street, leaving a tableful of half-empty pints sweltering in the heat.

I rang Ryan. I told him where I was and what I was thinking and he said, Give me fifteen minutes. In the meantime, I slipped over to the table where the tourists had been sitting, poured the beer they had left into two empty pint glasses, and settled in. The sun wasn't as powerfully hot as it had been, the breeze tested the backs of the scantily dressed, but it was a decent night, people were in good form. I didn't watch them so much as try to catch them out. It's always the way, any time I'm on my own in a crowd like this, I think everybody's looking at me. That's where the nervousness comes from: not knowing what to do with myself, not knowing how to act. I need somebody to bounce off, otherwise I have to get on like I do this all the time. That's why I cracked up at Ryan for taking so long.

Where were you? You said fifteen minutes.

I'm here now, aren't I?

He was wearing denim shorts with aviator sunglasses and looked like the kind of holiday rep who would shake your hand and call you a legend while trying to ride your girlfriend. He swiped a Guinness from the table next to ours and took the seat facing me.

What's this I hear about you picking up dog shite? he said.

Who told you?

Nobody told me nothing, I just heard.

He was mates with those PR lads, he'd had them back to the flat a few times, and I knew that one of them, the one Ryan was closest to, was called Simon.

Was it him? I said, and Ryan laughed.

Simon's a good lad, he sorts the boys out.

He did, to be fair, and always with words in the ears of bouncers who had kicked us out. Not that we had been kicked out of a lot of places, but we had got into enough scrapes around town for us to have cultivated a bit of a reputation. The fact that we both worked for the same nightclub didn't help. Bar staff talked. Floor staff too. Bouncers even, but most of all managers. Managers gossiped like aul dolls at their front doors, they were all mates with each other, and that didn't bode well for anybody falling out of favour. The amount of people we knew who had been sacked from one place only to find there was no work anywhere else in town. Hardly anybody had a contract. The few people that did were the type to do whatever they had to do to keep themselves sweet, which was why I wanted to know who had opened their mouth: I wanted to make sure they kept it shut.

Ryan's eyebrows appeared from behind his sunglasses.

You hear anything about your man?

What man?

The man, the fella you hit.

He wasn't a man. He was our age.

We're twenty-two, Sean. We're men.

Right enough, we were. But I couldn't work out why the word still felt wrong.

What're we gonna do? Ryan said.

Dunno, what do you wanna do?

We looked around. It had been a while since anybody had got up and left, and even longer since somebody had gone without necking their drink. And it was getting late. The shops were closing soon, and although we knew that the sensible thing to do would be to pack it in and head back to the other side of the town, to work, it seemed an awful shame to waste what was left of the good weather putting in a shift on a Saturday night, especially when the night before had ended the way it had, with no gear, no party, and the two of us in bed with each other rather than somebody else. We needed this, and the only way we could think to get to where we wanted to go was to follow the direction the ball was rolling, towards Ryan's granny's house, in Divis, where Ryan tapped her eighty quid he promised to pay back next week. His granny chucked the notes across the kitchen table.

This is the last time, she said.

I had known Ryan since I was a kid, we grew up together on the same street. We went to the same primary school as well, and the same secondary school, only Ryan left when he was sixteen. He did this because he had been told it was the only option for him, our school had steered him that way even though he was as smart as anybody. He could've stayed on and did his A Levels, no sweat. But because he acted out and struggled to pay attention, the school did what they always do and dumped him with the rest of the headcases in the bottom class. He got into fights, he lashed out at the teachers, and one day, when Mr O'Hare tried to make him stay behind after school, he threw a chair across the room and smashed a window. Then he stopped showing up, and I'm not just talking about going on the beek. He stopped going to school altogether. The school tried to tempt him back. They told him he didn't have to do eight GCSEs any more, that he could do three, the bare minimum. Ryan told them to shove their GCSEs up their hole and went to tech, got himself an apprenticeship, and started out as a plasterer.

Two years into his trade, the recession hit. Ryan was laid off. It was shite because he was doing well, he liked the work, and he only had a year to go before he was fully qualified. It made all those months he had trailed himself out of bed at seven o'clock in the morning for dick-all money feel like a waste of time. Sometimes, when his head was melted about how things had turned out, he talked about going to Australia. Loads of our mates were over there, having the time of their lives, and we were stuck in Belfast, working in a nightclub four nights a week, with no prospects, and no chance of anything better coming our way. The flat was good though. Not having to pay rent was a dream. But it was no Bondi Beach. It was no Gold Coast. It was a stroke of luck we made the most of every night we had enough cash for a bottle of vodka, but it was getting old. There's only so much partying you can do, and when there are fewer and fewer people to party with, it starts to feel like there's nowhere else to go. You're stuck in this hole with the same three or four faces for the rest of your life, drinking, taking gear, hanging around the local until there's no one left to talk to.

I stuck my hand out for a taxi at the top of Albert Street. It was one of those old clapped-out models that sounded more like a washing machine than a car, everything was rattling, and the sound it made as it went up an incline was like someone getting choked out. Black taxis were cheap though, and dead handy if you were stuck. Two quid gets you from the town right up to Twinbrook, and you can bounce out anywhere you want along the way. But it's always touch and go, you never know who you're going to end up sitting beside; anybody can wave a black taxi down, as long as there's space, and when there's five people squeezed into the back it can get a bit awkward, especially if one of those people have had a few pints and need to stick their head out the window. We were lucky that day. It was only us two, and two women who sat at either end of the back seat. One of them had a bunch of flowers. She knocked the glass partition between the front and back and got out at Milltown Cemetery. I watched her walk through the gates with the sun coming down behind her and wondered who she was going to visit.

Forty each then? Ryan said.

Aye, whatever you reckon.

He handed me two twenties from the eighty quid his granny had given him. I folded them up and put them in my wallet.

I'll get the meat, you get the swall, I said.

This wee girl's torturing me.

Who?

He showed me the messages on his phone. One of them said, *your mate's a scumbag*.

I laughed. She mates with your man?

Nah, she just knows him. Apparently they kept him in overnight, in the hospital.

Serious?

Aye, so she says anyway.

We got off at the Kennedy Way roundabout and walked over to Asda. It was packed. There were prams everywhere. Screaming babies. Wee girls in strappy tops burned to a cinder. At the fridges, I filled my basket with all sorts, steaks and all, then I headed for the pasta and the porridge, the milk, the ham and cheese, the packets of biscuits we'd go through in a day, and met Ryan at the self-checkouts. He nodded at the kid keeping watch. He looked about sixteen.

Wee buns, he said.

The trick was to start with the cheapest items first: I scanned a loaf of bread, a carton of milk, a jar of jam, and set them into the bag in the bagging area, as you do. Then I lifted a steak, seven quid a touch, and pretended to scan it by turning the barcode away from the scanner, and dropped it into the bag.

I heard Ryan's station behind me:

Unexpected item in the bagging area . . .

The kid keeping watch did what every member of staff would do and swiped his card across Ryan's screen without checking what the unexpected item was. The message stopped. He did the same with my station a second later and I thanked him. The station next to mine went off too, and before the kid could go back to his spot, Ryan's went off again, then mine. A man at the top of the queue asked for a Bag for Life. I dropped half a kilo of chicken. The kid stomped over and swiped his card. It was that easy, and in the end we walked out of there with fifty quid's worth of shopping we paid less than twenty quid for. The security guards hadn't a clue. They were too busy watching the cameras for people picking things up and putting them straight into their bags. That's what made it so good. Even if you were to get caught, all you'd have to do was act stupid and say you thought you'd scanned the things you were swiping, it was right there on CCTV, and there was nothing they could do. They had to let you go.

When we got back to the flat, Ryan pulled the litre bottle of vodka out of his bag. It still had the security tag on it. I fancied myself as a bit of a schemer, but he was on another level. He demonstrated this with the lie he told our manager to get us out of going to work that night.

Dee, you're not gonna believe this, someone broke into our flat –

It was a masterclass, that's all I can say. A real performance. The way he came out with it, like he had just walked into the flat and seen the state of the place, the shock in his voice. Our manager lapped it up.

Give me a ring if you need anything, he said.

We knocked that litre bottle into us. Then Ryan hooked his phone up to the Bluetooth speaker. Green Velvet had just dropped 'Bigger Than Prince' and he turned it up full whack. We strutted around the living room with our chests pushed out, stomping our feet, hyping ourselves up for a big night. It's the best thing about going on a mad one, getting ready, listening to tunes, asking does this look sweet or what? We took our time as well, it was important that we looked our best, and that meant ironing our shirts, washing ourselves over the sink, having a shave.

At ten o'clock, Finty McKenna picked us up in a taxi. On the motorway, the arguments started: we hadn't decided where we were going. Finty was barred from the Box. Ryan was barred from the Beachclub. All three of us had to steer clear of Limelight since that night we got into a scuffle with a crowd of metalheads who couldn't take a joke. And we couldn't go near Thompson's – too many people knew our manager. It was a toss-up then between M-Club and Mono. Both places were rough as toast, but the drink was cheap and the tunes were good, and there was always a few loose ones floating about, looking for a party. Ryan said Mono. Finty said M-Club. I said, Is there nowhere else?

There's the Bot, Ryan said.

That was it, settled. We went to Mono.

2

There was a lot of smoke, a lot of bass. Every tune was a banger and that was the problem. Big drop after big drop, it didn't help that every track sounded the same, that even when the drop came, it did so with the effect of having already happened. Even the girls flicking their hair next to the DJ booth wondered if it was worth the blisters. They winced as they took their heels off, stared vacantly across the club. By midnight, I could hardly see who was standing in front of me, only a white shirt: Ryan in the middle of a group of lads singing oi, oi, oi fucking oi. I tried to get him to go somewhere else, this place was a shithole, but he was having none of it. I couldn't for the life of me work out why, then an arm came around my neck. Finty McKenna planted his lips on the side of my face.

Got you a wee present, he said, and dragged me into the toilets.

It was a bag of gear. Pure gear too. The kind of stuff that goes through you faster than a bullet.

Lethal, isn't it? Finty said.

Aye, mate. Brilliant.

The smoking area was supposed to give me respite, it was supposed to clear my head, but as soon as the air hit me, something slipped; I dropped my drink. It was a plastic cup, so it didn't break, but my vodka splashed all over some girl's feet. She looked at me like I better get down on my hands and knees and lick it off.

Are you fucking serious? she said.

I told her I was sorry, it was an accident, and she turned to her mate.

This place is full of dickheads, she said, and that brought it all back. The argument the night before. The girl who pushed me, who sounded exactly like this one who was having a go at me now, uppity as fuck, and proper stuck up her own arse, in that way they are, like they could say anything. I had to walk away. I went over to the other side of the smoking area to talk myself down, and as I was standing there looking at the crowds of people huddled around the heat lamps, this one beefcake with a flicked-up fringe barging about the place with his shoulders squared, it dawned on me: I couldn't remember what the lad I hit looked like. I tried my best to think but all I could see was the shape of him on the ground. Blue lights. If he came up to me now, I wouldn't know any different. I would drop my head and step out of the way like I did with everybody else.

Ryan emerged from the crowd with a baggie of white powder pinched between his index finger and thumb.

Couple of keys, if you please?

I felt like I'd been doing this half my life. Padding myself full of vodka, tooting keys in cubicles, throwing it on to girls who looked at me like I was dirt, and rightly so. I shifted my weight and tried to snap out of it, but everywhere I looked I saw people I didn't want to be around, and it tired me out. Being constantly on edge, constantly watchful. Moving out of the way of that fella with the flicked-up fringe before he barged into me. All he needed was for me to say something, and God I wanted to say something. I wanted to smash a bottle over his fucking head.

I was halfway down the stairs, gunning for the doors, when somebody grabbed me by the arm. I panicked and tried to pull away, but they clung on to me, and they were saying my name.

Sean. Sean, where are you going? It's me. It's Mairéad.

I stopped. Stared at her.

Mairéad? Mairéad Riley?

She laughed. Threw her arms around my neck and hugged me.

What're you doing here? This place is a shithole, she said.

Ryan's idea, what's your excuse?

You're still knocking about with Ryan? Jesus Christ.

The crowd had bunched up around us. People were pushing and shoving. Mairéad took my hand and brought me over to the bar. She knew someone working there and got us sorted with vodkas we didn't have to pay for, then she led me to a booth at the back of the club. We sat next to each other because the music was loud; Mairéad's voice was gravelly and she struggled to shout. She looked well though. She suited the shorter hair; the fringe that used to come down to her eyebrows had been trimmed back. There was more of her face now. She leaned with her elbow on the table and asked me about Liverpool. I told her I moved back home last September, as soon as I graduated, and she slapped me on the arm.

Why didn't you message me?

I didn't think you'd be arsed.

She had gone to Queen's. Her social media was filled with pictures of her hanging around beer gardens with a different kind of crowd. I said this to her, and she made a face.

I can have more than one set of friends, she said.

She said friends instead of mates. I don't know why that stood out for me, it wasn't like she was speaking another language.

Surely there are better places to go on a Saturday night? she said.

She said *surely* just like that, like *surely* I should know.

Finty's here, I said, defensively. He can't get in anywhere else.

Finty McKenna? Oh my God.

What?

Nothing, it's just –

She drank her drink and looked away. Something was off, the music was too loud, and there were these silences, when everything sort of slowed. All this madness was happening around us and the two of us sat there like spectators, watching it. When we finished our drinks, I asked if she wanted another one, fully expecting her to say no. She plucked an ice cube out of her glass and sucked it.

Get me a double, she said.

I asked for two doubles, and when the barman turned his back, a couple of girls squeezed into the space beside me. One of them looked at me and I looked at her and her eyes narrowed. She whispered something to her mate and her mate gave me a dirty look. I apologized and stepped out of the way, thinking I was taking up too much space.

You were at that party last night, weren't you?

What party?

You attacked our friend. You punched him in the face.

Punched who? What're you on about?

I was there. I saw you.

She was short this girl, no higher than my shoulder in heels, yet the fury in her face rooted me to the floor.

Your head's lit, love. I wasn't at any parties.

Don't call me love, ya fucking dickhead.

Heads turned. Conversations were cut short. People were watching. The girls sensed this and started ramping it up, screaming at me. Backing me into the corner with their pointed fingers.

You could've killed him, you know that? He could've died!

I'm sorry, I said. I didn't mean to . . .

Then Ryan came whaling in, blocked out of his head, telling them to get away and leave me alone. The girls went nuts.

He attacked my friend. He snuck up behind him and punched him.

So fuck, Ryan said. He deserved it, now fuck off.

One of the girls pushed him. The other tried to throw her drink over him and missed. Finty moved to calm the situation, but it was too late: Ryan tipped his pint over the short girl's head. There was an uproar. Some lad who had nothing to do with anything got chivalrous and swung a dig. Ryan dipped his head and tackled him into the bar. One of the girls dived on Ryan's back. I tried to pull her off, but her mate was on him, scratching his face with lethal-looking nails.

Bouncers came rocking in. They grabbed the girls by the arms while Ryan and the other lad were stuck in headlocks. I thought I was sweet, I didn't throw a punch, and then an arm came around my neck. I saw light bending through smoke, an exit sign above a door, and suddenly I was on the ground, in an alley out the back.

Ryan's nose was bleeding, but you could flick Ryan's nose and it would bleed. It had been like that his whole life and he still didn't know how to stop it. What was all that about? he said.

They were at that party last night.

The cheek of them. He wiped his nose with the back of his arm and smiled bloody teeth. Thompson's? he said.

No chance. You'll not get in.

Who won't?

You won't. Look at the state of your shirt.

He looked down and frowned. My favourite shirt too, he said.

Mairéad was standing with Finty at the top of the alley. Ryan didn't recognize her. He thought she was just some girl I had pulled; he had no reason to talk to her. Then he did a double take.

Mairéad Riley, what the fuck? Has she been with us all night?

I'm standing right here, you can talk to me, Mairéad said.

But Ryan was too hyped up, the adrenaline was horsing through him, and the coke. He had taken a lot of coke. He bought a bottle of water from the burger van outside Mono and used it to wash the blood off his face. Then he put Finty's jacket on to hide the blood on his shirt and checked his reflection in the windows of the Urban Outfitters round the back of Victoria Square. He was laughing, shaking his head, recounting every detail about what had happened. Thankfully, he left out the part about those girls being at that house party the night before, and he didn't say a word about the fella I hit. He kept that on the shy. Not because he was trying to keep me sweet; he was just too busy boasting about his own scrap to care about mine.

Mairéad looked at her phone. Have you any plans? I said.

Nah, not really. I need to eat.

Me too. Do you wanna grab something?

Aye, why not?

We walked with Ryan and Finty round to Thompson's. It took ages, they kept stopping for another key. Ryan held one out for me, but I said, No, I've had enough. He looked at me like, what? Then he did the whole eyebrows raised, nod in Mairéad's direction thing. Yous two have a lovely night sure, he said, and headed on down the alley.

Mairéad looked at me quizzically. He's a dick, I said, and she agreed.

He's always been a dick, she said.

I let that one go. It wasn't worth the hassle.

Where do you wanna go then? I said.

Dunno, where's open?

McDonald's?

Aye, may as well, she said.

The white lights were ruthless, everybody looked like they had been dragged through a ditch, and there was a real gnarly atmosphere, cruel, like the canteen in school, except everybody's steaming and thinks they're a geg. Those poor bastards at the tills got it the worst. I actually felt sorry for them. It isn't like working on a bar, you don't have the music to block it all out, and people can be dicks when they're drunk. They don't mean any harm, most of them are just trying to have a laugh, but when you've been on your feet since noon and it's two o'clock in the morning, the last thing you want is some drunken arse-hole winding you up about how long they've been waiting for their Big Mac. Witnessing it is enough to make you hate people.

Then we saw something class. The security guards tried to kick a homeless man out and everybody stood up and was like, No, leave him alone, he's not doing any harm, and the security guards backed off. That was enough to restore my faith in humanity, but not enough to persuade Mairéad and me to eat in McDonald's itself. We took our grub round to that stupid onion ring sculpture they had built in the middle of Arthur Square where all the buskers and street performers played music at the weekend. We sat there, on the base, and talked about university.

Mairéad had studied English Lit, like me, but did a joint honours with Film Studies, which was what she was really into. All those mad art house films with subtitles, she loved that stuff, it was what she wanted to do. But it wasn't an easy trade to get into, not if you didn't know anybody. And if you couldn't afford to get by with no wages, there was no point going for an internship or anything like that – they didn't pay, and that left Mairéad with no choice but to keep working in a clothes shop in town. She had been there since she started at Queen's, and although it was destroying her soul, she only had to do it for another few months, then she was moving to Berlin.

I was surprised. People we knew went to America or Australia. They got working visas and stayed there for a year. Some of them came back. Most didn't. In that way, Berlin didn't make sense to me. I pretended it did.

That's class, fair play, I said.

Aye, well, there's nothing for me here so.

She dipped a chicken nugget into that sweet curry dip they do and ate it whole, without nibbling off the batter like I did with every single nugget.

You're like a wee mouse, she said.

I stuck my front teeth out and she giggled, held the chip carton up over her mouth and drank the crumbs. She had the same jet-black hair, the same grey eyes, but she dressed like somebody who listened to a lot of live music, all in black with Doc Martens and a mandala tattoo on the back of her left hand. Her arm was completely covered. She caught me staring and pulled her vest top down to show me her shoulder.

What's yours? she said.

I rolled my sleeve up to show her my tribal tattoo.

I've a Celtic cross on my back as well, I said.

No way. Let me see.

I hardly had time to turn around before she had her hands on my shirt and was pulling it up.

I like the Claddagh, she said. I used to have a Claddagh ring, years ago.

So did I.

Which way did you wear it?

With the heart facing away from me, like I was supposed to.

What about when you were going with me?

We were only thirteen.

Did you not love me though?

I did when I was sixteen, but you wanted fuck all to do with me.

Mairéad laughed. I had other things going on, she said.

She helped me pull my shirt down again. I turned round to face her and she told me how nice it was to see me. She had said this a few times that night, usually when we ran out of things to say. I told her it was nice to see her too and she laughed.

Look at us getting all weird and soppy, she said.

There's nothing weird about getting soppy.

There is if you're sober. Are you sober, Sean?

Not even a wee bit.

Good, have a nugget.

She fed it to me. I nearly choked. Stop being a wuss, she said.

I hadn't been called a wuss since I was a kid, and probably by Mairéad. It was the kind of thing she would've called me if I wasn't feeling up to doing whatever she'd planned for us, which was usually something stupid. Like that time we were on the beek, she took a notion to get a bus up the Shankill to see what it was like. She could call me a wuss all she wanted, but she was daft if she thought we could dander about the Shankill Road in our school uniforms and not draw attention to ourselves – we may as well have been wearing sandwich boards with I'M A TAIG written across them, in big green, white and orange letters. I said this to her and she told me to stop being a fruit. I told her to suck my balls and she said, Get them out. I didn't. That's the way it went. It was stupid, but it was part of our history, and that was how we knew where we stood with each other; we couldn't say anything worse than we already had. That must've had something to do with why Mairéad felt like she could speak to me the way she did that night, about Berlin, but also what she had been doing in Mono. It hadn't crossed my mind to ask why she had been there on her own. I just thought her mates had headed on somewhere else.

My mates wouldn't be caught dead in that place, she said.

What were you doing there then?

I was selling shots.

I stared. You're a shot girl?

Don't look so fucking surprised, Sean.

I'm not, it's just —

She didn't have the look of a shot girl. Not that she wasn't good-looking; she really was, just not in an eyelash extension, full face of make-up kind of way.

Mairéad took this as a compliment.

The girls I work with are stunning though. Really. And lovely people. They deserve every penny they get for the shit they've to put up with.

Do they make a lot of money? I said.

Aye, if they know what they're doing.

Do you?

Mairéad grinned. She leaned forward to open her bag and I saw something black and silky, some kind of outfit, a pair of heels. She pulled out a wad of five- and ten-pound notes; ninety quid she counted, for four hours' work.

I think I have an inkling, she said.

That ninety quid really played on my head later on, when Mairéad told me she wasn't going back up the road. She was going to her mate's gaff on the Ormeau. That was the opposite direction from where I was going; there was no case to be made for sharing. Not that

I would take advantage in that way, but it wouldn't have cost her anything to drop me off at the flat on the way back to Twinbrook. It was right there, on the motorway, and when you've just spunked your last tenner on a large McNugget meal and a bacon double cheeseburger, you have to take what you can get while it's going.

I'll order two taxis sure, she said.

I told her not to worry about it: I'm gonna walk round to Castle Street and get a taxi from there. Mairéad thought this was strange for about a second, then booked one for herself. The whole time we waited, I thought about asking her for a lend of a tenner; a tenner would get me back up the road no sweat. I just couldn't bring myself to. When her taxi came, she hugged me.

I'll give you a shout sure, I said.

Yeah, do, she said, and that was it, she was gone.

I headed round to Castle Street. The place was empty, there was nobody about, and the shopfronts had that eerie feeling, like they had been cleared out. There was a taxi depot two doors down from Cosgrove's, but the drivers were bastards. They wouldn't take me anywhere unless I paid up front. Then my phone died. I had no way of contacting Ryan or Finty, and I didn't know where they were, if they had gone back to the flat or what.

I sat on the kerb and tried to work out what to do. I'd two quid to my name, the black taxi depot wouldn't be open for another few hours, and my head was splitting. I shouldn't have touched that gear. I said this every time, it was my go-to when I was coming down. But seriously, it messes with your head. It makes you blame yourself for everything that's gone wrong in your life. Now I was stuck in the middle of the town with no cash and no way of getting back up the road, unless I walked. I could've walked. Instead I closed my eyes and listened to the breeze nudge the rubbish piled along the entries. When I opened them again, I could see Divis Tower, and behind it, the mountain like a cold shoulder against the sky.

The peelers had me down to the station at eleven o'clock on a Tuesday morning. They brought me into an interview room and questioned me about what happened that night I knocked your man out. They tried their best to catch me out, but I stuck to my story. I had been rehearsing it for days and was feeling good about how the whole thing was going until the man, the peeler man, who was the same peeler who had questioned me at the scene, whipped out a folder full of statements given by people who had witnessed the alleged assault and set them on the table in front of me. His wee blue peeler eyes locked on me as if to see how I would react.

He told me five witnesses had made statements against me, outlining an unprovoked attack on the victim, Daniel Jackson. This one from Gemma Hatfield said: *Man about six foot tall, short black hair, well built, wearing a blue shirt, came up from behind Daniel and punched him in the face, knocking him unconscious.* Another, from Kirsty Malone, said: *He pushed me so hard I nearly fell and then he punched Daniel in the mouth. Daniel fell and hit his head on the ground . . .* Joanna Porter said I was wearing a black jacket over my shirt and that I tried to hit Daniel's mate after Daniel. Rachel Henderson said the same thing – they must've been mates – and Gareth Waters said I started fighting with him before I hit Daniel: *I was outside trying to calm everything down and he started throwing punches at me. Daniel didn't see him coming. He came from behind Daniel and hit him.*

Daniel Jackson was still unconscious when the ambulance arrived. His statement said: *I can't remember what happened. I was standing with my hands in my pockets, then I woke up in hospital and there were nurses all around me.* The report from the doctor on call that night said that the patient was knocked unconscious with a blow to the mouth: *Mr Jackson suffered a deep laceration to the upper lip requiring musculature suture with absorbable sutures, and the overlying mucosal surface sutured with absorbable sutures.* His lip was sliced open, and it was very likely that Mr Jackson would have significant facial scarring. The peeler held the pages up in front of me and said, The fact that Mr Jackson's face has been cut and that the wound is as severe as it is means that the charge being brought against you is Assault with Actual Bodily Harm. Do you understand what this means?

I said I did, even though I didn't.

Every one of them have given different statements, I said. They've all said things that didn't happen, and not one of them has said a word about how Daniel Jackson and his mate came at me first.

The peeler leaned with his elbows on the table. Mr Maguire, it's important for you to understand that this particular charge is for the assault on Daniel Jackson. Whatever happened in the lead-up to the incident is circumstantial, unless evidence can be given to prove otherwise.

Evidence?

Do you have any witnesses?

Maybe. I don't know. I didn't know anybody there.

I stepped out of the peeler station that afternoon feeling like I hadn't seen daylight in days. I shielded my eyes with my hand and looked both ways before crossing the road to the bus stop. The bus pulled over and I stepped back to let the woman with the pram on first, then I treated myself to the front seat on the top deck. The view was great up there; I liked being able to look down at people going about their day without them knowing I was watching. For some reason, I thought about school. I thought about how I had tricked everyone into thinking I was hard, that I could handle myself, without ever having to throw a punch. I could wing bottles like a champion, and I was always getting into trouble with the teachers, and that somehow translated into me being able to have a dig. That's how it worked at my school; tell the teacher to shove his Bunsen burner up his hole and everybody thinks you can scrap like fuck.

If kids started on me in the street I would run into my house and hide. I would stare out my bedroom window and pray for them to go away. Sometimes they did. Other times my ma would hand me a hurley and tell me to get stuck into them. I didn't have it in me. My brothers saw this and did what they could to toughen me. They would trail me out on to the street and tell me to hit the kid I had to fight, and I would, because they were there and nobody had the balls to hit me back – my brothers had fought their whole lives and were good at fighting – yet there I was, the only one out of the three of us who was stupid enough to get caught.

I got off the bus on Wellington Place and dandered around that side of town for a while, looking at stuff, thinking about things, but not paying much attention to where I was going until I found myself standing across the street from the clothes shop where Mairéad worked. I could see her at the front of the store, hanging clothes on the sale rail. She looked calm, peaceful even, the way she slipped each hanger under the hem, her hands working automatically, without conscious effort. I wondered if I should pretend I was going upstairs to the men's section and bump into her accidentally on purpose. Instead, I messaged her: *I'm in town if you're about*, and headed round to the bookshop.

I didn't plan on stealing anything that day. I just went in for a look. Then I spotted a copy of Knut Hamsun's *Hunger*. It had an introduction by Jo Nesbø, who I hadn't read, and an afterword by Paul Auster, who I had. It seemed right up my street as well, anything that said 'existential novel' in the blurb was always a winner, and sure your man who wrote it won the Nobel; there was no way it was going to be shite. I slipped it under my arm and pretended to look for another book, and I really had to sell it. I had to make it look like I had already paid for the book I was carrying around so that if they were to catch me sauntering out the doors I could say, shit, sorry, I was in a world of my own there, and crack a joke like I had completely forgot. People do it all the time, and let's be honest, nobody wants to phone the peelers. They don't want to go through all that crap. They just want to get through their shift as quickly and painlessly as possible, with no aggro. No additional paperwork. The one thing I had going for me was that people walk in and out of bookshops with books in their hand all the time, and there's no way of telling who's paid for what. The trick is to make it look natural, and the best way I could think of doing that was to stop right outside the doors and act like I was in no hurry to go anywhere. When I was sure that nobody was going to call me back into the shop, I sauntered on down the street with the book tucked under my arm.

People were on their lunch break. They sat out the front of the City Hall and watched the pigeons and the seagulls squabble over their crusts. I found a seat in the sun, on a bench facing away from the road, and read the first page of my new book. I hadn't been able to get through more than a few pages of anything in months. But there was something about the sunshine and the heat and the crowds of people lying on the grass that appealed to that part of me that used to dander around Liverpool with a pocket-sized Moleskine journal tucked in the inside pocket of my coat. I had a lot of thoughts back then and I took them very seriously. Then I finished my degree and moved back home. I hadn't written anything since.

Was that you standing outside my work?

I looked up but it was very bright, and even though I couldn't see, I knew it was Mairéad. She had a big leather bag slung over her shoulder. Her wrist was bent all the way back.

You're gonna get sunstroke, she said. Look at you.

There was a tree behind us with plenty of shade. We sat under there for a while, me with my back against the trunk, gulping from the bottle of water Mairéad had given me. She was wearing jeans with a black vest top. Her shoulders were sunburnt and she smelled like aloe vera. How'd you know where I worked? she said.

I didn't. I was just walking past. I was gonna call in and say hello.

So you just stood there like a creep, watching me?

I'm no creep. You were right at the front of the shop.

Just don't do it again, okay?

I held my right hand up to God. I'll never walk past your shop again, I said.

Mairéad glared at me. You're not even funny, she said.

I wasn't going to tell her about the interview with the peelers, I didn't know how she would take it, but I was nervous, and I didn't know who else to talk to. She listened, and when I got to the part about hitting the lad outside that house party, she looked me dead in the eye and said, You're an idiot. I asked why, and she said, I thought you would've wised up, I thought you would've knocked that shit on the head. I told her there was nothing I could do about it – two lads came at me, they were gonna knock my ballicks in, but she was sceptical. Not about whether or not I was telling the truth, but whether I was right to raise my hand the way I did.

Like, sitting here now, do you think hitting him was worth it?

I thought for a second, then I said, Aye, I do.

Why?

Because fuck him, Mairéad. He came at me.

Did he though?

Of course he did, why else would I hit him?

Mairéad didn't answer. She watched a group of girls doing cartwheels on the grass. They wore leggings with crop tops that rode up their bellies as they spun. At the front gates, a fella in an Adidas top and cargo shorts had set up shop with a mic and a speaker and was shouting about sin and salvation. Two wee lads who were sitting on the bench closest to him stood up and walked away. They were hold-ing hands.

The fucking state of it, Mairéad said, seeing what I had seen. I can't wait to get out of this place, swear to God.

When do you go, right enough?

September, October. As soon as I've enough money, I'm gone.

You nervous?

Mairéad laughed. Not at the question, but the way I had asked it. I'll be all right, she said. I've a few mates over there. She picked a blade of grass and wrapped it round her finger. I don't want to rely on them too much though. I want to make my own way, you know?

And then what?

Then I'll just breathe.

Across the way, the girls doing cartwheels were making eyes at a group of lads sitting close by. I glanced at Mairéad and saw that she was watching them too. She had this look like she remembered some-thing, and for a second, it was like she had gone somewhere else.

Can you not breathe here? I said, and Mairéad shook her head.

No, she said. I can't.

She stretched her arms out in front of her and lay with her head back on the grass. She had worked forty hours that week, and she was selling shots again that night, from ten o'clock till two o'clock, then she was in the clothes shop first thing in the morning for a ten-hour shift her manager was making her cover for a girl who had phoned in sick.

I could do with a day off, she said.

I looked down at her and could see the freckles on her nose and cheeks. Above her lip, on the right side, she had a mark from a pier-cing she did herself with a needle and an ice cube. I asked if it was still open and she leaned on her elbow and said, Give me that bottle of water. She took a gulp but kept the water in her mouth and, using the air to push the water into the space between her front teeth and upper lip, spurted a little stream through the hole and across the grass, dribbling on my jeans.

Party trick, she said, and lay back down.

I went on Mairéad's Facebook that night and looked at the photos she had been tagged in. Nights out in the Limelight and Stiff Kitten, the after-parties, the messy student houses down the Holylands where everybody's taking Es and having a good time. Mairéad in the middle of it all as usual, slotting in with the kind of crowd she would've started fights with when we were kids. The hippies and the emos who stood out the front of the City Hall, listening to Nirvana. Cutting themselves. Calling people like me smicks and spides.

I scrolled down to the bottom of the page, back to Mairéad's first few weeks at university, and realized I couldn't go any further, that she had set up her profile when she had already moved out of Twinbrook and got rid of the tracksuit bottoms and the big gold earrings. Like this one picture I found of her standing in front of her wardrobe door mirror. She was wearing a pleated skirt with fishnet stockings. Her skirt was rolled up short, like when she went to school. It made me think about that day we were on the beek, years ago. I asked Mairéad if she wore knickers under her tights and she pulled her skirt up to show me. It was raining. We were standing round the back of the flats, in the alcove under the steps. She used her thumb to pull her tights down. There was a wee bow. Later, in my room, I had a wank over that wee bow. Then I got into bed and lay there for a long time, thinking about what I had done.

4

There was no word from the peelers, nothing about my statement or what they were going to do with it, until I got a phone call from my ma a few weeks later telling me there was a letter for me, from Courts and Tribunals. I knew by her voice that she had already opened it, and she knew I knew, but she still asked if she should read it.

It's saying you're up in court, Sean. It's saying you're the defendant.

Three days later, I was sitting in a solicitor's office, a dusty little cupboard of a room taking up the floor above a hairdresser's in Dunmurry. The man himself was a big fella, broad shouldered, with the kind of paunch that afflicts middle-aged men who don't go to the gym as much as they used to but still cut an imposing figure.

Have you thought about your plea?

Not guilty, I said, and he looked doubtful.

I should tell you that if the verdict goes against your plea, your sentence will be more severe.

How much more severe?

It can be the difference between a suspended and a custodial sentence.

What like, jail? You serious?

He was. He told me to think very carefully about how many statements had been made against me and how extensive each of them was. The fact that every person who made a statement just so happened to be Daniel Jackson's mate had nothing to do with it. When it came to court, it was their word against mine, and if there were five of them and one of me, the odds were stacked.

I tried to explain this to my ma, but she struggled to get her head around why anybody would press charges in the first place.

It was a bloody fight, what kind of person presses charges for a fight?

She was sitting on the stool in the middle of the kitchen. She had an easel with a canvas board in front of her, a paintbrush in hand. Beside her, on the breakfast counter, her paints and brushes in cups and glasses of water.

Tell me the truth now, is it crap? she said, turning her easel round to show me.

It wasn't crap. It wasn't great either. It was a copy of a photograph she had found on the internet of two horses running along a beach. She had the photograph open on her laptop. I've been at it all day, she said. Since eight o'clock this morning. See the ears? I worked on them for two hours straight. I haven't over painted them, have I?

They look like a good set of ears to me, I said, and she grinned.

You've always had an eye for art. Even when you were a child, you were always looking at the paintings.

She dipped into her dollop of black and paid a lot of attention to the horse's nose, her tiny brush bending as she dabbed. She spent hours every week copying these pictures she found on the internet, and then tried to sell them. Sometimes she did all right and sold one or two a year: Madonna, Gerry Adams, someone's Alsatian. It was good for her, being able to make a few quid to pay the bills that working four days a week cleaning somebody else's house didn't cover. And it gave her the incentive to keep painting and get better, which she was, I suppose. I tried to get her to take classes, but she couldn't cope with being in a room full of people she didn't know telling her what she was doing wrong – her nerves couldn't handle it. She wasn't as anxious as she used to be, but there was a time in her life when she couldn't do the shopping without breaking out in a rash or cross the road without shaking herself sick at the thought of getting knocked down. Living where she did didn't make it any easier; that house she was in now was right in the middle of Dunmurry village, and it wasn't like she had neighbours or anything like that: there was a credit union on one side, a barber's on the other. There was a Spar across the road, and next to the Spar, a wee loyalist bar called the Dunmurry Inn. They had their bonfire on the eleventh night in the car park out the back of my ma's house every year. She didn't mind, she said it was mostly kids. But there was that one time they tried the handle on her front door. She thought they were coming in to kill her. I would too if I'd grown up where she did, on the Falls, and lived through the things she had.

She was only seven when the curfew started. She remembers helicopters hovering over the road, the sound of gunshots in the night. Having to sleep on the floor in case stray bullets came through the window. She'd been on Valium since she was a teenager. Back then, she couldn't walk down the street without being pushed up against a wall. She had to stand there and take it, quietly, while the Brits frisked her, their hands going down between her legs and up. No wonder she couldn't sleep. All those dreams she had about lying flat on the ground while bullets whizzed overhead. The sound of my granny's voice in her ear: It's gonna be okay, it's gonna be okay.

I watched her paint. The brush scratched the canvas board.

What about that room? I said. Is it cleared out?

Most of it, aye. There's still a bit to go.

There was more than a bit; the wee room was filled with stuff my ma didn't have enough space to put anywhere else. There were no windows, and if you stood in the middle of the room and held your arms out lengthways, you could touch both walls with your fingertips. It was only a matter of time before we were kicked out of the flat, and if I didn't find a new gaff with Ryan, this was where I'd end up.

Is there no bed? I said, from the top of the stairs.

Your granny has a spare mattress.

Single or double?

You wouldn't get a double in there, son.

I looked in from the hall. It was dark even with the door open.

Can I bounce into the shower? I said.

Go ahead. There's towels in the hot press.

I must've been in there for about twenty minutes. I had my ma's loofa on the go and everything, and it was great, the warmth, the heat, the coolness of the steam rising up. It was the first shower I'd had in a month, since the last time I called in to see her, and I felt like a new man.

Back downstairs, my ma was stressing herself out.

You think those legs are okay? They don't look a bit skinny, do they?

She had painted the horses' legs so that each of their knees disappeared into the water, even though the water was only supposed to be a couple of inches deep. She couldn't get the hooves right. She had spent ages but they looked terrible.

Nobody will notice, will they?

The horses don't have any feet, mother.

For God's sake.

What? Would you prefer if I didn't say?

She glared at the canvas board.

You're right, she said. You're always right about this stuff. Worst thing is, I know myself. I know fine rightly. I just pretend I don't, to make it easier.

When I was a kid, my ma had this art book that came with brushes and tubes of oil paint her best mate Mary bought her for her birthday. She hadn't painted anything since she was a teenager but had always said it was something she wanted to do. My da laughed at her. He told her she'd be as well cutting her ear off, she couldn't paint a wall. My ma took it to heart. She pulled me up on to her knee one night my da didn't come home – he did that from time to time, out of spite – and told me to pick a picture for her to paint. I chose a dog, a foxhound. It had floppy ears and a long neck, brown patches on a white coat. My ma cut the back off a Cornflakes box and used it as a canvas board. Even at that age I knew she was doing something that meant something to her, and I could see it coming together in front of me, the nose and the mouth, the shadow around the ear. I was put to bed before it was finished, but when I saw it the next morning, I thought it was the best painting I'd ever seen. My ma smiled. She knew it was good, and she showed my da who also knew it was good, but would never admit it. Not until she finally got away from him and he demanded to take me with him, and the painting. He wanted the painting.

I wondered if that was why she kept doing it, if she was still somehow trying to prove him wrong.

Where is that dog, right enough? I asked her.

Your granny's. Have you called into her? She was asking about you. She's always asking about you.

She had finished painting for the day and was cleaning her brushes. It was a slow process, she had to squeeze the paint out of the bristles and dip them in turps to rinse them, and she went about it methodically, one brush at a time. It reminded me of those mornings I would sit with her on the settee, before school, and watch her do her make-up. She'd be there from seven o'clock in the morning putting all this stuff on her face, beautifying herself, she'd say, in case she bumped into someone on the way to work. She was in no hurry, she had been following this same routine since she was a teenager, and it showed. On her way out the door, she would check herself in the mirror at the bottom of the stairs. She would see something that wasn't the way it was supposed to be and get herself into a whole panic. It was too late to do anything about it though: she had to walk down to the Malone Road and scrub the shit off somebody else's toilet seat. That's what she had been doing for the last fifteen years: cleaning other people's mansions for six quid an hour.

Remember Mairéad from down the street? I said. Mairéad Riley?

Ach, aye. Mairéad. I haven't seen her in ages . . .

Her voice trailed off. She had seen something in her painting and had to turn the easel towards the light coming through the kitchen window. She's my friend on Facebook, she said, absently. She always comments under my paintings.

Aye, well. We've met up a few times.

Is that right? She peeled her eyes away from her horses and looked at me. Her ma isn't well, is she? she said.

Nah, she isn't.

And Mairéad, is she okay?

What do you mean?

Well, it can be passed down, you know. Addiction. It's a disease.

I had heard her saying this before about other people and didn't know if it was true, but it annoyed me.

She isn't an alcoholic, I said.

I'm just saying, son, you've always had a wee thing for her.

I didn't deny it, but I didn't admit to anything either.

She's moving to Berlin, I said.

Ach, she's not, is she?

In the next few months, aye.

My ma sighed. This kind of thing really got her down.

I always thought there was a sadness in her, she said. I think you did too. I think you felt a bit sorry for her.

I laughed. I thought it was the other way round, I said.

It was like a plate had been dropped on the floor. My ma went stiff. I could see the emotion rise up in her, out of nowhere. The guilt.

Why would she feel sorry for you? she said.

She doesn't, I was only messing.

Then why'd you say it?

It was a joke, mother. I was only joking.

The moment passed. My ma grabbed a box of fish fingers from the freezer. She took four out and put them under the grill, grabbed the butter from the fridge, and knocked the kettle on.

Have you heard from Anthony? she said.

No, why?

He hasn't been answering his phone again.

I'm sure he's all right. He's probably working.

I don't think he is.

She lifted her easel by the legs and set it by the back door, then she cleared the strips of kitchen roll she had used to clean her brushes and packed her tubes of paint away. Her face was blank, closed as a grave, as she emptied a cup of murky-looking water into the sink.

I didn't tell you, she said. But he stole Bernice's car.

What do you mean he stole her car?

She told me Anthony had got up to his usual lark and disappeared with his mates to a party somewhere in Twinbrook, only this time he sneaked back into his house in the early hours of the morning, took his wife's bank card and disappeared with the car, leaving her with no money, no food in the fridge, and no way of getting the kids to school. Bernice had to put the kids into a taxi and drive round to the gaff she had heard Anthony was partying in, but he wouldn't come to the door; he wouldn't even acknowledge that his kids were there. He dropped Bernice's keys out the window and slammed it closed.

Could you not give him a ring or something? my ma said.

What for? What am I gonna say?

Just talk to him, I don't know.

I'm the last person he'd want to talk to, mother.

No, you're not. He'd listen to you. He'd listen to you more than anybody.

She took her fish fingers out from under the grill and set them on a plate with two rounds of toast. It was the same thing every night: fish fingers and toast. Salad if she was feeling fancy. She carried it over to the settee with a pot of tea and sat with her feet up on the coffee table. I'm gonna put something on now, she said, meaning the TV.

That was my cue to go.

I bent down to give her a kiss and she grabbed me by the hand. You wouldn't take any of those drugs, would you, son? she said. They're wrecking our Anthony's head.

Aye, I know.

There was a crowd of lads with their tops off standing around an Astra at the bottom of Summerhill Drive. They were on the beer already, and they had the tunes pumping. The kind of hardstyle that makes you want to fight. It was sunny too, every other garden had a barbecue on the go, and there were kids everywhere. They played football and chased each other with sticks. You couldn't walk ten yards without one of them running up beside you and asking for money. I told them I didn't have any change. Prove it, they said, and I stopped in the middle of the street and turned my pockets inside out.

It was like I had been on holiday. Nothing had changed, but everything felt different. The way people looked at me. What're you doing here? those looks said. I headed on over to Gardenmore Road, where my granny and granda lived. I wanted to grab that painting my ma had done of the dog, but there was nobody in, and they didn't leave their back door unlocked like they used to when I was a kid. It only took one wee dick from about the estate to try the handle and everything would be gone. I sat on the bench in their front garden and watched a woman across the street water her plants. Her house was the end house, and on the gable wall there was a mural of Bobby Sands. It was the same portrait they used for everything else, the one where he's wearing the red jumper with the white collar. My ma always said it didn't look anything like him, and she would know. He lived round the corner from her when she was a wee girl.

On the day of his funeral, a hundred thousand people lined the road from Twinbrook right down to Milltown Cemetery. My ma couldn't go. She was eight months pregnant with my oldest brother, Gerard, and was worried that something would happen. Instead, she stood across the street from St Luke's chapel and watched the coffin being carried out. The thing she remembered most was the size of the crowd, and the quiet. You could hear a pin drop, she told me. Then all of a sudden, there were helicopters; it was like the volume had been turned up. Through the crowd, my ma stared at the doorway of the same chapel she had walked out of a few months before, hand in hand with her new husband, in a hail of confetti. She was seventeen. That's how it was back then. Didn't matter how young you were, if you fell pregnant, you were sent down the aisle in a rented dress before your belly started to show. At nineteen, she had Anthony, and at twenty, the family moved to New York. It was supposed to be a new start, they had a foothold with a well-to-do aunt who put them up for a few weeks until they got jobs and a place to live. Three months into their two-year stint, Gerard and Anthony's da came home from the bar one night and beat her. It was her twenty-first birthday.

I left my granny's and headed over to Summer Hill, where we used to live. It was warm. The sun prickled the back of my neck, and as I walked along the road past St Mark's, I remembered what my ma had told me about when she came back to Belfast. She was twenty-two. She had tried to make it work with Gerard and Anthony's da, but there had been more drinking, more coming home late at night and hitting her. Moving back a few weeks ahead of him allowed her to do something about it; she went to the priest and asked for an annulment. The priest said he would do it, no problem, if she gave him five hundred quid. My ma didn't have that kind of money. Nobody did. The priest told her not to give her husband any excuse to raise his hand, and sent her on her way.

That's why she never went up for Communion. You're not allowed to take Communion if you're living in sin, and my ma had to get a divorce. She had another kid with another man too. My da. He lived with us for a few years after I was born, and then she was on her own again, now with three boys, in a housing executive house she wouldn't have got if the local Sinn Féin councillor didn't go out of his way to help her. Now I was standing outside that house, our house, but it belonged to new people who had done it up nice with flowerpots and hanging baskets. There was a bench too, and a tree they had planted in the corner of the garden. I leaned with my hand on the wall and pretended to tie my laces. The blinds were open, and on the windowsill there was a plant with leaves that had darkened and turned yellow.

We should've still been living there, it was our house. But the housing executive turfed my ma out as soon as I moved to Liverpool. They said she didn't need all those bedrooms any more; her sons had grown up and moved out. She was put on the waiting list with everybody else and told to sit tight. That's how she ended up in my granny's spare room. She was stuck there for a year before she took matters into her own hands and found a place to rent, in that house in Dunmurry. It cost a fortune, and she had to take on more cleaning jobs to keep herself ticking over. She wasn't young any more though. She was nearly fifty, and she struggled to keep up the pace her employers expected of her. Her back was wrecked with sciatica, and she took these kidney infections that knocked her off her feet for whole weeks at a time. My brothers did what they could to help her, but they had their own kids to worry about, and I wasn't making enough money to pay my phone bill never mind anything else. That's why painting was good for her. Even if she only sold one or two a year, it made a difference.

I cut down the alley round the back of Danielle Porter's house and came out on to the main road. I was heading over to the River Path, to loop back round to Gardenmore Road, but I got distracted by the crowd standing on the grass at the bottom of Aspen Walk. They were watching a man who had climbed up a ladder and was trying to fix the sheet they had hung over the mural for Carol Ann Kelly. I asked what was happening and a woman told me the mural had got damaged a few years ago, in a storm. Now they were unveiling a new one. At the back of the crowd, there was a group of wee lads standing on the pavement, watching. One of them was on a scrambler. He leaned with his elbows on the handlebars and picked muck out from under the chassis. I recognized Finty McKenna's wee brother. He had his hood up even though it was roasting. The sun was beaming down and he was dressed like he was ready for snow.

Well, Seany, he said to me. Have you any fegs?

Nah, no fegs.

Any dope? Give us a bit for a joint.

I shushed him and moved closer to the crowd. Deirdre Mulholland was at the platform they had set up there, with a mic and an amp. She was a local councillor for Black Mountain. It was her job to say a few words about the mural and the artist, and why it was important to keep Carol Ann's memory alive: Often it's the most vulnerable people in our communities who suffer, and they shouldn't be forgotten any more than our prisoners and volunteers, she said. Then another woman got up. She was involved with the Relatives for Justice group. She thanked Carol Ann's mother for all the work she had done for the campaign, and her brother and sister. They were standing at the bottom of their ma's garden; the mural was directly facing her house.

It all came back to me then, the stories my ma used to tell, and this one in particular about Carol Ann Kelly coming down the entry one day with a bottle of milk. She had gone to the shop for the aul fella who lived next door; he would slip her fifty pee for her troubles and away she'd go. She got to the bottom of the aul fella's garden, she was about to open the gate when a jeepload of Royal Fusiliers pulled up and fired two plastic bullets. Carol Ann was hit in the back of the head. The ambulance was called, and they got there as quickly as they could, but the Brits told them that nothing had happened, it was just a bit of unrest, and wouldn't let the paramedics cross the cordon. That's what made all the difference. Those minutes that passed while Carol Ann drifted in and out of consciousness, when her ma held her in her arms and screamed at the Brits to let the paramedics through.

By the time she was rushed to hospital and put on life support, it was too late. She died on 22nd May 1981. She was twelve years old.

Imagine the mother's panic when she ran from her home to cradle her child as she lay dying on the ground, the woman from Relatives for Justice said. Imagine the heartbreak as the family kept vigil at her hospital bed while she was on the life support machine. Imagine when it had to be switched off.

I looked around the crowd and saw men and women who would've been the same age as Carol Ann when she was murdered, who probably knew her and played with her on the street. They had brought their kids with them. Their grandkids too, and there was no messing about. They watched solemnly, and when the mural was unveiled, they tilted their heads to the side, curiously, as if trying to work out where they recognized her from. I moved up to the front for a better look. The mural was similar to the one that had been there before, only this time Carol Ann was smiling with her lips closed, shyly, as if she didn't want to say cheese. There was a round of applause. People came out of their houses with tea and sandwiches they handed out over their garden fences. Kids climbed down off their daddy's shoulders to play with their mates on the grass.

I headed across the road to the River Path. The path was peppered with glass that glittered in the sun, and the grass was scorched black from all the bins that had been stolen and burned. It was the kind of place people only walked through during the day, when it was safe, but at the weekends it belonged to the young ones from about the estate. We drank our barrack busters down there when we were kids, smoked weed. Listened to Happy Hardcore on boom boxes that needed new batteries after every other song. Now the young ones were at it just the same. I saw them hiding in the bushes along the riverbank. Finty's wee brother with his mates huddled close, their hoods up, taking turns on a dip they held up to their mouths and sucked. We weren't any different at that age, but still. It landed differently. The whole estate did.

I crossed the road to St Luke's chapel. It was small and square and didn't look like a chapel, there was no steeple or anything, and if it wasn't for the cross on the roof, you would think it was part of the school. There was a memorial garden round the side of the building, the Celebration of Life Garden. For all the people from about the estate who had killed themselves. I stood there for a while, looking at the flowers. Thinking about how young they all were. Out of the corner of my eye, I saw a fella with a ladder slung over his shoulder walking along the path towards me. It was our Anthony's mate, Marty. I hadn't seen Marty since before I moved to Liverpool. He had picked me up from Thompson's one night in the taxi he drove for a while after he lost his job at Bombardier – they laid off half their staff a few years ago, when the recession hit. Now he was cleaning windows.

How's it all going? I said. You ticking over?

Fuck sake, Sean. Ticking over? I'd be lucky to have enough for a flutter at the end of the week.

You still up in Poleglass?

No, fuck. Got a wee flat in Glasvey. Mon round, I'll show you.

I was going to head back down the road, but Marty was insistent. He handed me his bucket and extension pole and made me follow him towards the houses at the other side of the square, him leaning to one side under the weight of the ladders, all five foot four of him, looking like a character from a slapstick with his jeans falling down around his arse, his Nike Air Max squelching as he walked. He told me he had twenty houses to do the next day, and he had a meeting with a fella about a block of flats in Dunmurry. It was a big job, enough for two people, and if all went well, he'd be able to take his brother on with him. His brother had been out of work for a year. He had a child and everything, and Marty didn't want to let him down. I took the ladder off him and watched as he popped the padlock and opened the shed out the back of his flat. The ladder was shoved in with the bucket and the squeegees, the extension pole, and the bottle of vinegar he used with the window cleaner. On the inside panel of the shed door hung a pair of weatherproofs, two high-vis bibs, and a hard hat from when Marty was a plasterer. He showed me his toolbelt. He took it off the hook and held it out for me to see.

Got that when I was an apprentice, he said. Smasher, isn't it?

Inside, his flat was small, barren-looking. The kitchen smelled of bleach, and the few dishes he had – one big plate, one small plate, and a bowl – were arranged neatly on the dishrack. In the living room, he had a framed photograph of Ian Rush, signed, hanging on the wall above the TV. There was a CD cabinet, and on top of the cabinet was a football trophy: PFA PLAYER OF THE YEAR 1997: MARTIN CAFFERY. No photographs, no art, the emptiness of the flat would've depressed me if I didn't know that this was exactly how Marty liked it.

I'm gonna bounce in the shower. Do you wanna cup of tea?

Nah, I'm sweet. I'm gonna head on, I said.

Wise up, fuck sake. I'll be two seconds.

He came out of his bedroom ten minutes later wearing jeans and a shirt he buttoned up as he walked around the room. Then he twisted the lid off the tub of E45 he had sitting on the table and slathered his hands with it. The skin around his knuckles peeled sorely. I asked him if he'd seen our Anthony recently and he said, Nah, kid. Not in a while. I steer clear of all that madness.

He's been going bucko, I said.

Aye, so I hear.

He stood in front of the mirror and brushed his hair forward at the temples. The wet-look gel he used to slick his fringe had hardened. I could see his scalp. You know me, Sean. I'm not one to run about mixing reports, but I'm dreading seeing the cunt here, he said.

Who? Anthony?

He's up in the Laurel Glen sure, is that not where you're going?

I thought about it for a second, then I said, Aye, may as well, and waited for him to finish fixing his hair.

5

The Laurel Glen was smaller than I remembered, and dark. The main source of light came from the snooker table, which glowed like a floodlit field in the corner of the room. Taking turns around the table were two wee lads in Celtic tops. They moved through the light like they could see things nobody else could, and chalked. The bar was next to the fruit machines, and the woman behind the bar was talking over the taps to Anthony. Marty tapped him on the shoulder. Anthony turned and stared at me for a second, as if trying to work out who I was. Then he erupted. Slung his arm around my neck and pulled me into a hug.

There he is, the wee bro. Back with the big boys. What do you want, a pint? A vodka? A bag of toot?

All three, I said, and he laughed.

Is that my wee brother or wha?

He bought me a pint. He bought the aul lads sitting there a pint as well. Then he asked Marty what he wanted, but Marty said, Nah, I'm all right, and Anthony looked at him.

What do you mean, you're all right?

I've work tomorrow. I'm taking it easy.

Anthony was taken aback. Can you believe this cunt? Tightest bastard I've ever met in my life. I'm getting this round, Marty. What're you having, a pint? Get him a pint.

Anthony, seriously —

Shut the fuck up and take a pint, will ye?

Three pints were set on the countertop, and a round of shots.

No way, Marty said. I'm not doing it.

Ach, go on. Just one.

No chance.

He took his pint and went next door, to the bookies, leaving me with Anthony at the bar.

He had got bigger since the last time I saw him. His face was puffy and swollen, and his belly was massive. Too big for the shirt he wore, and his bootcut jeans, which were torn at the knee and stained with what looked like blood. His voice was gone too, and everything he said came out the wrong way. Four days on the trot will do that. It'll push your body to a place it doesn't want to be. You could see it in the way he held himself hunched over, with his hand on the back of the stool, blinking heavily.

What has you up here anyway? he said.

I told him I had a meeting with my solicitor. He looked at me like he didn't know what I was on about, then he grinned, slung his arm around my neck, and dragged me over to the fellas standing by the snooker table. The wee bro's knocking cunts out now, he told them. University educated and he's laying them out, isn't that right, kid? Tell the boys what happened.

I didn't make a song and dance about it, these fellas weren't the type to be impressed by that kind of thing. I just said it like it was: I got into a fight at a house party and knocked some cunt out. Anthony thought it was brilliant. Who does that sound like? he said, and they said, You. It sounds like you. He pulled me into him and kissed me on the side of the head.

I fucking love this kid. I'd die for him, wouldn't I?

I agreed that he would, and he looked at me like he was going to cry.

Instead, he bought another round of shots and tried to get Marty to take one. He had come back from the bookies with a handful of dockets and was watching the screen above the bar, waiting for the next race.

What about a wee blast of this? Anthony said.

He pulled a bag of gear from his pocket and twiddled it in Marty's face.

Get that away from me.

Or wha? What're you gonna do?

He grabbed Marty into a headlock and wrecked his hair.

Fuck sake, Anto. Knock it on the head, will you?

I felt bad for Marty, he clearly didn't want to be there, and Anthony was torturing him. Look at this cunt in his Ted Baker shirt, he said. Showing far too much cash, isn't he, lads? Come here till I hit you a slap. Sean, hit him a slap. Tell him to wise up and take a line.

I didn't know why Marty had even come. The Laurel Glen isn't the kind of place you go for a quiet one. Not with headcases like our Anthony about. I'm away for a sniff, he said, and staggered off to the toilets. Marty looked at me. Anthony had rung him earlier that day, he said, and told him that if he didn't go up to the bar and have a drink with him, he was coming down to Marty's flat. I'll wreck the place, he'd said, and that left Marty with no choice but to go up and sit with him. Let him run out of steam, and hope that at some point Anthony would finally fade and go back home to his wife and kids. But it was six o'clock in the afternoon and Anthony was showing no sign of going anywhere.

He doesn't stop, Marty said. He just keeps going.

I could see it dawning on him, the very real prospect of being stuck with Anthony for the rest of the night, taking his stick. Doing everything he could to pull him out of this spiral. Because chances were that Anthony would be looking for somewhere to go as soon as last orders were called, and if you had a gaff just sitting there empty, with no wife, no kids, he was coming home with you. No two ways about it. It made drinking with Anthony when you weren't on his level feel like you were being subjected to some kind of torture. His mission then was to bring you down to his level. That was what redeemed the whole experience, because when you got there, it could be the best craic in the world.

Anthony appeared beside me. Tootski? he said, waving the baggie.

I thought you'd never ask, I said.

There were two cubicles in the men's toilets and both of them were taken. Nobody went near the urinals, and not one person in the queue said a word about how seven fellas needed to take a dump at exactly the same time. Then one of the cubicle doors creaked open. The man who stepped out handed something to the man at the top of the queue. The same thing happened again with the other cubicle, except the man who stepped out handed something to the fella in front of me. Everybody saw what was happening and laughed. When it was my turn to step to the front, the lad behind me tapped me on the shoulder and said, Here, somebody's looking you. I turned to see what he was talking about and realized too late that he was trying to cut in front of me.

There's a queue here, mate, I said.

Aye, and I'm at the front, what're you gonna do?

He pushed his head into my head, his fist was cocked at his side, and over his shoulder I saw his mates watching, waiting for me to swing. I backed down. I held my hands up and said, Right, no problem, and let him take my spot. His mates laughed. The men around me laughed too.

You've come to the wrong place, big lad, they said.

When I went back out to the bar, a crowd of people had gathered around the snooker table and were chanting, Par-ty Mar-ty, Par-ty Mar-ty, Par-ty Mar-ty. Marty was up on top of the snooker table. He had his shirt unbuttoned and was dancing with his hands up in the air.

We got him, Anthony said.

What do you mean, you got him?

He picked up his pint and showed me how he had spiked Marty, with an E.

That's him out for the week, he said.

Anthony used to bring me up to the Laurel Glen when I was a kid. He'd buy me a Coke and a bag of crisps and I'd sit with him and his mates and watch them play pool. John Boy, Buzz, Speedy, Rabbie Duck and Pigeon. Marty Caffery. These were names you'd see written on fences and walls all over the estate, and they were famous in that way, for the madness they got up to. The shows they put on in cars they stole from posh estates in Lisburn. I was only a kid, about thirteen, and crowds of us would gather along the road in the middle of Twinbrook, cheering them on. We loved it. The buzz we got from watching it. The screeching tyres, the smoke. The smell of burnt rubber. It was like the road was being torn up. Then the peelers would come in their big lumbering meat wagons. They hadn't a chance, the hoods were too fast for them, and we had our bricks and bottles and we pelted them until they took off out of the estate. There was no better feeling than watching them go. It was like we were running them off our turf. Then the stolen car would be driven on to the pitches and burned. The drivers would disappear into the night. We would gather around with our hoods up and watch the seats melt into the flames.

They were the people I looked up to when I was a kid. They were who I wanted to be. The mad bastards, the ones everybody knew and talked about when we stood at the shops: Remember that time Speedy pulled up in a brand-new Audi TT? He stole it from some arsehole on the Malone Road. Broke into their gaff in the middle of the night and lifted the keys right off the bedside table. He was there that day, in the Laurel Glen. He was standing at the fruit machines, dropping pound after pound. I tried to bend his ear about those cars he used to fly about in, but he was quiet, he kept reaching into his pocket for more shrapnel. I noticed the scar running from the corner of his mouth to his ear and remembered how a crowd of men from down the road broke into his house one night and tried to cut his face off. There was a scar on the other side too; it started from his eyebrow and went right down to his chin. He didn't look like himself any more. Anthony slung his arm around my neck and guided me back to the bar.

Leave him be, his head's lit, he said.

Marty was there, he was leaning with his back against the counter, cursing the world and everybody in it. His shirt was still unbuttoned. His pudgy belly hung out over his jeans.

Your brother's a cunt, he said.

I agreed. The woman behind the bar agreed too. She had caught Anthony taking coke off the countertop and was shouting at him.

Do it in the toilets, for fuck sake, she said.

Anthony giggled. Take a wee toot sure, he said.

Get that out of my face.

Go on, Veronica. Let the hair down. Me and you, we'll run away.

Slugger, he's trying to get me to take that badness.

Slugger looked up from his phone. Is he not barred? he said.

He's been barred for months. Doesn't stop him.

I'm not barred. Who's gonna bar me? You?

Slugger glanced at Veronica and Veronica glared at him as if to say, *will you bloody do something?* For a second, Slugger looked like he was contemplating it. But then he saw how Anthony was looking at him, and his head dropped.

Nah, Anto. I wouldn't do that, he said.

See? We're all friends here, aren't we, Slugger?

Aye, all good.

That was the effect Anthony had on people. They knew his reputation and no bouncer on the road was stupid enough to test it; he was a different beast. I had seen it for myself plenty of times, outside bars and clubs, on the street. It was what made me feel safe in places other people wouldn't. All I had to say was, Do you know Anto

Quinn? and that was it. The hardest men at house parties became my best mates. They shook my hand and told me, Your Anto's a legend, tell your Anto I was asking about him. Here, take a beer. Take a line. Take anything you want, just make sure Anto knows. That was how it was that day, in the Laurel Glen. The fella who started on me in the toilets saw who I was with and went completely pale.

Here, mate, I didn't know who you were, he said. I know your brother –

I could've smacked him. I could've punched the head clean off him right in the middle of the bar and nobody would've done anything about it. Not his mates, not the bouncers. Not even Veronica. And I could've made a complete dick out of him. I could've said something like, Where's your mates at now, big lad? and pinned him up against the wall. Made him feel as small and weak as I did when he got me in the toilets, and I could do it in front of everyone, the whole bar, with Anthony standing there, cheering me on like he did when I was a kid.

Go on, Sean. Hit him. Knock his ballicks in.

Instead, I let him shake my hand. It was better to let it go.

Anthony gave me twenty quid and made me swear I'd come back, as soon as I finished my shift. I'd get another taxi back up the road.

Give me an address and I'll be there, I said.

I had no idea how geared-up I was. I had taken a lot of coke.

The taxi driver knew. He stared into his cupped hand.

Have a good night, he said.

There was a queue from the doors to the end of the car park. The downstairs lounge was packed. I grabbed what I needed from the stockroom and carried two crates of mixers up to the top floor. There were usually eight of us working on the bar up there, but two people had been sacked the weekend before and nobody had been taken on to replace them. The mood was tense. Thursday nights were mad even with a full team, and there was a lot of prep to do before the doors opened: fridges needed to be stocked, limes cut, ice buckets filled, beer mats laid, spirit bottles plugged, cases of Red Bull spaced between the plastic cups. All this in the fifteen-minute gap between starting our shift and the nightclub doors opening, and with no floor staff to give us a hand – they were in the lounge getting their heads melted before the worst of the night had even started. And as annoying as it was to be given so little time to organize ourselves before we got hit with a wave of six hundred-odd students mooching for a double vodka, it was working out well for me that night, to have everybody running about in a panic, too distracted to see that something wasn't right with me, my eyes. If it wasn't for Anthony giving me what was left of one of those baggies that were being passed around the Laurel Glen that day, I would've crashed, and that would've made the whole thing worse. Having to work through a swarm of eager students leaning all the way over the counter, waving their fivers at me trying to get my attention.

I gave you a twenty, one of them said, acting a maggot.

Don't even try it.

I did. Swear to God –

They were always at it, those GAA top wearing wankers. Slapping handfuls of shrapnel on the soaking wet countertop, looking at me like I was some kind of dickhead when I told them to pick it up and hand it to me. The countertop was laminate. Trying to lift a bunch of 10 and 20 pees off a laminate countertop when it was wet was impossible unless you'd a good set of fingernails on you, which I didn't. They could give me as much stick as they wanted, all I had to do was tell them to fuck off, you're not getting served, and move on to the next customer, who had seen how things had gone for the last arsehole with an attitude, and fell immediately into line, with a please and thank you to boot.

It was midnight before I got the chance to duck into the staff toilet. I took two keys, then another one for good measure, and when I checked how much was left in the baggie, I was tempted to hoof the rest of it, just so I didn't have to worry about having it on me. Back on the bar, I was getting into it, the music and the lights, the girls making eyes at me over the countertop, and I was working hard, serving three and four people at a time, cracking jokes, laughing, running about the place wiped off my nut. I had no idea Dee was standing behind me. He could've been standing there the whole night and I wouldn't have noticed. The gear had got to me in that way. It blurred everything.

Come out here for a second, he said.

He took me into the stockroom and tried to have a go at me about something his da had said about him being an arsehole to his staff. There had been a complaint, and I think he thought it came from me. But it was tricky with the PR girls sitting there in the corner, on crates they had turned upside down. Dee had to lower his voice so they wouldn't hear him, but he also had to speak loudly enough that I could make out what he was saying over the music. I hadn't a clue what he was on about, and I could see that it was doing his head in – he kept running his hands through his hair and glancing at the girls. Then he quiet-shouted at me, through his teeth, and that doubled me over; I was in a wrinkle, laughing. Dee thought there was something wrong with me. He checked my eyes and everything.

Are you on something? he said.

Me? No.

You sure?

He came right up into my face.

Don't do that, I said.

What?

Don't get in my face like that, Dee. Seriously.

Or what? What're you gonna do?

His chin was sticking out. One short sharp clip and that would be him, out like a light. He was lucky those PR girls were there. One of them stood up and was like, What's the craic here, are you gonna send us home or what? Her name was Ciara, she was six foot tall in heels. When she walked towards you, you crumbled. Dee was no different. He tried to take his phone out of his pocket and dropped it on the floor.

What does it say on the rota? he said.

I was supposed to finish at twelve.

Yeah, me too, another girl said.

I'm not even supposed to be here.

All right, give me two minutes.

Dee took one last look at me, and was gone.

The bouncers were our mates that night, they were in as much of a hurry to get out of there as we were, and they worked ruthlessly, snatching drinks out of people's hands as soon as the lights came on, looming over anybody who lingered, herding them out the doors and into the car park where they were left to their own devices. The only hope we had of leaving any time soon was to make sure the club was clean enough for Dee to let us go, which he did, after checking everything had been done properly, including the smoking area, where we spent twenty minutes picking up feg butts that had fallen into the gaps between the decking, hooking them out with our fingers.

The bar staff and the floor staff and those PR girls I had seen in the stockroom earlier in the night were waiting in the lounge, scrolling through their phones, drawling about what they were going to do when they got home, the food they would eat, the sleeping they would do. Word started going around about a party in Jokey's house in Carrick Hill. Nobody was interested, it was only the start of the weekend, and having a comedown going into Friday night was never a good move. Then somebody said, Fuck it, and bought a ten-glass bottle of vodka from behind the bar. There was laughter, a few sidelong glances. Big Billy from East Belfast jumped up and was like, Sure why not? The mood shifted. People were like, Are you going? Are you going? I'll go if you go. Even the PR girls, whose feet were cut to pieces from the heels they had to wear, started dancing to music they played on their phones.

Somebody book taxis, they said.

How many do we need?

Five? No, six.

Ryan came running up to me; he had been working in the VIP bar that night so I hadn't seen him. You going or what? he said, and then he looked at me: Holy fuck.

I shook my head from side to side and the whole room moved with me.

I need to go home, I said.

Somebody was sitting on the kerb out the front of the flat. I didn't know who it was or what they were doing there until the taxi stopped and the person shaded their eyes with their hand – Mairéad. She was wearing a short black dress with heels she had taken off and set on the kerb beside her, next to her big leather bag, which she had been using as a shield to protect her legs from the rain that dotted the windscreen of the taxi driver's car.

I brought her into the flat, thinking she was looking for a party, and handed her a beer, sat down next to her, and started talking shite about the state of me trying to get through my shift after taking a fuck-ton of gear in the Laurel Glen that day. I was laughing, shaking my head, blithering stupidly about how nobody had caught on even when I came back from the toilets that second time, wiped off my nut. Mairéad took her phone out of her bag and said, Do you have an iPhone charger? I told her, Nah, I don't even, and she said, Lend me your phone. I need to get a taxi.

She was going over to the Ormeau. The person on the other end of the line told her they were all booked up. She tried another depot and they said there were no drivers available in the area.

This is ridiculous, Mairéad said. What's going on?

It didn't make sense to me either, she had only just got there. I said this to her and she said, Aye, I know, and stood up as if to leave even though there was nobody coming to get her. She slung her bag over her shoulder, and then, feeling the weight of it, dropped it on the floor.

You all right? I said.

No, not really.

She took a breath to steady herself. Then she sat down, fixed her skirt.

Some bastard pulled my dress up in work, she said.

They did what?

She told me she was selling shots that night, in Mono, and she was doing her usual lap around the dance floor when some dickhead she had told to get away from her earlier in the night snuck up behind her and pulled her dress up. She couldn't pull it down again, she was carrying a tray of shots, and although she acted like she didn't care about people seeing her arse – It's only an arse, she said – she had to walk across the dance floor in front of everyone with her dress stuck up around her waist, set the tray down, and fix herself.

I should've smashed the tray over that bastard's head, she said. She rubbed her hands on her thighs and pressed her knees together. Know why I didn't? Know why I stopped myself from really flipping out?

Her chin wobbled. I thought she was going to break.

Because I would've had to cover the cost of the bottle.

The bottle was ninety quid. Mairéad would've had to work the entire shift just to pay it back.

She used her hair to hide her face and turned away from me. Her bag was on the floor at her feet, and all around it, a puddle had spread out. I went into my bedroom and got a pair of sweats and a hoodie I liked to wear around the flat and gave them to her. She went into the bathroom and came out again with the hoodie on but not the sweats, they were too big.

How long were you waiting out there? I said.

Not long. I didn't finish work till two.

Wait, you finished your shift?

Not only did she finish her shift, she carried on working without telling anybody about what had happened, not even the bouncers, who I thought would've trailed the lad out by the throat. Then she told me who the lad was: he was the owner's brother. She had drunk-kissed him a few weeks ago, at a house party. He had been melting her head ever since.

What's his name? I said.

Don't even go there, Sean.

But I was already there. Waiting for him outside Mono, like a dick.

Are you gonna go back? I said.

Of course I am. I need the money.

She pulled my hoodie over her knees and hugged her knees to her chest. She used to do this with her school jumper, back when we hid in the bushes in the corner of the fields, those days we beeked school. I remembered the rain coming down and the smell of the rain in her hair, and when it was really bad we would hold our blazers up over our heads, and smoke.

I wouldn't have come here if I had somewhere else to go, Mairéad said.

It's all right, you can come here any time.

I know, it's just . . .

Her voice trailed off. I pulled the purple throw from the back of the settee.

Will you stay here with me? she said.

On the settee?

Just till I fall asleep.

Aye, okay.

I climbed into the inside and let her have the outside because she was smaller and it was easier that way. We lay there for a while, holding each other. Not really saying anything. Then Mairéad saw the brightness coming through the blinds and groaned.

What am I doing with my life? she said.

I woke up and Mairéad was gone. She had left my hoodie and sweats on the settee, folded neatly, with a note she had written on the back of a receipt:

Thanks for letting me stay x

I had two missed calls from Anthony at six in the morning, and a video he'd sent at seven. I opened it and there was Marty with his shirt off, in his trunks, shadow-boxing in the middle of his living room. He was like lightning too, throwing jabs and hooks. Setting up the uppercut. People were laughing, cheering him on. Go on, Marty, they shouted. His hands flashed out in front of him, and he made that *ts, ts* sound boxers make. I thought it was a geg, he was really going for it. Then I remembered what he said about the meeting he had that morning, the block of flats. The work he hoped to get so he could bring his brother on with him.

I messaged Anthony and asked if he was still on it.

He replied with a picture of Marty with a rolled-up tenner stuck up his nose. I turned my phone off and went back to sleep.

6

My solicitor was doing my head in about witnesses. He wanted me to get someone to go down to the peeler station and give a statement, and he wanted them to give evidence in court as well, in the witness box. I asked Ryan if he was up for it, thinking he could spoof his way through it like he did with everything else, but sure he didn't have anything to do with it, he hadn't even been there that night, and it wasn't worth risking it in front of a judge; he could end up getting done too. The solicitor wouldn't leave it alone though. He kept ringing me and leaving voicemails. I can contact witnesses on your behalf, he said. But I didn't know anybody at the house party that night, they were all Daniel Jackson's mates, and there was no way they would back me up.

The weekend before I was due in court, I went on the rip with a few lads from about the estate who knew the craic, they had been in and out of jail since they were no age, and they told me I'd nothing to worry about. I was a first-time offender, no criminal record or nothing. The judge would hit me a slap on the wrist and send me on my way. So I wasn't losing any sleep about how it would go, I hardly even thought about it. The only reason I couldn't get over the night before was because I was used to going to bed at four o'clock in the morning, after work, and I knew I'd to be up early for court.

I turned my lamp on and tried to read, but I couldn't concentrate. All these thoughts kept sneaking up on me like they always did in the early hours, when I could hear the work vans coming and going from the industrial estate at the bottom of the road. It was like I was talking to myself, my voice was in my head, but it was all over the place, jumping from one thing to the next. The way Daniel Jackson had spoken to me in the kitchen that night. I was just standing there, trying to have a good time, and him and his mates started winding me up about where I was from – they were posh pricks from the Malone Road and thought they could get away with it. One of them was like, You best be careful, his dad's probably in the IRA, and that cunt Daniel Jackson piped in and said, Sure he doesn't know who his dad is, he's from Twinbrook. The kitchen erupted. It was like one of those rap battles you see on TV, when one of them lands a belter and everybody goes ooh, fuck, and throws their hands up in the air. I couldn't come back from it even if I wanted to, the whole room was against me, and they kept mimicking me, my accent. No matter how many times I told them not to, they couldn't help themselves. They had the numbers, they had the room, and the room was saying they could take the piss out of me as much as they wanted. There was nothing I could do.

I reached for my phone and typed my da's name into the Facebook search bar. He was twelve years older than the last time I saw him. His hair was grey. His face was flat and wide, and he was dressed in those country hacker clothes he used to wear when he picked me up at the weekends: the corduroy trousers and Barbour coats, the flat cap he used to hang from the banister at the bottom of the stairs. No pictures of his wife or his daughter. Only him. His dog. Standing in fields at working tests, watching somebody else's retriever dash across the grass with a floppy-necked pheasant clutched between its teeth. He looked awkward. He didn't know what to do with his face, and his shoulders seemed to shrink in a way that made him look weak. Turn the camera on him when he isn't looking and see him striding purposefully across the field, his arms wide, watching where he's going with a walking stick he holds loosely, with one hand.

The last time I saw him he took me to get a pair of football boots for my tenth birthday. I was gunning for Adidas Predators, the black ones with the red tongue Zidane used to wear. My da looked at the price and was like, No way, not a chance, and tried to tempt me with a brutal-looking pair of black Umbros. But I knew he had the money, the same way I knew he would say no before saying yes, which he did, after a barrage of stuttered curses, and brought me to the till. When he dropped me back home later that day, I leaned over to kiss him on the cheek like I always did and he told me to fuck away off.

What age are you? he said.

I got out of the car and crossed the street with my string bag slung over my shoulder. My da called me back. Come here over, he said, through his open window. I walked towards him and he spat at me. I jumped back and spat at him and he laughed, revved his engine, and spun away.

The train came at quarter past nine that morning, and at ten, I was emptying my pockets into a container and walking through the metal detectors at the entrance to Laganside Courts. There was a lot of waiting around, and my barrister, some watery-eyed weasel in a two-piece suit, who was full of the kind of useless energy I had only ever seen on a five-a-side pitch, when that one poor bastard who doesn't want to be there is stuck in nets, kept apologizing on behalf of no one in particular for something that was completely out of his control. He brought me into a room down the hall and made me tell him about what had happened that night. He had all the statements laid out on the table in front of him. There was panic in his eyes.

Have you thought about your plea? he said.

I told him I wasn't guilty. He said, No, of course not, but if you decide to argue your case, you'll likely face a harsher conviction –

So, I should say I'm guilty?

I can't tell you what to say, Mr Maguire. I can only give you advice.

Is telling me how to plead not advice?

The solicitor smiled. I knew what he wanted me to say, and I knew there was an easier way to go about this, but I couldn't, not when I knew I wasn't.

Fuck it, I'm not guilty, I said, and watched his shoulders slump.

I'll try my best, he said.

Back in the hall, people waited to be called. I watched the younger lads, the repeat offenders, the ones who had been there plenty of times before, saunter back and forth from the vending machines. They made a point of wearing their Peter Storm coats and their Nike Air Max because fuck putting on a shirt and tie for some judge who had already made up their mind, it would hardly make a difference. The first-timers with their minor offences looked at them like they had lost their minds, the way they carried on, laughing, joking, winding each other up about how long they were going in for this time. But they couldn't see what was happening. They were too worried about making a good impression to think about how the whole thing worked.

I messaged Mairéad:

You better visit me in jail

You're not going to jail. Don't be saying that
I finish work at 12, wanna meet me after?

aye where abouts?
City hall?
I don't feel good about this

you'll be all right
you'll be in and out in no time

it reminds me of school

what does?

My name was called. My barrister came at me with a stack of fold-ers, he told me what to say and what not to say, and while he was talking, pages fell out of those folders and on to the floor. He bent down to pick them up and dropped another one, and another, so that as we walked into the courtroom, he was dipping down and popping up like some sort of jack in the box. Those cunts who were pressing charges against me were in a kink. They saw the hack of this fella bumbling into the room with me and knew I hadn't a chance. I had to sit with them in the gallery at the back, and it wasn't like I had backup; I was there on my own. They saw this and tried to intimidate me, leering at me all disapproving like I was some kind of lowlife. It wasn't right. I said this to my barrister and he looked at me dimly.

The judge will ask you to stand, all you have to do is state your plea, he said.

I did what I was told and said, Not guilty, Your Worship, loudly enough for the old fart in the black robe lording it over the courtroom to hear. The man himself glared down at me through glasses that had slid down his sweaty nose, and told me to approach the witness box. A woman in uniform, a peeler or a security guard, I couldn't tell, handed me a laminated page and asked if I'd like to take an oath or an affirmation. I saw the words printed in large font and said I'd take the oath even though I wasn't religious, I didn't believe in God, yet I held the laminated page out in front of me and recited the words as clearly and piously as I could. My barrister stepped out from behind the table in the middle of the room and read my statement out. Any time he needed me to clarify something, he turned to me and said, Is this correct? I said, Aye, it is. When my side of the story had been told, he went back to the part he wanted to talk about, when those two lads sitting in the gallery started winding me up in the kitchen.

It says in your statement that things escalated, how did they escalate?

I glanced at the judge. He was watching me, closely.

They started getting aggressive, I said.

In what way?

There was some pushing and shoving. Your man squared up to me in the kitchen.

Were you concerned for your safety?

Yes.

And did you express this to Mr Jackson?

I told him I didn't want any trouble and he laughed at me.

What happened next?

I rang a taxi. The woman in the depot told me it would be half an hour. I sat on the kerb across the street and waited.

How did you feel about having to wait so long?

Not good. I wanted to get out of there.

Tell the court what happened next.

Your man and his mate came out of the house looking me.

This is Daniel Jackson and his friend, Gareth Waters?

Aye. Both of them.

And you felt threatened by them?

Aye, I could tell they were gonna hit me.

How could you tell?

Their fists were clenched, and their heads were pushed forward, like this.

I showed my barrister what I meant. He looked at his pages.

You said in your statement that Mr Jackson tried to hit you first.

He did. He swung a few punches. I moved out of the way, but there was two of them and one of me. I threw a punch to protect myself and he fell to the ground.

Did you know he was unconscious?

No, I thought he tripped over the kerb or something. I looked at my hands, then at the laminated page. I didn't mean to hurt the wee lad, I said.

Do you have any previous convictions, Mr Maguire?

No. I've never even been in a fight before.

This must've been quite an ordeal.

Aye, it was, I said, and looked at the floor.

My barrister told the judge he had no further questions. I was feeling good about how the whole thing was going. I had conducted myself well, I thought. Then the prosecution barrister stepped out from behind the table in the middle of the room and calmly, calculatedly, slipped his hands into the pockets of his pin-striped trousers.

Mr Maguire, your statement states that my client, Mr Daniel Jackson, attacked you on the street outside the house party you attended on Tate's Avenue on the 20th of July of this year, is this correct?

He came at me, yes.

What do you mean he came at you?

He came towards me aggressively.

So you punched him?

No. He tried to hit me.

Don't people walk towards you all the time, Mr Maguire?

They do, aye. On the street.

And do you punch them in the face?

No. I don't.

What do you mean when you say, 'he came at me' then?

I mean he squared up to me, I said, hesitantly.

Squared up to you?

Like, came towards me like he was going to hit me.

This is your justification for punching my client in the face?

No. I mean, he tried to hit me first.

So, he came towards you, then he tried to punch you?

Aye, well. I saw him coming towards me and he swung a few punches.

The barrister looked confused. You said you've never been in a fight before, Mr Maguire, yet you knew how to elude a barrage of punches and were able to counter those punches with your own punch and knock Mr Jackson unconscious?

I had to protect myself. I just swung my hands.

But he never hit you?

No.

So you could've moved and would have essentially been out of harm's way?

He was coming towards me. There was nothing I could do.

But it says in your statement that you hit him more than once, Mr Maguire. You hit him a left and a right –

Yeah. It was a fight.

And you won this fight, didn't you, Mr Maguire?

No, that's not how it is –

But the barrister had sat down. Was that it?

The judge told me to go back to my seat. Those arseholes at the other end of the gallery leaned forward to look at me, and when I sat down, Gemma Hatfield was called. She was the girl who came flying at me after I knocked Daniel Jackson out, screaming, calling me all the bastards of the day. Now she was all dressed up in a pencil skirt and blazer, and she was wearing those thick black glasses people wear to make them look smart. She picked up the laminated page and recited the oath like she was taking a pledge of abstinence, and she was dead earnest about it, like she was doing God's work. Nobody knew who he was, we didn't even want him there, she said, even though nothing whatsoever was said to me at the time. In fact, everybody at the party was sound, offering me a beer, talking away to me in the kitchen, having a laugh, and that was what really got to me. The way every single witness stood up in front of the courtroom and made me out to be some kind of scumbag, intimidating everyone, coming off with all this guff about me being abusive to the lads that were there, calling them names, then going mad when I was asked to leave, as if I was some kind of leech who couldn't take a joke and ended up running about the street like a lunatic, screaming. Telling people I was going to knock their ballicks in, and all of them with the same snotty voice, uppity as fuck, getting on like their sheltered lives had been blown apart by this terrible act of violence I had committed.

Where were you when the confrontation happened?

I was standing on the kerb.

I was across the road.

I was at the front door.

And they were at the other side of the street?

Yes.

You could hear what they were saying from that far away?

I could. They were shouting.

At each other?

Yes.

But not arguing, or verbally abusing each other?

No, just like, telling him to calm down kind of thing.

He was very upset.

Yeah, he was so aggressive.

I've never seen anybody lose their temper like that.

It was terrifying.

Daniel Jackson was the last person to go up to the witness box. I saw how small he was compared to me and knew the courtroom noticed it too, and the judge. His barrister made a point of telling him it was okay, don't be nervous, and Daniel nodded gratefully. He was such a timid wee fella, sitting there with his hands clasped between his thighs, his shoulders all bunched up. He couldn't remember anything about what had happened. One minute he was standing on the street, minding his own business. The next he woke up in hospital with no clue how he got there. He had to get surgery on his lip. He spoke so meekly that I sensed the mood of the courtroom shift.

I keep thinking it's going to happen again, he said. I don't go out. I don't do anything. I just stay at home and watch TV.

His barrister let that hang in the air for a second. Then he said, No further questions, Your Worship, and sat down.

My barrister stood up. He flicked through Daniel Jackson's statement, dropped a page, bent down to pick it up and dropped another.

Tell me this, he said, after he had recovered himself. What happened in the kitchen?

Daniel wasn't stupid, he knew what he had to say. It was the same thing they had all said: just a bit of banter, no harm in it, and when somebody said something about me not knowing who my da was, I went ballistic and tried to grab Daniel by the throat.

Why you? my barrister said.

He thought I said it, but I didn't.

Who said it then?

I don't know why it matters.

Even if you and your friend attacked my client on the street?

Nobody attacked him, he's lying about that.

Answer the question, please.

What's the question?

Did you and your friend, Gareth Waters, attack my client?

Daniel looked confused. No, he said. He attacked us.

That was it, that was the best my barrister could do.

Instead of going the long way around to avoid walking past me, Daniel Jackson headed straight towards me, with his eyes locked on me. My head dropped. When I looked up again, my barrister was crouched down next to me. There was panic in his voice.

You went to university, didn't you? What did you study?

English Lit. Books.

Is that what you want to do?

Books? Aye, why not.

The barrister scribbled this down. Anything else I could use?

Use for what?

To plead your case. I have to plead your case.

I didn't understand why he was getting himself into such a state. I'd had a meeting with my probation officer the week before and she told me I was looking at a few hours of community service, a suspended sentence at the most. There was no talk about jail or anything, and when I asked, the probation officer shook her head and said, No, that's not something you should worry about. My barrister seemed to think it was. He was pleading with the judge to consider my level of education, my future as a writer, my hopes of one day publishing a book. Sean has no prior convictions, he said. He has no history of violence, or criminality. He acknowledges his wrong and sincerely regrets any trauma he's caused. As he said himself, he didn't mean to hurt Mr Jackson. He was quick to co-operate and acknowledge his mistake, and he has openly expressed his wish to compensate, by way of an apology, in a letter or in person –

Oh, there will be compensation, the judge said. I'll tell you that.

He pushed his glasses up his nose and glared at me from across the courtroom. There's nothing in Mr Maguire's nature, as far as I can see, that suggests to me that he is anything more than a bully and a thug, he said. He saw that this young man's back was turned, took his opportunity, and pounced. What's worse, he continued, and, if anything, more infuriating than the fact that Mr Maguire viciously attacked this young man for no reason beyond his own indignation, is that he has the gall to come into this courtroom and profess his innocence. Taking this into account, and the fact that we could have been looking at a much more serious situation than the one we are confronted with today, I am inclined towards exerting my full judicial powers and convicting with the most substantial custodial sentence permitted for this crime: seven years in prison, if my memory is correct?

It was like my stomach had been punctured with a needle and the air was slowly leaving my body. One of the barristers sitting at the tables in the middle spun round to look at me. The whole courtroom was looking at me, and I realized with a cold feeling that I wasn't who I thought I was to them. They were on the outside looking in, and the person they saw wasn't me.

Please, Your Worship, my barrister said. It would be such a shame for someone who has come from where Mr Maguire has, and done as well as he's done, only for it to be taken away –

The judge batted his hand. He had made up his mind.

Taking the evidence into account, and the transparency of the statements presented here today, I'm convicting Mr Sean Maguire of Section 47 Assault with Actual Bodily Harm. Your sentence will be two hundred hours of community service, and a six-hundred-pound fine. Failure to comply with the terms of your community service order within a period of twelve months will result in a summons back to court, and further charges being brought against you, do you understand?

I said, Yes, I do, and that was it. I was free to go.

7

I rang my ma as soon as I got to the City Hall. She'd been worried sick, saying prayers all morning. My granny had lit a candle.

You told granny?

Of course I told her. Who else am I supposed to talk to?

Don't tell her about community service. Just say I got a fine.

How can Anthony and Gerard fight their whole lives and never get a peep from the peelers, and the one time you do, this happens?

I didn't know. I had done all the things I was supposed to do. I had stayed on in school, gone to university. Got my degree. Now I was being pulled up in front of a judge who called me a bully. I had never bullied anybody in my life. I got suspended from school for headbutting someone for picking on Christopher Wilson because he was gay. How could I be a bully?

You're not a bully, Mairéad said. You're not like that.

She was in her work clothes, or her normal clothes – it's hard to tell with somebody who's allowed to wear their normal clothes to work. She didn't for once have that big leather bag slung over her shoulder. Instead she had a smaller bag with loads of zips, strapped across her chest. She saw me looking at it and patted it proudly: It's like a fanny pack, but for your tits.

She took a packet of paracetamol from the front pouch and swallowed two without drinking any water. She'd been out on the swall the night before and looked like she was feeling it.

I should've just said I was guilty, I said.

Why didn't you?

Because I'm not.

Mairéad laughed, thinking I was joking. She got up off the bench and ran her hand through her hair. Mon, we'll go for a pint, she said.

I don't have any money.

I have money. I'll get you one.

I shook my head, stared at the ground.

You wanna seen the way that judge looked at me, I said. He looked at me like he wanted to spit on me.

He probably did, the pervy bastard. He probably goes home and beats the meat off himself over the thought of locking wee lads like you away.

I'm not a wee lad though, am I?

You are to him. You're just some wee ballroot from about the road.

I smiled. Mairéad held her hand out and I took it.

We headed towards Royal Avenue. Mairéad wanted to bring me to this bar she liked, The Sunflower. It had a good beer garden, and people were allowed to bring their dogs. She thought that would cheer me up. On the way, we bumped into Finty McKenna. He was running up and down the street outside Primark trying to get bums on seats of those open-topped buses you see driving about all over the place. He had the red tie on, the black trousers, and the white shirt with the sleeves rolled up, showing off the terrible tattoo he got when he was too young to know any better: FINTY, written in big black letters, in Olde English script, right in the middle of his forearm. I asked him how the new job was going and he told me it was sweet as long as he played it right and didn't get into too many scraps. There were four different bus tour companies, each of them had squads of lads working the busiest spots, and they were all fighting over the same customers. There had been digging matches and everything. Only the day before, Finty tried to poach twenty-four Italians straight off a cruise ship that had come in that morning. You're talking a hundred quid a head, and that's not counting the cash they spend on site, he said. The lads he was trying to poach from didn't take it well. They called their mates from across the road and chased Finty down High Street.

They tried to jump you? I said.

Oh aye, about ten of them. Happens all the time, doesn't it, Steeky?

Steeky was the fella he worked with; he was standing in the shade. He was ginger and the heat was killing him.

All the time, he said.

I thought he was saying it happened all the time to everybody who worked for that company, but no. He meant that it happened to Finty. There were rules, guidelines that had been agreed on so there were no conflicts – apparently it was worse a few months ago, people from different bus tour companies were punching the head off each other all the time, in the middle of the street, in front of tourists, and the tourists weren't happy about it. The rules were brought in to enforce some kind of ceasefire. But Finty couldn't help himself. He broke every rule in the book, and they kept going after him.

What's it like, Steeky? I have them tortured, don't I? Finty said, proudly.

Steeky shook his head. He's fucking nuts, he said.

He didn't have to tell me. I had known Finty since I was a kid. Mairéad had too. We knew exactly what he was like.

If you're ever looking for a job, come to me, he said. I'll get you sorted.

I don't know why he thought chasing tourists around the town nine hours a day for no fixed wage was something I'd want to do. I'd rather be on the bru, I said, and he nudged me with his elbow.

Aye, but sure, you love a scrap, don't you?

Nah, not really. Why would you say that?

Wee birdies tell stories, he said, winking.

Who? Who's telling stories?

But Finty had turned his attention to Mairéad. He had just recognized her.

Mairéad Riley, Jesus Christ, what happened to you?

I stopped knocking about with dipsos like you, Finty. What about it?

Finty grinned, loving her cheek. What're you doing with this cunt then? he said.

We didn't plan on drinking as much as we did that day, but the weather was good and there were plenty of bars with decent beer gardens that got busier as the afternoon wore on. That meant we could save a few quid and swipe whatever pints were left behind by people heading on somewhere else. Mairéad wasn't sure at first, it seemed a bit miserly to her, and she didn't know what kind of germs could be festering around the rims of other people's glasses. Then she began to work around her reservations, leaning more towards drinks left behind by women, or good-looking lads. Strictly no nose pickers or arse scratchers, no sweaty older men, and nothing that had been left in the sun too long. Not until later in the afternoon, when Mairéad's inhibitions fell away completely. She planted herself next to a group of middle-aged men and said, You gonna drink these pints or wha?

Two buffed-up bouncers in short-sleeved shirts guided us out the doors.

Roid heads, Mairéad shouted. Protein-drinking cunts.

We got a pizza from Little Italy and ate it on the steps outside the Europa. It was great, the two of us just sitting there, gnawing crusts, catching mozzarella, fighting over the garlic dip. Sitting at the other end of the steps was a group of women mixing vodka with Coke they drank straight from the bottle; they were all steaming. One of them smiled and waved in my direction. I thought she was waving at me and was about to wave back when Mairéad grabbed me by the arm and said, Look. I twisted round in my seat and watched as a blue car with a mad-looking contraption built on to its roof drove along Great Victoria Street.

Is that a camera? I said.

It's the Google Street View car. We're gonna be on Google Maps.

We went for a piss in the train station toilets, then we paid for two singles to Balmoral, with plans to go back to the flat and drink the beers we bought from the off-licence across the road. We got very cosy on that train, the two of us slouched with our feet up on the empty seats, joking around, messing about. Flirting, like when we were kids. Neither of us realized where the train was headed until Mairéad saw the sign at Central Station, the opposite direction from where we were supposed to be going, and jumped out of her seat.

Oh my God, we're going to Holywood, she said.

We may as well have got off the train in a different country, it was like a holiday resort up there, with the promenade and the waterfront and the beautiful houses overlooking the lough. We were half lit, walking along the stony beach, staring around like what the fuck are we doing here, and laughing. Mairéad with her jeans rolled up, paddling her feet in the water, telling me to come on, take your shoes off, it's great, and stepping hesitantly forward. I looked across the lough at the hills, then I looked towards the city and saw the yellow cranes in the distance. Mairéad waded further out, then she stopped and came back, pulled her jeans and her top off and went in in her underwear.

Mon, she said. Stop being a wuss.

What about our stuff?

Just leave it, it'll be sweet.

It's freezing, Mairéad.

No, it's not. It's lovely. Come on.

I pulled my trousers off, then the shirt and tie I had worn to court, and waded into the shallows in white boxers I regretted wearing as soon as the water came up over my waist. I wasn't much of a swimmer. I said this to Mairéad and she came back from the deeper water and swam up and down beside me. I moved from foot to foot and sort of flapped my hands around, but I was splashing all over the place and felt a bit stupid. Mairéad climbed up on to my back and tried to dunk me, but I wouldn't let her. She ended up just sort of hanging there, with her arms around my neck.

This water's stinking, she said. Take me back to the beach.

She wrapped her legs around my waist and refused to climb down until I had carried her all the way back to her clothes. She pulled her top on and dried herself with her jeans. I dried myself with my shirt and put my trousers and socks on. For a while we sat on the sand, drinking those beers we bought. Mairéad hugged her knees to her chest and watched the sun ripple across the surface of the lough. The few dog walkers I could see were further along the beach, close to the park. There was nobody else about.

I thought I was going to jail, I said.

Mairéad looked at me. The sun was in her eyes; she had to squint.

Swear to God, I thought that was it. My barrister was talking all this shite about my education and all, he was begging the judge not to put me away. He said I had a degree and that I was gonna write a book —

That's what saved you, Mairéad said.

I sighed, stared at the sand between my feet. I should've just stayed in Liverpool, I said.

You don't have to be in Liverpool to stay out of trouble.

I reckon I do.

Mairéad sucked air through her teeth. Well, I was worse than you and I can tell you, you don't, she said.

It was true; if there was anyone I thought would end up in jail somewhere down the line, it was Mairéad. She was mad as fuck when we were young, always fighting, always getting into all sorts of trouble with the peelers, and she had the stickiest fingers in Belfast — the wee girl couldn't walk into a shop without swiping something. It was mad that she had ended up in Queen's. It was even madder that she had turned out the way she had, with the tattoos and all, and all the things she was into, the films, the music. No Happy Hardcore any more. No 'Donk In The Dark'. It was all Bob Dylan and Joni Mitchell. How did that even happen? I said, laughing.

Mairéad shrugged. She leaned with her hands in the sand.

I made new friends, she said.

The walk from the train station to the flat was long and cold – our clothes were wet from the beach and we were shivering. Mairéad made me put my arm around her. Then she tried to slip her hand into my pocket for warmth. My instinct told me she was going for my balls and my body reacted accordingly: I jumped backwards out of the way. Mairéad thought it was hilarious. She was all, What's the matter? Have you got the tickles? and tried to reach again. I yelped and pulled away; it was a reflex. She killed herself laughing.

I already saw it anyway, she said.

Did you fuck.

I did. The cold water didn't do you any favours.

It never does.

Mairéad giggled. Want me to warm it up?

Warm what up?

She reached again, less aggressively. I pulled away.

What? My hands aren't cold any more, she said.

If I did that to you, it would be a different story.

Would it?

We had stopped outside the block. Mairéad was staring at me.

Go ahead, she said.

What?

Touch me.

Your bag's in the way.

I didn't mean my tits.

I moved my hand, but couldn't. Mairéad took it and placed it between her legs.

Rub it, she said.

You're nuts.

Go on. Do it.

I did what I was told. She closed her eyes. The street lights made her face yellow.

You're getting hard, she said.

Her hand was on it and she was squeezing softly. I moaned, tried to kiss her, and she turned her head away.

None of that now, she said.

She took me by the hand and led me into the block. It was like we were kids again, when we would lie in the long grass, touching each other. Making ourselves come. We had no idea about anything back then, we were too young, and it was all curiosity. Now it was something else.

The hallway light was broken. I dropped my keys on the floor.

Gimme, I'll do it, Mairéad said, and sure enough, she found the keyhole easily, with no effort at all, and stepped into the flat, kicked her Converse off and strolled into my bedroom. By the time I finished digging through my drawers for the comfy clothes she demanded, she had taken her clothes off and was standing next to my bed in her bra and knickers. I didn't know where to look, if I should look. Not that I'm shy, but the way she stared at me from the other side of the room made me feel like I was doing something wrong.

Let's just get into bed, she said.

We lay for a minute without saying anything really, then Mairéad turned to me. This can't be anything other than what it is, she said.

That's okay.

Okay. Well.

She kissed me. I kissed her back and it was awkward, our arms clamped around each other, then we broke apart.

It's like being a kid again, isn't it? she said.

Yeah, it is.

She rolled on to her back and stared at the ceiling, then she reached behind her and said, This is doing my head in, and unhooked her bra. She pulled it out from under the blanket and dropped it on the floor.

Come here, she said.

For a while that was how it was, Mairéad guiding me carefully through, then she said, Fuck me, in a way that was neither an instruction nor a command. More a sigh of approval I took literally and acted on in a way that could've gone horribly wrong, but didn't.

I need a towel, Mairéad said, when we finished.

I handed her one from the radiator and she used it to wipe the come off her belly. It was funny, the way she lay there with both hands on the towel, breathing heavily. She smelled like the sea.

I need to set an alarm, she said. I need to go to work.

She started work at nine but had to be up earlier so she could go back to her mate's gaff and get a shower. She wouldn't wash herself over the sink even when I boiled the kettle at seven o'clock in the morning and carried it into the bathroom for her. She didn't think a cowboy wash was a proper wash, and when I told her it was sweet, I've been doing it for about a year, her mouth fell open.

When was the last time you had a shower?

About two weeks ago, I said, and she heaved.

You need to sort that out, Sean. That's unbelievable.

I went back into my room after Mairéad had gone and saw that she had left that leather chest bag hanging off the back of my desk chair. Inside it was her make-up, a stick of deodorant, a bottle of hand sanitizer, a Muji pen and a Moleskine that was the same as the one I used to have when I lived in Liverpool, but smaller. The pages were filled with lines she had written and then scribbled out, reconfigured into other lines, and gathered into poems. I read one after another until the sun glared through the window, then I fell asleep.

8

One day, early in the morning when Ryan hadn't weighed home from the night before, when I had just woken up and wasn't sure if getting out of bed was a good idea, the door knocked and I answered without thinking to a woman in a suit. She looked at me then looked at the number on the door as if to make sure she had come to the right place. She had, and she told me who she was: so-and-so from something-or-other. A bank maybe. She asked if I lived there and I said I did.

Been here a year, I said.

Are you paying rent?

Of course I was paying rent. Five-fifty a month, I lied.

The woman explained the situation like she was breaking the worst news. The property is to be taken and closed off at the end of October, she said. Do you have somewhere else you can go?

Not really. No.

The woman shrugged, plucked a pen from her inside pocket, and asked my name. I said the first name that came into my head and forgot what it was the second she confirmed how much rent I'd been paying and for how long.

Can I ask if you're employed?

Aye. Well, self-employed. I'm a writer.

So you're not receiving any benefits?

No.

I expected her to ask me about the kind of things I wrote about.

Instead she handed me a card with the number of the man who would be doing the repossessing. She told me to speak to him, he might be able to hold off for a week or two if I needed more time. Then she tucked her clipboard back under her arm and, with one last glance at the number on the door, turned on her heel, and was gone.

That day in court, when the judge closed my case, my barrister told me I needed to be careful not to reoffend. I hadn't really listened to him – I was still trying to recover from the whole thing – but I wasn't stupid. I knew how close I'd come, and there was no way I wanted to be pulled up in front of that judge again. Then Ryan laid it out for me. We had less than a month to source enough cash for rent and deposit for a new gaff, we were talking the guts of a grand here, and that was for the few places that weren't asking for bank statements and references and proof of employment. There was no way we were making that much money on the bar. Even if we put ourselves forward for every day shift going, we would still fall short, and it wasn't like we could tap someone – we owed everyone we knew money, including our mas. The only hope we had was to dip into the tills in work. This was Ryan's idea. Out of the two of us, he had the most to lose. His ma wouldn't take him in. Neither would his da. His granny might, but there was no guarantee. I tried to talk him out of it. We could try and get another job, I said.

There's no jobs going, Sean. We've looked everywhere, and even if we found somewhere that would take us on, by the time we get paid it'll be too late. We'll be out on our holes.

What if we get caught though?

The worst they can do is sack us.

They might press charges.

Nah, too much effort. They wouldn't be arsed.

Dee would. Dee would go out of his way to fuck us over.

Ryan thought about this, but it wasn't enough to put him off.

I know a wee trick, he said. You don't even have to dip the till, and they've no way of knowing what's happening, they can't see it on the cameras. Trust me. I'll show you how it's done.

Thursday nights were student nights. Ryan and I took our usual tills at the end of the bar and worked our way through the swarm of baby-faced punters squealing over the countertop. Girls dolled up to the nines with their hair and their eyeshadow leaned with their chests across the sticky counter, all beautiful, all there to dance and laugh and maybe sneak a kiss. At midnight, I poured four vodkas for a weary-looking lad in a chequered shirt. He handed me a tenner like it was a high-five, but I didn't ring it into the till. I didn't even acknowledge taking it. I scrunched the note into my hand, held it with the two fingers I didn't use to hook the neck of the vodka bottle, and moved on to the next customer, whose order I took as I plucked a napkin from the container beside the straws and blew my nose even though there were no snots to be blown. I buried the note in the napkin before slipping it into my back pocket, and that was it. That's all I had to do. The till wasn't down, and anybody watching the cameras – nobody was ever watching the cameras – wouldn't pick it up.

An hour before the lights came on, I sneaked into the toilets and transferred the cash from my pocket to my sock where it felt like a tumour growing out of my ankle. All through clean-up it was there, itching as I mopped the floor. When we were finished, we had to sit in the lounge and wait on Dee counting the tills. He refused to let anybody leave until everything was in order, and he made a point of bollocking people every time their tills were down. Most clubs overlooked the odd ten or twenty quid. Not Dee. He made a point of docking it from people's wages, if he could trace it back. That night was no different. He stormed out of his office at three o'clock in the morning with a receipt that was so long it dragged along the floor.

Tills are down two hundred quid, he said.

There was an intake of breath. Two hundred quid was too much to pass off as a mistake. You couldn't undercharge that many people if you tried. Dee was livid. He went around the room one staff member at a time and made us empty our pockets. Didn't matter which floor you were working on, he had everybody turning their wallets and their purses inside out. The first person to refuse would become a suspect, and if they didn't cave under the pressure, Dee would send them packing whether they had stolen the money or not, simple as that. One after another, we did what we were told, and it was getting tense, people weren't happy about how they were being singled out. Then it came round to me. I took everything out and set it on the table in front of him. There was a ten-pound note, a few coins, my wallet, keys and phone. Dee stared like he was trying to connect the dots, and then he moved on to Ryan, and as soon as Ryan took his hand out of his pocket I knew he was caught; you could see it right there, fattening his wallet. Hundred and fifty quid, cash. He counted right in front of Dee, calm as you like, and said he won it on an accumulator. I actually won four hundred and sixty, he said. But sure you know yourself. Big weekend.

It was hard to tell even when you knew, Ryan was that good at lying, and the way he just threw it out there, like you could take it or leave it, somehow made him more persuasive.

Dee wasn't biting. I don't believe a word you say, he said.

Fair enough, don't. But this is my money.

Ryan picked the cash up off the table and put it back in his wallet. Check the cameras, he said. See for yourself.

Oh, I'll be checking the cameras, and if I see anything –

At that moment, one of the supervisors came out of Dee's office and told him she had done a recount. The tills weren't down, there had been a mistake. She showed him the till-read. People cracked up at Dee for accusing them, the floor staff especially, who didn't even have access to the tills but had been made to empty their pockets like everyone else, and that distracted him from Ryan, who sauntered towards the doors with a big smile on his face.

What'd I tell you? he said to me. Wee buns.

*

Finty whaled into the flat that night at four o'clock in the morning. He was blocked out of his head, steaming like, and he was in one of those states where everything he did took twice as much effort. Buttoning his jeans after taking a piss, putting his phone on charge, opening the case of beer that was already open – all he had to do was pull the flap back. Inside the box was one bottle of Bud. He popped the lid with his teeth.

Now, he said, with a smile. Who would like some cocaine?

I knew this was Ryan's doing, he had been planning it all night, and he never said a word to me about it because he knew I would say no. I had been saying no a lot lately and it was melting Ryan's head. He wanted to bring people back. He wanted to stay up all night getting wiped out. I told him we'd never save enough money for a new place if we kept going on the rip. But Ryan couldn't think that far ahead. He only saw what was in front of him, and that night it was a big bag of gear. He had it chopped up nicely and was holding the plate out to me, like a gift.

Wee toot? he said, grinning in that way he did, like he knew.

In my head, I was raging at him. He knew I was trying to stay off it, and I knew he was trying to make me cave for that exact reason. It was like that time Finty was on the straight and narrow, when he was doing deliveries for Golden Bell. We ordered a delivery to Dootzy's flat one night we were on the rip, and when Finty came to the door, we dragged him in and filled him with gear. He got the sack for not showing up for the rest of his shift, but it was a lethal night, we had a ball. The same thing was happening now. What I had forgotten was how funny it is when somebody breaks, when they see the gear cut up all lovely and neat like that and think, fuck it, why not?

I took the plate and hoofed the biggest line I could see. Just like that, it was party time. Ryan connected his phone to his Bluetooth speaker and put on some nineties dance music. He turned it up as loud as it went and listened with the kind of misty-eyed nostalgia that would make you think he was there, in 1994, bopping it out to Altern-8 and Praga Khan.

Remember this one? he said.

The first mistake I made was taking the gear. The second was sending Mairéad a message telling her what I was doing:

You never stop wee lad
Who you with? the reprobates?

Oh aye
Your best mate Finty's here
he said mon up and party with us

tell him no thank you
id rather drown

lol
what you doing up at this time anyway?

She didn't reply, and after a while, she went offline. I kept checking anyway, just in case.

She has you by the balls, Ryan said.

Does she fuck. We're just mates.

Mates my hole. Every time your phone goes you near jump out of your seat.

I'd jump out of my seat for Mairéad Riley any day, Finty said.

She's stuck up as fuck, Ryan said. The way she carries on. Look at the hack of her profile picture. He showed Finty, and Finty raised his eyebrows. What's the craic with the black and white?

She thinks she's a model, Finty said.

Still would, wouldn't you?

Oh, aye. I'd buck the hole clean off her.

You'd buck a hole in the ground, I said, and that made everyone laugh.

You know who she's living with though, don't you? Ryan said.

I knew by his voice that the obvious answer was the wrong one, so I waited for him to tell me. He was more than happy to, as soon as he poured a vodka he took his time to dilute with orange cordial and, with a smack of his lips, sank in three large gulps. Ahh, he said, and then: She's been living with some posh wank from her course, down the Holylands.

How do you know?

You know yourself, wee son. Word gets about. Isn't that right, Finty?

Finty nodded pensively, as if Ryan had imparted some great wisdom.

You're not wrong, mate. No smoke without fire.

And there's a lot of smoke, Ryan said.

How do you know she's not living in her ma's?

Because she hasn't stayed in her ma's in months, has she, Finty?

I haven't seen her and I live across the street.

That's because she's down the Holylands, getting bucked.

Finty choked on his beer. Getting bucked, he said, shaking his head.

I told Ryan he was talking shite. He chuckled and said, Aye, right, okay, and rolled his eyes. I tried a different tack.

Just because she's living with a lad, doesn't mean they're riding, I said.

There was a staggered silence, then Ryan and Finty burst out laughing.

What else do you think they're doing? Ryan said.

They could just be mates.

This buckled them. They were holding their stomachs, tears streaming down their faces, laughing their balls off. Fuck me, Sean, Ryan said. For all your education, you can be a dopey bastard sometimes.

*

We talked our way into the morning. The same stories with the same punchlines we told the last time we were on the rip, and the time before that. And it wasn't like we didn't know that we were repeating ourselves. In fact, having already told the stories before contributed to the buzz we got from hearing them again. We helped each other out, correcting details, reminding the teller of certain events, but also, and most importantly, we were coked off our nuts. Didn't matter what anybody said really, as long as the subject matter was consistent: stupid stuff we got up to when we were kids, fights we'd been in, football teams we'd played for, and of course, the serious stuff. The early-morning heavy talk we hadn't got round to just yet, but which was on the horizon. I sensed it when Finty started talking about his da. He had a reputation as a bit of a hard man, and all the stories Finty told lived up to the things we had already heard: that he was somebody you didn't fuck with. We were in awe of him in that way. Then Finty told us about the time his da caught him sniffing glue and beat him so badly he broke his arm.

He broke your arm? I said.

Aye, fuck sake. Clean break.

How old were you?

About thirteen, wasn't I?

Aye, thirteen, Ryan said. It wasn't long after that kid threw himself off the footbridge, remember?

You okay like? I said, and Finty, looking aghast, leaned over the plate and cut more lines.

I'm sweet, are you sweet?

He glanced at Ryan. Ryan chuckled and tried to sling his arm round me. I shrugged him off and said, Stop mucking about, will you? He held his hands up defensively, as if I had threatened him, and backed off to the other end of the settee.

Do you still see your da? I said.

Do I fuck. He's paranoid out of his mind. Goes to bed with a hammer and everything.

A hammer?

He's convinced the Brits are coming to get him, the nut. I came home one night and he was walking up and down the living room, mumbling all sorts of madness about some screw from Long Kesh.

Was your da in Long Kesh?

My da? Fuck sake, Sean. Do you even know me?

I only knew what I had heard, and what Finty had alluded to every once in a while, but he never spoke about it.

My da did seven years for possession of a weapon, he said.

He was serious now, and he was sitting very still.

Does he talk about it? I said.

Does he fuck. He locks himself in the bathroom and cries.

Finty leaned forward to take a line, but he was all over the place, shaking, and he couldn't find his nostril. Ryan had to help him. We laughed about it, but it wasn't good. Finty was in a bad way.

They can shove their United Ireland up their hole, Ryan said.

Here, no call for that now, Finty said.

What? They saunter about the place like they're heroes.

Are they not?

Fuck sake, Finty. Can you not see for yourself?

Finty chuckled, but he looked confused. My da's a doorman, he said.

What about you, Finty? What do you do for a living?

I chase tourists about the town and push them on to buses, and I sell a wee bit of toot to keep me ticking, he said, with a wink.

But you shouldn't have to sell gear, should you?

Why not? Easy money, isn't it?

Ryan agreed, it was. He came at it from another angle.

Look at how many of our mates were two or three years into their apprenticeships and got laid off as soon as the recession hit. They didn't go to Australia because they wanted to, they had to, fuck sake.

I was a bricky, Finty said.

Exactly, and every taxi driver on the road used to be a foreman.

What's that got to do with anything?

Ryan turned to me and said, Look at Sean. He went to Liverpool and got his degree, and fair play to you, there's no chance I could do that. But like, you thought that was it, you got your education and all, but sure what difference has it made? And it's shite because you did well, and I'm not trying to be a dick here, you got further than any of us could. But you're no better for it. You're exactly where we are, and sure where the fuck are we?

Nowhere, I said.

Exactly, so what chance do we have?

Finty agreed, we were all fucked, but he couldn't get past what Ryan had said before, about the Provies. Ryan had to explain that he wasn't having a go at his da for what he'd done during the conflict, but he hated what the war had done to him, and hundreds of people like him, men and women who had fought for all that time, who had done things they would have to live with for the rest of their lives, and for what? The same settlement they were offered back in 1973, Ryan said, pointing with his finger now, getting all riled up. That's what they signed off on in 1998, the same shite they wouldn't have wiped their arses with forty years ago, and you wonder why people call the Shinners sell-outs? The cunts settled for the status quo, and look where it's left us. Look where it's left your da, and everybody else's da. They're all fucked in the head. Go into any bar about the road and you'll see them sitting there, nursing pints. Talking all sorts of balls about what they did for their country, and no wonder. The shit they've seen. My da's just as bad. You know yourself. Paranoid out of his mind. Can't leave the house without thinking someone's gonna kill him. He lost two brothers, fuck sake. What do you expect?

Finty shook his head and looked away. Ryan told him to forget about it, change the subject. But he was all right. He had just remembered something his da told him, years ago, about how he would hear footsteps coming along the corridor outside his cell and pray the screws weren't coming for him. That was the worst thing, all that dread that hung over him, then hearing the door unlock and not knowing if he would be trailed down the hall like he was every other day, and beaten. That's what keeps Finty's da up at night. He still hears that sound, the footsteps coming along the corridor, the keys in the door.

My da was only sixteen when he was brought in, and they targeted the younger ones because they thought they could break them so . . .

His voice trailed off. His eyes dropped.

Do you reckon he regrets it? I said.

There was a pause. Glances were exchanged, but not with me.

Regrets what?

Like, the things he's done to you. Breaking your arm and all.

Finty shrugged. His eyes had gone all heavy. He had that deadened look you see in people who have been through some bad stuff in their lives, when it all just sort of sits there, in your head.

Right, that's enough of this morbid shit, Ryan said.

I looked at Finty and could tell he agreed with Ryan but wouldn't say either way because that's the way he was. I said, Right, okay, and apologized for bringing it up. I also said, There's nothing wrong with talking about things, and Ryan agreed, As long as it doesn't ruin everybody's night, he said, which made Finty laugh. It annoyed me, the way they did that. I had hardly said a word. I was just sitting there, listening, but they were getting on like I was to blame. That's why I never said anything, because any time I did, I had the feeling that they didn't want to hear it. So I went quiet. I drank vodka, I took lines, but I hardly contributed, and it carried on that way right through the morning. At nine o'clock, Ryan was waffling on about the conspiracy theory documentaries he had become obsessed with after watching a film about Bob Lazar one night he was stoned out of his head. He fell into a YouTube hole so deep he came out the other end convinced the moon landings didn't happen. I closed my eyes and heard his voice as if from the other end of a tunnel. The tunnel was long and dark. I felt like I was being pulled through.

There's no stars. Look for yourself, they're not there.

Too right they're not, it's daytime, Finty said.

The blinds were open. I squinted to check the mountain for messages but it was too bright.

Is there anything written up there? I said.

Ryan pushed the blinds aside. Do you want me to spell it out for you?

Aye, go ahead.

Y-O-U-R-G-A-Y.

You spelled it wrong, I said.

Listen to Mr University here, giving me English lessons now.

At ten o'clock, Finty put on 'Joe McDonnell'. The three of us were sprawled across the settee with our arms round each other, singing every word. When it came to the part that said, 'And you dared to call me a terrorist while you looked down your gun,' we staggered to our feet in the middle of the living room and belted out the chorus. That was the start of it, and for the next hour, Finty played one rebel song after another: 'Come Out, Ye Black and Tans!', 'A Nation Once Again', 'The Broad Black Brimmer' and of course 'Grace', which we sang with tears in our eyes, and big lines of coke we blasted during the second verse.

By noon, we had settled down again. There was hardly any gear left so we started taking keys to ration it out. I went for a piss, and when I came back, Ryan had a pen and paper and was writing something down.

What're you doing? I said.

We're trying to remember everyone who's bucked Mairéad Riley.

He held the page up to show me. The list was long. It went right down to the bottom line. I snatched it off him. He held his hands up as if to say, *wow, take it easy*, but he was laughing.

Come on now, Sean. She stole half the virginities in Twinbrook, he said.

What's that got to do with anything?

Nothing. Doesn't matter.

No, seriously. Why do you keep going on about it?

Take it easy, Finty said. He's just saying –

He's just saying what? What're you saying?

Mate, I hate to be the one to tell you this, but the wee girl's a slut.

What?

Mairéad. She's a slut.

He was smiling, as if daring me to do something about it, so I lunged across the settee and grabbed him by the throat. Finty tried to pull us apart, but he was out of it, he could hardly stand, and we were on the floor now. Ryan was on top of me; he was strong as fuck. We rolled into the table and knocked everything over: bottles, glasses, plate. Finty was squealing, Watch the gear, watch the gear! I don't know how I got him, it happened fast, but also in slow motion – that's the way it is when you're fighting, you can see every-thing. He tried to pin me down with one hand and punch me with the other, but I pulled that hand away and used it to push out from under him. He took two digs, one that busted his nose, another that glanced off his forehead. But before I could do any real damage, Finty got a good grip around my waist and trailed me backwards across the room.

Ryan jumped to his feet but stayed where he was behind the coffee table. His nose was bleeding, there was blood all over his chin. There was no call for that, Sean, Jesus Christ, he said, looking down at his shirt.

No call? You've been acting a dickhead all night.

I have? Fuck sake, Sean, you've been itching for a scrap since we sat down.

Itching? You're lucky I don't break your fucking jaw.

I called him outside. Let's go, fair dig, I said. But Ryan, as if he knew how much I would regret this, looked at me with amusement, then a kind of pity.

Take it easy, he said. It's done.

He lowered himself on to the settee with his head tilted back to stop the blood from gushing down. Finty was on his knees with a bank card, scraping, trying to gather up the powder that had been spilled. But the floor was stinking, there was gear everywhere.

We may get another bag, he said.

9

I woke up feeling like I had been pulled out of somewhere deep. The door was at the wrong side of the room. I reached with my foot to find the ladder and realized I didn't have the bunk bed with the settee under it any more, and this wasn't my childhood home. I saw my coat hanging from the back of the door and had to turn the lamp on to make sure it wasn't a man standing there, watching me. I was shaking. I couldn't remember falling asleep, and that freaked me out. The hours that had gone by, a whole afternoon on my own in the empty flat.

I dragged my blanket into the living room and let the TV laugh for me. Then I rang the Chinese at the top of the road and ordered a chicken curry with no peas or onions, half chips, half fried rice, a portion of prawn crackers and a tin of Coke. I ate what I could, but my stomach was in bits. I had diarrhoea, and then the shakes got worse. I curled up under the blanket and shivered. My heart was going like mad, the sweat was lashing off me, and I kept getting shooting pains in my arms and legs. That's when I started to panic. The room was like a hole in the ground that I had fallen down into. There was no rope, no ladder, and no matter how much I tried to dig my hands into the mud, the earth wouldn't hold my weight. I fell back down into the darkness. When I woke up, I was overcome with emotion. I sat up on the settee and took deep breaths through my nose and out my mouth.

Through the blinds, the sky had darkened. The minutes leading up to what was supposed to be the start of my shift ticked slowly by. I'll sort it out tomorrow, I told myself. I'll make up the kind of excuse that would turn Dee's rage into sympathy – some kind of accident, someone close to me dying.

I didn't expect him to ring me. His name flashed across the screen.

DEE WORK

I could say my battery had died. I could say that ringing him was the last thing I was thinking while this terrible thing that had happened was happening. I could say any number of things, but the amount of times I'd been food poisoned, or injured at five-a-side. It didn't matter how much I hated the job, losing it would leave me worse off than I was now.

I held my phone to my ear. I could feel my heart at the back of my throat.

Dee, you're not gonna believe this. I was driving down the road with my brother there and a car pulled out and rammed into the back of us. I'm in A&E here. I'm okay, but he's wrecked his neck. Think it might be whiplash.

What about Ryan? Was he in the boot?

I haven't heard from Ryan.

Right, well. You tell Ryan when you see him that he's sacked.

Look, Dee, I'm really sorry. I should've rung –

No, Sean. You should've come into work. That's you done.

Please, mate. Swear to God, this is the last time. I'll come in. I'll leave the hospital right now and get a taxi down.

But Dee had hung up.

I messaged Ryan and told him. He tried to ring me, but I was on my knees on the bathroom floor puking up clumps of undigested rice. I splashed my face with water and leaned with my hands on the sink. I was sweating, but I was cold. My lips were chapped to bits.

Did he definitely say I was sacked?

                                            Aye definitely

ah well
Hows the head?

                                                      Sore
                              you rabbit-punched the fuck out of me

I think you broke my nose

                                    you deserved it ya cunt

Lol
You coming up
we've a bag of pure here

                                                  where r u

finty's
mon

                                        I'm in a bad way

He didn't message back.

I didn't want to think about this stuff, it wasn't good for me, and
the more I thought about it the worse I felt. I replayed the night
before, all the things I had said and done looping around me like a
tightening rope, leading me back to that morning after my ma's
thirty-eighth birthday. My granny woke me up and told me my
granda was going to drive me home even though my house was
only round the corner. I had just turned ten, and I was sitting in the
passenger seat watching the sun coming through the trees, wonder-
ing if someone had died.

My ma was waiting for me in the living room. She was wearing a housecoat over the clothes she had worn the night before, and she was hugging her knees to her chest. The living room smelled like fegs and drink, and as I walked across the lino floor, the bottoms of my guddies made a sound like Velcro. None of this made sense. The house was usually spotless for me coming home. Didn't matter how big the party had been the night before, my ma would be up at the crack of dawn destroying all evidence that anybody had been there. She did this because I was still a child and it was important for her to keep the house looking the way it was supposed to. But she was just sitting on the settee that morning, sniffling, dabbing her eyes with tissue. Ignoring the mess around her.

I sat on the chair closest to the window and waited for her to steady herself. As I waited, I imagined what it would be like if somebody close to me had died. To be that person in school who carried an aura of tragedy. The boy every teacher paid extra attention to, whose identity hinged on this one defining instance of loss.

I need to ask you something, son, and I want you to tell me the truth, okay?

Okay, I said, confused now, uncertain about how these conversations went. Nobody had ever died before so there was nothing to refer back to, no blueprint.

My ma looked at me like the sight of me physically hurt her.

I need to know if your daddy has ever done anything to you, she said. Has he ever hurt you in any way?

I had to take a second and wrap my head around the question I was being asked. Did my daddy hurt me? No. He shouted and he bawled, but he only ever raised his hand threateningly. Why was my ma asking about that though? What did it have to do with death?

He's never done anything else, has he? my ma said. He hasn't laid a hand on you?

No, Mummy.

Are you sure? Are you positive, son?

I shook my head, no, then I realized what I was doing and said,

Yes, I'm positive. At the other side of the room, the kitchen door was open. The light coming through the window made a shadow on the floor.

Your daddy did terrible things to Anthony when Anthony was a wee boy, my ma said. He touched him, and . . . She trailed off. That word, 'touched'. I knew what it meant. It couldn't mean anything else. I swore nothing like that had ever happened. I held my right hand up to God.

Are you sure? Are you definitely sure?

She covered her face with her hands and her hair came down over her wrists. I'm sorry, son, she said. But your daddy, you can't see him any more.

The door to the hallway opened. Anthony stopped dead.

Did you tell him? Jesus Christ, what'd you tell him?

I had to, son. I had to know.

What the fuck did you say?

I didn't say anything. I just asked him. I didn't tell.

She was in a state, crying, and that annoyed Anthony for some reason. Fucking stop, will you? he said, but my ma couldn't. She was in bits.

I'm sorry, son. I'm so sorry.

It was Anthony who told me to go upstairs to my room, he needed to talk to our ma, he said. He wouldn't look at me. Even when I stood up and walked past him, he dropped his head, turned away.

I closed my bedroom door behind me and stood for a while with my back against the wall, listening to their voices below, then I turned my PlayStation on and climbed up on to the top bunk, to the bed, and played *Metal Gear Solid*. It was my favourite game, I had clocked it eight times, and now I was trying to do it without shooting anybody, just sneaking. Disposing of my enemies through stealth. I was hiding under a box, waiting for the right moment to pounce, when my bedroom door opened. Anthony walked over to the ladder and took the first step so he was level with me.

You all good? he said.

Aye, all good.

What're you playing?

Metal Gear Solid.

Let's see.

He climbed up on to the bed next to me, and for a while he just sat there, watching me. Then he put his arm around me and kissed me on the side of the head.

You're good at this, he said.

PART TWO

The junk is sinking back into the sleech and muck.
Ciaran Carson

10

The night before my first shift at community service, I was up all night thinking about what I would do if someone broke into the flat and tried to kill me. I tried to imagine what I would do to save myself, and because I was thinking about this with my eyes closed, I saw a man coming into my bedroom, and the gun – it was always a gun. Then it was, what if I jump out the window? What if I hide under the bed? What if I push past him and there are more men outside, waiting on me?

I ran through every possible outcome. It never ended well.

In the early hours, I heard the rain against the window. All my work clothes were laid out: the high-vis bib and weatherproofs my probation officer had given me the week before, my steel toe-capped boots, which I put on over a pair of thick black socks. I splashed my face with water and tried to put contact lenses in, but no matter how much I fiddled around with them they wouldn't set. I ended up walking up the road at half seven in the morning wearing glasses I couldn't wipe on weatherproofs that weren't the right material; the rain had them soaked, and every time a car drove by headlights gleamed through the raindrops and made everything yellow.

It took ten minutes to walk up to Milltown, and when I got there I didn't know where to go. There was a yard round the side of the building at the front of the cemetery and in the yard was one of those huts you see on building sites, the green ones that look like shipping containers that have been fitted out. The door was open, but it was dark inside. I could just about make out the shape of a man sitting on a bench with his back against the wall.

Is Joe here? I said.

The man didn't say anything. He was sitting very still.

I was halfway across the yard, gunning for the gates, when the Portaloo door swung open. A tall, skinny man with a head like a pinball stepped out. He was wearing jeans he hadn't bothered to button and an orange high-vis coat with a hood that bunched up around his neck. Who're you? he said to me, and when I told him, he glared at me and said, Who told you to come here? I told him my probation officer had, Wendy. He took me into his office and made a real show of leaning all the way back in his leather high-backed chair.

How many hours? he said.

Two hundred.

Have you been given all your gear?

Think so, aye.

Boots?

I looked down at my feet.

Aye.

Don't come anywhere near this site without them.

Okay.

There were some forms I had to sign, then he brought me back to the hut. The man I had seen sitting in the dark had been joined now by other men. They staggered into the rain like they had been ordered to their deaths, and lifted litter picks and black bin bags from the wheelbarrow Joe had parked in the middle of the yard. It was a mixed crowd, old and young, and they all had that same jaded look about them, like they had been there half their lives.

Right, let's go, Joe said.

I followed the lead of the other men and kept my eyes on the ground, picking up crisp bags, empty bottles, old pieces of knotted string, my black bag bunching up and twisting in the wind. The rain was in my face. It was hard to see with my glasses on, but then the rain died down and it wasn't too bad. Joe let us do our own thing as long as we didn't stray too far. I stuck to the pathways as much as I could; I didn't feel right about walking over the graves. I vaguely remembered going to a funeral when I was a kid and being told this was something you weren't supposed to do. I stretched, leaned with my hand on the closest head-stone to reach a bunch of plastic flowers that had been chopped to pieces and were scattered all over the grass. On the headstone there was a picture of a man who had died in 1992. There was a tricolour on a plinth next to it, and beside his name, the word *Óglach*: young warrior.

We were given a smoke break at ten o'clock. Fegs were lit, drags taken. The man sitting closest to me was halfway through his second smoke by the time everyone else had finished their first. He flicked his butt into the grass and leaned with his elbows on his thighs.

So what'd you do? he said to me.

I just cleared down around those graves there, the one with the angel –

I mean to get here, what'd you do?

Oh, assault. I got done for assault.

Who'd you assault?

Some fella at a house party.

The man spat on the ground between his feet. I looked down and saw blood.

See that? he said, pointing. That means you'll be clearing the rub-bish from my grave soon. He saw the look on my face and laughed. Don't worry, he said, wiping the slabbers from his mouth. I'll have plenty of company.

He sparked up another feg, that was his third in ten minutes, and you could smell it on him, that horrible smell heavy smokers carry.

Have you any relatives buried here? he said.

Think my great-granda's here, and my great-aunts.

Nobody close to you?

Nah, not yet, I said, and he leaned in to me.

You've all that to look forward to then, he said, with a grin.

Across the way, the graves were facing the same direction we were so that the backs of the saintly statues fixed on top of the more elaborate memorials looked like they were congregating across the field to witness some kind of event. I asked the man what he had done to end up there. He blew smoke through his nose and stared across the cemetery.

All sorts of things, he said.

There was another smoke break at eleven, and at twelve we headed back to the hut for lunch. I sat in the corner and watched as the other men pulled their weatherproofs off and hung them above the electric heater. The kettle was boiled, cups of tea handed out, and Joe, popping his head in to make sure we were all there, told us we wouldn't be going out again any time soon. The rain was back on, the roof of the hut was getting pelted, and the wind made the windows shake. I closed my eyes and tried to sleep like the rest of the men, but I couldn't get any heat into me. Didn't matter that I had three layers on; the draught whistled through the rusted corners of the hut, and there was nothing you could do but drink your tea, stretch your feet out as close as you could to the heater, and breathe into the neck of your coat.

At two o'clock, my phone died. I glanced at the man sitting closest to me, but he had pulled his hood up over his head and was fast asleep.

Has anybody got an Android charger? I said.

Nobody answered.

There was a stack of newspapers on the table in the middle of the room. I picked up the *Sunday World* and read a story about a man who went over to his mate's house to fix his smoke alarm and ended up killing him with a samurai sword. It was one of those mad stories you hear about every once in a while, when some psychopath who used to be in the UDA takes something the wrong way and snaps. They had been drinking all day these two fellas, they had known each other for years, and they were enjoying themselves, having a good time. Next minute, your man took the sword out of his boot, calm as you like, and walked back into the house. Nobody heard the screams. Not one neighbour, and I'm not talking about a big street here. I'm talking six houses in a square in the middle of East Belfast. The neighbours must've known. They must've seen who it was and thought, no, we better not. Say nothing. In the meantime, the man with the sword drove home to his wife and told her.

I killed so-and-so, he said. Nobody's going to fuck me over again.

Across the room, at the other side of the hut, the man who had spoken to me earlier was sitting with his feet up on the bench. He had a can of Harp tucked under his coat and his eyes were locked on the door.

Do you reckon we'll get sent home? I said.

The man took a chug and burped loudly but politely into his hand.

I'm dying, he said.

I called into Asda on the way back to the flat and did the trick at the self-checkouts with some sausages and bacon for dinner. I got some tuna as well, for my packed lunches. When I got back, Ryan called me into his bedroom. He was on his knees in the middle of the floor, struggling to get his suitcase closed.

Gimme a hand, will you? he said.

I sat on top of the suitcase and leaned with my weight down on it. The bed had been stripped, the mattress was bare, and the pillows, which had turned yellow. It was the first time I had seen Ryan since that night with Finty, and that was two weeks ago.

Where you going? I said, and Ryan, surprised, said, Moving in with Finty sure, aren't I?

Since when?

We told you that night we were all here sure, remember?

They didn't say a word to me. He was full of shit.

Have yis got a place sorted and all? I said.

Finty got a bru drop. Hundred quid a month. I thought I may as well, seeing as we're getting turfed out of here any day now, you know?

He got the zip closed, finally, and lugged the suitcase up on to the bed. I glanced around the empty room. It looked bigger now with nothing in it. The mould was bad though. It came right up to the windowsill and darkened the bottoms of the blinds.

Be sad to go like, we had some craic in this place, didn't we? Ryan said.

We did, aye.

Some parties.

Aye.

You'll have to come up for a few swalls some night, he said.

I said I would, sounded good, and followed him as he staggered with his suitcase through the hall and down the stairs. Finty was waiting outside. He had his da's van. It was one of those wee white ones you see people flying about in, when they're first starting out. He waved at me.

House-warming next weekend, Seany-bo. See you there?

Aye, see you there, I said.

Finty started the van, dropped it into first, revved the van until the engine squealed, then lifted his foot up off the clutch and let the wheels spin until there was smoke.

Ye-ha, he shouted. Up the Ra!

The smell of burnt rubber hung in the air after they were gone.

I don't like doing things I've never done before in front of other people in case I do it wrong and make a dick out of myself, so I watched as Joe showed me how to lift the choke and pull the starter cord, then how to change the wire and hook the strimmer to the harness, which lightened the weight, making it easier to lean with my elbow on the handlebars as we trooped through the cemetery, me and five men I didn't know – people came in on different days – and the fella who spoke to me on my first shift. He walked alongside me with a feg sticking out of his mouth, puffing great clouds of smoke without a care in the world about the petrol tank he had tucked under his arm and how easily the fumes could catch.

What'd you do, kid? he said to me.

What?

To get here, what'd you do?

Told you last time. I got done for assault.

Aye, but why?

I dropped my head and quickened my pace but no matter how fast I walked, he was right there, dragging his boots behind me.

Joe had a leaf blower strapped to his back and was stalking between the headstones like some kind of Ghostbuster. He led us to a patch down the back where there weren't many graves but the waterlogged grassland had drawn swarms of midges that bit every inch of exposed skin. I didn't want to fall behind the other men, and I didn't want to look like I didn't know what I was doing, but my eagerness to keep up made me cut too close to the ground, taking chunks out of the muck, splattering my chest and arms, my face shield even, making it difficult to see past the mud seeping through the already mucky mesh. Before long, I was twice as dirty as the other men and hadn't cut half the grass. My arms were sore, and the bottom of my back. The harder I tried, the more awkward the strimmer became, juddering as it did under my arm, the shaft wobbling with the momentum of the spool, butchering the field.

The first smoke break couldn't come quick enough. I slumped on to the kerb of the nearest grave and lay back to look at the sky. It was so clear and blue and lovely to look at that I held my phone up in front of me, but instead of taking a photograph, I flipped the camera round and took a selfie. My face was specked with muck and my hair was damp with sweat, and in the background of the picture, dandelions leaned with their big heads to the side. I sent it to Mairéad, thinking it would give her a laugh. One of the men sitting closest to me saw what I was doing and said, Jesus Christ, he's worse than my wee girl.

Who is?

He is. Taking pictures of himself.

How old's your wee girl?

The men laughed. No call for that now, Fra, they said.

Sure he can take it. He's a big boy, aren't you, Samuel?

The man called Samuel nodded, but his eyes were locked on the ground.

When the smoke break was over, Joe led us back towards the middle of the cemetery, to a field where the grass was lush and green and far easier to cut. I was starting to get the hang of it, swinging the strimmer more from the hips now, rotating from side to side, and it was hypnotic, the sound of the strimmer wire slicing through the grass, the grass spraying up into the air. I didn't have to think about what I was doing. I didn't have to think about anything. The engine drowned everything out, and my hands, tingling with the tremors, started to feel like they didn't belong to me, that they were being carried by the motion of the strimmer itself and, as if by magic, the work was getting done. It took us half the shift, right up until after the lunch break, to finish the field, and when we did, Joe treated us to another ten-minute smoke break. We plonked ourselves on the grass and swigged from bottles of lukewarm water handed out by one of the younger lads who had been sent across the road. Your man who kept asking me about what I had done, whose name was Fra, was sitting close by. He leaned with his hands on the grass behind him and surveyed the field.

Know why there are no headstones on this field? he said.

I didn't answer. I knew he wanted to tell me.

This here isn't just a field, kid. This is the poor ground. You know what the poor ground is?

I did, but I humoured him.

Eighty thousand people are buried under your feet right now, he said. Eighty thousand, and that's just on this patch. There are three patches. See that field over there, and that one there? You're talking over two hundred thousand people, and not one of them has a name. They lost their names because they couldn't afford to buy their own plots, then the sick people got chucked in on top of them, the ones who keeled over with typhus and influenza. Now they talk about 'The Disappeared'. They wanna know where all those people are when they've been disappearing people themselves for years and years, and they're right here. They're under this grass. Now you tell me who's in the wrong.

I knew exactly who was in the wrong, but I was afraid to say in case Fra didn't want to hear it. I just sort of agreed with him, hoping he'd leave me alone. He didn't.

You know who else is buried here? he said.

There were so many people buried in that cemetery. I hazarded a guess with Giuseppe Conlon, thinking that would be somebody he would want to talk about, but no.

You ever see *Darby O'Gill*? he said.

I hadn't. I wasn't even sure what *Darby O'Gill* was.

The main character's buried here, Fra said.

In the poor ground?

No, for fuck sake. Here, in the cemetery.

I didn't know if I was supposed to be impressed or what. I just nodded along, it was that kind of conversation, and Fra kept talking, about the film, and the main character in the film, who was played by a man called Albert Sharpe. He was from the Falls, he grew up on Iveagh Parade, and that seemed to mean something to Fra – maybe he was from that neck of the woods himself. I tried to ask him if that was the case, but Fra was in full flow, telling me this story about how a man showed up at Albert Sharpe's door one day, looking for him. This was back in the fifties. Nobody had much of anything back then. Working in the mills was hell on earth, and there was no steady work at the docks. Not if you were a Catholic. Fra made sure to emphasize this as he described the man standing at Albert Sharpe's door that day, all dressed up in a suit and a hat, and shoes that were so shiny that the kids in the street stopped playing their games and crowded round to watch.

It was Albert Sharpe's wife who answered the door. She was in her apron, and she saw this well-dressed man standing in her doorway and thought she was being evicted. The man sensed her panic and told her he wasn't looking for any trouble, he wanted to speak to her husband, Albert, and she paused. His accent threw her. Who're you? she said, and do you know what the man said?

Fra paused for effect.

Walt Disney.

That's mad, I said.

Isn't it? Walt Disney showing up at his door on the Falls.

Did Albert Sharpe's wife not invite him in?

Of course she fucking – why're you busting my balls?

The other men had overheard and were laughing.

Are the little people buried here as well, Fra? they said.

I laughed along with them, it seemed like the thing to do, and then Fra looked at me and I went quiet. He had that effect on people, and it seeped out to the men sitting around us. Suddenly everybody was looking at their phones, smoking their fegs, and staring off into the distance. It was eerily quiet, and Fra had this grin on his face like he knew, he had me, and all he had to do was lean over my shoulder and whisper.

Who's your da? he said.

My da?

Aye, who is he?

It was like being cornered on the street and asked if I was a Catholic or a Protestant. The last time was about ten years ago, when I was walking through an area I shouldn't have and got dragged down an entry by three lads who would've done a lot worse if the man from the taxi depot hadn't come out from behind the counter and said, All right, that's enough now, boys. Let him go.

His name's Seamus, I said. Seamus Maguire.

Seamus Maguire? Did he drive a taxi?

Dunno. I haven't seen him since I was a kid.

One of them ones, aye?

Aye, one of them ones.

The rest of the afternoon was spent doing more of the same. It was trickier, more deliberate work trying to navigate between the graves, and the amount of strimmer wire I went through. It blunted the more it dug into the ground, or hit stone. I knocked the strimmer off and used my finger to clear the muck out of the spool, then I slipped the new wire through the wee holes in the head. As I did this, I looked back at the clumps of spicy-smelling grass piled across the field; I couldn't believe how much work we'd done and in so little time. In reality, hours had gone by, an entire day, and I hadn't once looked at my phone. Not since Mairéad replied to the picture I had sent earlier that morning.

Six hours of my life gone in a blink, a grand total of twelve hours in the bag and another hundred and eighty-eight more to go. I trudged with the rest of the men back to the hut, my petrol strimmer like a mine detector guiding me to the gates, which opened on to the road, and cars passed smoothly from sight, one after another receding into the distance.

I went looking for my da again that night. I wanted more than I could find on his Facebook page, which wasn't much, and that meant combing through dozens of forums and local newspaper archives. Then I fell down a rabbit hole scrolling through message boards of people reminiscing about where they were from. My da was from the Market, and there were loads of people posting about the lives they had growing up there, the people they knew. The only mention I could find of anybody with the same surname was a man called Peeps Maguire, who played guitar for a band called Terry and the Tokens, back in the sixties.

I posted a message anyway, at one o'clock in the morning:

Does anybody know Seamus Maguire? He had a sister and a brother, Christine and Peter. Not sure which street they lived on, but he grew up in the Market, his da lived there his whole life. If anyone knows anything about him, I'd love to hear.

Then I found an interview he did for an Irish country sports magazine. He had won a clay shooting competition, a few years back, at a ground outside Ballymaloe. It was a serious event, people from all over the world took part, and seeing as my da had no background in the sport, no family connections, the interviewer wanted to know how he had got started.

My da told him he moved to the countryside thirteen years ago with his wife and daughter. He didn't know anybody, they were in the middle of nowhere, and he was trying to get used to this new way of life when a fella from down the road called in with his missus one afternoon to say hello. Peter Scullion was a big deal in the shooting world, he had made it to the Olympics in 1988. He invited my da down to the clay ground and offered to show him the ropes. My da tagged along for a bit of craic, and he was hopeless, he couldn't make a shot to save his life, but he got an unbelievable rush off it. By the end of the following week he had applied for a shotgun certificate.

The first gun he bought himself was a Webley & Scott he still dusts off the odd time, when he's feeling nostalgic. It won him his first registered shoot. I remember watching him cleaning it when I was a kid, the noise it made when he rolled the barrel off the action. That gentle clicking sound, like when they reload guns in films. He would take me out those weekends I went up to stay with him, before everything came out. We'd set up the clay trap in the field out the back of his house. My job was to load the discs, and sometimes he'd let me have a go on the gun. I'd feel his weight behind me as he guided the rifle in my hands, showing me how to follow the trajectory, and when the disc dropped, we would squeeze the trigger together, my ears popping with the sound.

One day there was a rabbit. My da spotted it moving along the hedges at the far side of the field. He crouched down, held his finger to his lips, and moved slowly forward, his boots sinking into the muck as he shouldered his rifle and lined up the shot. There was a snap. The gunshot rang out, and the crows took off into the sky. Later, when he finished skinning the rabbit at the table in his back garden, my da held the slippery pink carcass up for me to see.

That's our dinner, he said, smiling.

After that morning when my ma turned thirty-eight, I never saw my da again. My ma tried to make it up to me, making a fuss of me whenever she could, but I knew what she was doing and I didn't think I deserved it. Like that time she invited the whole family round for my sixteenth birthday, cousins and all. I locked myself in my bedroom and refused to go downstairs. She thought it was because my da had never tried to reach out to me, and to be fair, that did hang over me. But it was everybody going out of their way to make me feel better that made it worse. Reading that interview with my da brought it all up again, and it wasn't like I was trying to torture myself or anything like that. It was just hard to pull myself away when he was right there, on the internet, living his life with his wife and daughter somewhere in the countryside.

His daughter was called Aoife. She was only a child the last time I saw her; she had only just turned four. I hated being left alone with her. She'd stare at me for as long as it took for me to look at her, then she'd run around the room with whatever toy she wanted to annoy me with that day, and squeal. Now she was tweeting about her GCSEs: *so much fear trying to revise for topics I've never seen before in my life*. She seemed smart though. She went to a good school. People called it 'The Academy'. It had its own Wikipedia page and everything, and it had been around since the 1700s. I had an image in my head of kids in robes eating three-course meals for lunch. Aoife with that group of girls with wavy hair and HD brows, standing outside changing rooms with their bare feet crossed, holding medals they'd just won. Their dance instructor posted statuses about how proud she was, how hard her girls had worked, how they would learn from their experience and come back even stronger. I believed her. This wasn't just a phase – Aoife had been dancing from no age. One of her mates tweeted a photo of her when she was a child, about five years old. She was standing next to a glittery pink ballet barre with her hands raised up over her head, eyes closed, with the caption, *feel the music girlfriend*.

There were no pictures of her with my da, and there was nothing that suggested they were related beyond the fact that they shared the same surname, but I knew it was her. I could tell. She was my wee sister.

11

The next day, I went to the bru like I was supposed to every two weeks to sign on. The man behind the desk asked if I had recorded all the jobs I had applied for in the booklet they had given me, when I first claimed Jobseeker's Allowance. I told him aye, I had, and he asked me to show him. I couldn't because I hadn't brought the booklet with me, and he said, I'm going to have to give you a warning. If you don't bring your Job Search booklet with you next time, we'll have to cut your benefits.

I took his word for it. They were looking any excuse.

Instead of going back to the flat, I took my laptop with me to the sandwich shop in Andytown and spent the afternoon using their Wi-Fi to apply for jobs. Mairéad messaged me. She wanted to know what I was up to. I told her and she said she was on her way back up the road and that she would call in. I watched through the window as she climbed out the back of a black taxi with her carry-on luggage-sized bag slung over her shoulder. She looked tired, sort of worn out. Her clothes were all loose and raggedy, her jeans even, which were supposed to be skinny but had bunched up around her knees. She leaned over the job listings I had printed out and spread across the table in front of me. There was bar work, call centre work, the odd café or admin job, and then, lucky for me, a bookshop.

You gonna go for it?

I played it down and told her I might, even though I had already written the cover letter and was planning on spending the next few days filling out the application form, making sure it was good.

There's a job going in Queen's Street Studios as well, I said.

Mairéad raised her eyebrows. Bit arty farty down there, isn't it?

Too arty farty for me, you mean.

No, I don't. I mean for anyone.

She went to the counter and came back with a pot of tea. She looked pale, gaunt even, like she had spent the last few days sleeping on somebody else's settee. I asked if she had been out the night before and she said, No, why?

I don't know, you seem a bit—

What?

Tired. You seem a bit tired.

I got my flights booked. I'm moving to Berlin.

My stomach sank; I was starting to think she might not go.

When do you leave? I said.

Not until next month, I've still a few things to sort out.

She took her phone from her bag and showed me pictures of the flat she was moving into. I nodded and smiled and did the whole, That looks class, thing. Then she put her phone away and craned her neck to read the cover letter I had written for a coffee shop in the town. She shook her head and said, Hold on till I show you, and logged on to her emails, downloaded the CV that got her the job in the clothes shop, and told me to use it as a template; she had never not got a job she had applied for. She knew how to answer questions about how I had used my initiative to reach my goals, and she had a whole list of examples about how I had worked with other people as part of a team, making sure to explain how each particular situation had improved my skills as a team player. By the end of the afternoon, I'd applied for seven jobs. I thanked her and she batted a hand.

You want me to have a look at the one for the bookshop as well?

I did, but I couldn't let her see what I had written. How much I loved books. All the writing I had done and planned to do. Authors whose work had inspired me, and how I could combine my customer service experience with the knowledge I had acquired while studying for my degree. I told her not to worry about it, she'd done enough, and we left it at that.

Later, when the tables had been cleared and we were the only people left in the sandwich shop, one of the lads from behind the counter did a lap of the floor with a brush and scoop. Outside, the sun had dropped. The few clouds clogging the sky had reddened over the mountain. Mairéad took a picture on her phone and uploaded it to Instagram with the caption, *summer nights in the west*. I didn't say anything. I didn't even take the piss. I watched her slip her phone into the back pocket of her high-waisted jeans, and carried on walking down the road.

It was the first time I had seen Mairéad since that time we ended up in Holywood. I knew she had been working flat out – in the clothes shop, and in the nightclub selling shots. Trying to save as much money as she could. Still, I had the feeling that she had pulled away from me. I sensed it as we dandered down Andytown; the same studied silence she retreated into that night I came home from work and she was sitting on the kerb outside the flat. She had that big leather bag with her that night too, and she had it with her after Mono that first time, when we went to McDonald's. And then there were those things Ryan had said about her living with some fella in the Holylands. She had never mentioned the Holylands, and if she was living with some lad down there, why wouldn't she say anything about it?

We stopped at Kelstar and ate fish suppers at the tables out the front. Then we went to Fusco's and got ice cream. We sat outside, on the steps in the corner of the car park, and watched a couple of wee lads playing football against the wall. The sun had fallen behind the mountain now, the sky had turned pink, and all along the road, people were making their way home from work. Mairéad spooned the last of the honeycomb out of the corners of her tub and ran her finger around the rim. When she was finished, we went back up on to the main road and turned towards Casement Park.

Look, Mairéad said, pointing at the gates.

It was the first time either of us had seen them open since Casement Park had been closed off for a redevelopment project that had gone tits up a few years before. Mairéad wanted to go in. She grabbed me by the hand and dragged me towards the entrance.

It'll be like a wee adventure, she said.

I followed her down the lane, thinking we would have a peek and leave it at that, but no. She wanted to see if there was a way we could get through the barriers blocking off the pitch. We checked along the palisade fence right up to the stands, then we circled round the back of the stands. Between the wall and the section of the fencing that had been built around the floodlights, the bottoms of two poles had been popped and loosened. I only noticed this because they were sitting at an angle, in a way you wouldn't see unless you were really looking. I pulled them outwards and moved them to the side, making an entrance through the bottom of the rail. Mairéad slipped through. We climbed up the bank behind the bleachers and looked down at the pitch. There were full-scale bushes down there, weeds and flowers and thick clumps of undergrowth. The stands were empty. The windows along the stands were covered with grills that had rusted, and all along the walkways, old advertising boards lay where they had been ripped off the walls.

Mad, isn't it? Mairéad said.

Crazy.

We did a lap of the stadium, and when we got round to the stands, we walked up to the doors leading into the changing rooms and tried to see in, but it was dark. I said to Mairéad, Let's go back to the other side, it's better over there, and she agreed. She didn't like standing in the shadow of that empty structure either; it was like something from Chernobyl. We walked round to the opposite side of the pitch and sat on the concrete bleachers, right at the halfway line, and took in the view.

Doesn't feel right, does it? I said, and Mairéad shook her head.

It really doesn't.

I looked at that bag she had tucked under her legs, on the next step down, and said something like, What's the craic with you and that bag? as if that would get us on to the conversation I wanted to have. It didn't. Mairéad was busy scrolling through the pictures she had taken as we walked around the stadium. She paused over one of me standing in the middle of the bleachers, staring out over the pitch.

You putting that on Instagram? I said.

Do you not like it?

No, I do. It's good.

She leaned into me and let me watch as she cropped each of the pictures into a square and uploaded them. I was part of her grid now, and I was surprised by how much this meant to me.

Ryan's moved out then, has he? she said.

Aye, that's him away.

How do you feel about it?

All right, aye.

You're sick of all that shit though, aren't you? The partying and all.

I'd rather party than live with my ma, I said.

It'll be grand. Your ma's great. My ma, on the other hand —

She laughed. I hadn't realized she was joking.

What about your living situation? I said.

What about it?

Like, have you somewhere to stay?

I've loads of places to stay, she said, plucking a weed out from between the concrete blocks.

Do you have a place to live though? I said.

I will when I get to Berlin.

Across the field, at the other side of the stadium, a man had appeared at the top of the bank and was shouting over at us. There was no other way out, I had checked, and there was no point trying to run, he had a dog, so we stayed where we were and acted like we weren't doing anything wrong. The man walked all the way round with his big Alsatian traipsing along beside him. He was wearing jeans and guddies, an O'Neills jumper, and a high-vis bib that hung open at his belly. He was breathing heavily. His Alsatian was panting too, and the two of them were a sorry sight trying to make their way along the top of the bleachers. There were bottles and bricks and bags of rubbish to navigate around, clumps of nettles that pricked his jeans and made him stumble.

You're not supposed to be here, he said.

Sorry, mate, there was an opening in the fence.

That's my opening. That's so I can get in and out.

We patted the dirt off our arses and moved as if to walk back the way the man had come, but he said, No, you're walking round this way, and made us do a full lap of the pitch with him and his dog, on the route he must've taken every night, to make sure there was nobody hiding down the back. Only last weekend, he caught a crowd of young ones hunkered around a fire, drinking away, very irresponsible. It would only take for one of them to fall down those steps, he said, and we agreed, it would be dangerous, especially at night. The dog stopped for a piss and the man used the opportunity to take in the view. It's a terrible shame, he said, shaking his head. A terrible shame. There's a lot of history in this stadium. Lots of stories. Our county's home ground, and look what they've done to it.

How did it end up like this? Mairéad said, and the man explained how they were supposed to have started building a new state-of-the-art stadium by now, with a forty thousand seat capacity, but the planning permission had fallen through. There were all sorts of problems with the budget, and the people who lived in the streets around the stadium hadn't been properly consulted. But the thing that really annoyed the man was how the plans for upgrading Windsor Park were well under way, and that rugby stadium over east, whereas Casement had been kicked to the bottom of the queue as usual. The powers that be would rather drown themselves than see the GAA do well, he said. The local residents too. They want nothing to do with it.

Why not?

They don't want people pissing in their gardens, he said.

He walked us round to the gap in the fence and stood on the grass at the top of the bank, watching as we slipped through. Don't be telling anyone about this now, he said, meaning the gap.

We promised we wouldn't. The man gave us a thumbs up.

On the way back to the flat, I came right out with it and asked Mairéad if she needed somewhere to stay. I didn't want her thinking I had some kind of agenda, but Ryan's bedroom was just sitting there empty, and it wasn't like she would have to pay rent or anything like that – it was free, and as far as places to live go, it wasn't the worst.

Who said I needed a place to stay? she said.

Do you not?

Mairéad didn't answer. When we got back to the flat, I told her I could get rid of the damp for her, with a sponge and soapy water, and there was an extra fan heater knocking about somewhere, to keep her warm.

It gets cold at night, I said.

Mairéad looked at me. I thought she was going to say no, it's not a good idea. Then she sat on the edge of the bed.

I need to get some bedsheets, she said.

We went up to the Kennedy Centre that night to watch a Ken Loach film; they were doing a whole season for a festival they had running through September. We brought our own crisps and chocolate because we didn't want to get fleeced at the pick 'n' mix, and we got stoned in the car park before the film started. Mairéad had a bit for a joint stashed at the bottom of her bag. We used her earring to poke holes through an empty can and used it as a pipe. Ten minutes before the film started, we were glued to the claw machines. Mairéad nearly got one. The teddy bear she picked up hit the side of the chute and fell back into the pile. She leaned with her face right up to the glass. I made her stay where she was and took a picture.

Look, I said, showing her.

It hadn't come out well, but you could see her reflection and the side of her face, with the camera over her shoulder. She looked unreal.

Send me that, she said.

The film had just started when we got into the screen. Five minutes in, the main character gets sentenced to three hundred hours of community service. Mairéad leaned in to me and said, That's you. I laughed and the fella behind us shushed us. Mairéad shushed him back. I opened a box of Pringles and she took two and made herself look like a duck.

You're gonna get us kicked out, I said.

Me? An innocent duck?

The plot was a bit mad; the main character somehow finds himself in a whisky distillery with the man supervising his community service order. The people who are on community service with him get to taste some whisky, then the main character is handed a dram and asked to describe what it smells like. He does this very well, he has a real knack for it. His supervisor recognizes his potential and takes him to another distillery, later in the film, for a whisky tasting session. He's a kind man, he sees the good in people, and he wants to help the protagonist turn his life around. Mairéad nudged me and said, Is that what your supervisor's like? I said, Aye, that's exactly what he's like, and we went into convulsions laughing.

Later, when we were back at the flat, we talked more seriously about it.

There's this man in Milltown, I don't know. It's like he's following me.

What, like around the cemetery?

Sort of. He keeps asking me stuff. He wanted to know who my da was.

We were sitting on the settee in the living room. Mairéad had on the hoodie I had given her to wear about the flat. She had pulled it over her knees like she liked to do, and she was drinking red wine from a cup.

Maybe you look like someone he knows, she said.

I thought about this and remembered what it was that got to me. He asked me why I hit that lad. He was like, why did you do it? Mairéad tilted her head to the side. Why did you? she said.

He was trying to make a dick out of me.

In what way?

I told her it was hard to explain, you had to be there. There was five of them and they were all taking the piss out of me, in the kitchen at that house party. I was on my own. I had nobody to back me up.

Where were they from? Mairéad said.

Dunno, the Malone Road or something.

Mairéad leaned with her back against the arm of the settee. She was listening.

I can take a slegging, I said. I can give as good as I get, but they were posh as fuck, and I was outnumbered, everything I said sounded stupid. Then one of them was like, Don't be winding him up, his da's in the Ra, and your man, the fella I hit was like, Sure he's from Twin-brook, he doesn't know who his dad is. I just snapped. I grabbed him by the throat and pinned him against the wall.

Mairéad held her cup with both hands. She was sitting very still.

I told him I'd get him. I told him I was gonna knock him out, and I did. I walked across the street like I was gonna shake his hand and he put his hand out for me to shake and I smacked him. I hit him as hard as I could and knocked him clean out.

Jesus Christ, Sean.

I know.

What was his name again?

Daniel Jackson.

She went on her phone to see if she could find him on Facebook. Is that him there? she said.

Aye, that's him.

She scrolled through pictures of him on holiday a few years ago with his ma and his da and his wee sister, the four of them sitting around a table in a fancy restaurant, drinking those stupid-looking cocktails with the straws and the sparklers and the big chunks of watermelon stuck to the rim of the glass. Alcohol-free, I was sure. Those parents wouldn't let their well-reared children anywhere near a drink until they turned eighteen. I said this to Mairéad and she agreed, they looked like that kind of family, and for a while we just sat there, staring at them, trying to put together our own ideas about who they were.

The most Mairéad said about where she had been staying those last few weeks came later in the night, when I asked about Berlin. She told me she wasn't getting enough hours in the clothes shop and it was getting harder for her to cover her rent – she had been hired while she was a student and her manager kept treating her that way even after she had graduated. Then she got a text from her landlord telling her he was selling up. The people she lived with scattered. She was left with nowhere to go but back to her ma's. That was a whole other thing, she said, and I didn't need to ask why. Mairéad's expression said it all.

She decided on Berlin because she knew this girl from a placement she did in her final year. She was working as an editorial assistant for a production company over there, and she told Mairéad she would help her find a job. In the meantime, she got a gig in a call centre so she could save more money, but the hours clashed with her shifts in the clothes shop; they both wanted her to work weekends, and neither of her managers felt like accommodating her – they wanted flexibility, and that meant her being available whenever they needed her, not the other way around.

Mairéad packed that in after a few weeks and started working as a promo girl for a nightclub, handing out flyers around the town. It depressed her, she was going to quit, then one of the girls asked if she would cover a shift selling shots. She did it because there was thirty quid in it for her, and whatever money she made that night, which was fuck all. She was like Bambi on ice; she couldn't even carry a tray of drinks. People fired her a few quid because they felt sorry for her, and at the end of the night, she got a slap on the arse. That tipped her over the edge.

I locked myself in the toilet and cried, she said.

She started going a bit mad then, drinking a lot, partying, staying in other people's houses whenever she could, going back to her ma's those nights she didn't have a choice, then sneaking out the door first thing in the morning, before her ma woke up. She did more promo work, then she got roped into selling shots again, this time with two girls who saw that she was struggling and helped her. She got better at it, she started making a few quid, and although she wasn't partying as much, there were nights when she went home with people she otherwise wouldn't have because it was easier than going back to her ma's. Then she stopped going to her ma's altogether. For the last few weeks she had been moving between different places, sleeping wherever she could. I got the sense that she had done this without making it obvious that she had nowhere else to go, that she just followed the after-party and stayed wherever she ended up. It was usually a mate's house, but sometimes it wasn't.

You should've told me, I said. You could've stayed here.

Nah, that wouldn't have been a good idea.

This was at four o'clock in the morning, we had done some drinking, and we were both steaming, the two of us snuggled up on the settee, talking intensely, in that way people do at that stage of the game.

Why wouldn't it have been a good idea? I said.

You know fine rightly, Sean. Don't act stupid.

You afraid of us riding each other again?

No, Mairéad said. But I was afraid you would expect it.

I felt guilty when she said this, and a bit ashamed of myself.

Sorry, I said.

It's okay. It's just the way it is.

Later, when we ran out of things to talk about, and when Mairéad realized she had to be in work the next day, she pulled her hood down over her face and said, We need to go to bed.

Together? I said, messing her about.

She glared at me. Not funny, she said.

We gave each other a hug in the hallway, and it was nice, the way we were able to do that, with no awkwardness. No feeling that we were crossing any sort of line. Mairéad went into her room and I went into my room, and for twenty minutes, I lay awake, listening. Then the door swung open. Mairéad stood at the bottom of my bed.

That damp's wild. Can I stay in here with you?

Aye, bounce in.

Seriously now, this isn't –

I know.

She got in. It was a double bed, there was plenty of space, but she put her head on my shoulder.

What do you wanna do with your life, Sean? she said.

Dunno. Haven't really thought about it.

She sat up on her elbow and looked at me. There must be something, she said. What do you wanna do?

I wanna go to sleep.

Fine, don't talk then.

She rolled on to her side away from me, sighing like she was in a huff. I did what anybody would do in that situation: I tickled her.

Fuck off, Sean. No, stop. Okay, okay.

Her head was back on my shoulder now, she was out of breath, but she was watching me, waiting for me to say something.

I wouldn't mind getting back into writing, I said.

Really? Is that something you used to do?

In Liverpool, aye. I did a Creative Writing module. It was good.

Have you thought about doing an MA?

Dunno. Maybe.

You should. The one at Queen's is really good.

You love it down there, don't you?

It's been good for me.

In what way?

In the same way Liverpool was for you, she said. It got me away.

Mairéad was supposed to go to work the next day, at two o'clock. She kept looking at her phone, and the closer we got to the time her shift was supposed to start, the more reluctant she became. She moaned. She curled up on the settee and whimpered.

Phone in sick, I said.

What will I say?

Tell them you've come down with a flu. High temperature.

She chewed the inside of her bottom lip. Should I?

Why not?

I could get the sack.

Aye, only if you get caught.

She had to hype herself up, and she did this by walking up and down the living room and chewing the back of her phone. She had never phoned in sick before. She was a good worker, reliable. Never missed a shift. I told her that was all the better for her, they'd never suspect her. She took her phone into her room and came back five minutes later looking like she had committed a crime. I told them I couldn't come in for the rest of the week, she said.

What'd they say?

They said it was okay. They told me to let them know.

She grinned, nervously. What're we gonna do now? she said.

Whatever you want.

We went to Asda and stocked up on crisps and chocolate and food for the next few days. Mairéad paid because I didn't have any money and she wanted to contribute. When we got back to the flat, she made this meal with chickpeas and rice that tasted unlike anything I'd ever had. She told me her friend had shown her how to make it. She was vegan and had the best recipes. I made a joke about her mates from Queen's being in the Greens and she rolled her eyes. They probably would be, given half the chance, she said.

She finally came round to the idea of washing herself over the bathroom sink, when she had gone two days without a shower. I plugged the fan heater into the extension cord and filled the sink with hot water. She stomped into the living room twenty minutes later with a towel wrapped around her. Her hair was wet and there were droplets on her shoulders.

I smell like my wee brother, she said.

She pulled my hoodie on over the towel and slipped her towel out from under it. All my knickers are in the wash, she said, laughing.

I gave her a pair of shorts. She stood in the middle of the kitchen with her arms held out, showing me how big they were on her. I told her she could do a wash if she wanted and she pulled all the clothes she had out of her big leather bag. There was a pair of jeans in there, two tops, a jumper, some underwear, and a denim jacket that had been rolled up into a ball. How long have you been living out of that bag? I said, and she chuckled, but didn't say. It had always been that way, since we were kids. Silences hung like curtains around her. She plonked herself on the settee beside me.

Is it too early for a drink? she said.

12

The weather was miserable that week. Even with my weatherproofs on, I was soaked, and when Joe finally packed it in and brought us back to the hut, the cold was hard to take. Then the door swung open and Joe was like, Right, let's go, and out we went again, into the rain. That's when it really got to me, when I was staggering between the graves, freezing, sliding all over the place in the mud. I had a hundred and eighty-odd hours of this ahead of me, and it wasn't the summer any more. There would be more rain, more wind. More long afternoons spent sitting in the hut, shivering. Clinging with both hands to my warm cup.

Can you not ask to be moved to another site? Mairéad said.

Dunno. Don't think so.

What about a charity shop? Do they not do it in charity shops?

We were sitting in Mairéad's room, on the bed. She had washed the mould off the wall, and she had gone up to Asda and bought new bedsheets, pillows, and a lavender-scented candle she had lit on the bedside table. Next to the candle was Susan Sontag's diaries lying face down with the pages open. There was a pen clipped with its lid to the back cover, and underneath it the Moleskine journal Mairéad had left behind with the leather chest bag she wore that one time and never again.

There was somebody at the door this morning, she said.

Did you see who it was?

Some man and a woman. They got into a car.

She was sitting at the opposite end of the bed doing her make-up in the mirror she had propped up against the pillow. Her back was to me, but I could see her reflection over her shoulder, the pencil she used to make the wee points at the corners of her eyes flick out. She was going to a thing that night, an exhibition launch. Her mates from Queen's had written responses to the work on show, and there was a reading after, in a bar in town. She asked if I wanted to go with her but I knew what it was like to be around that crowd and wasn't sure I could hack it. I might just take it easy, I said.

You sure?

Aye. Long day.

She stopped doing her eyeliner and looked at me over her shoulder. There were little flecks of mascara on her cheek.

You scared? she said.

Scared of what?

Being around the university crowd.

Nah, it's not that. I just don't know anyone.

You know me.

I know, but you know what I mean.

What?

Are they not all posh as fuck?

Mairéad laughed. Some of them are, aye. But they're harmless like.

Harmless my hole, I said. Last time I was around people like that I ended up in court.

My friends aren't like that.

Are they not?

She turned back to the mirror and did something with a spongy thing on her face. I couldn't really see, her hair was in the way, and she had tilted her head to the side so that she could get a better angle in the light coming through the window. I'm a bit nervous myself, she said.

What for?

Nothing, really. I just get like this every time I've to go to these things.

Why do you have to go?

I don't have to, it's just nice to support your friends.

She was at her fringe now, brushing it with a comb. I stayed there for a while, watching her, and it was dead relaxing, the way she did everything so quietly. Then she stood up and said, I need to get dressed, and looked at me as if to say, *get the fuck out*.

I'll get ready then, will I? I said.

Aye. Go get ready and we'll look at some art.

Right, okay. Fuck it.

I took my weatherproofs off and stuffed them into the basket at the bottom of my bed, then I carried the kettle into the bathroom and filled the sink with hot water. In the mirror, my body was pale and chubby, but also weirdly thin; I looked fat and skinny at the same time. I needed to get back to the gym. When I was finished, I went into the living room to see what the craic was with Mairéad. She had her denim jacket on and was leaning with her face right up to her laptop screen.

We're not on Google Maps, she said.

I sat next to her and watched as she dragged the yellow man from the bottom corner of the screen and dropped him on to Great Victoria Street. The screen morphed into Street View, and there I could see the tables out the front of the coffee shop, all empty, with a man dressed in black standing in the doorway, having a smoke. Mairéad double-clicked her way from one end of the road to the other, making the images dissolve then reappear in a way that made me feel like I was being tugged forward.

Here, she said, handing me the laptop. I need to brush my teeth.

Her trust in me surprised me; everything was open, her Facebook, her emails. I clicked into Messenger and saw an unread message from a lad called Conor:

if you need a place to stay, you're more than welcome to . . .

I couldn't read the rest of the message without opening it, and I couldn't open the message without Mairéad knowing I had read it, so I extracted what little information I could from the few words I could see and clicked back into Google Maps.

You ready? Mairéad said.

Aye, that's me.

Okay. Let's go.

We crossed the road at the top of Royal Avenue and walked round to the place where the exhibition was happening. Outside, a group of people Mairéad knew were having a smoke. Mairéad introduced me. I shook their hands but didn't get to speak to them for long enough to know what they were like; Mairéad needed a drink. She lifted two glasses of red wine from the table, they were giving it out for free, and nodded for me to follow her to the other side of the hall. The few snippets of conversation we had were interrupted by her seeing somebody she recognized. She told me who they were and what they did – usually some kind of art – but she wouldn't go over and say hello. She was too nervous, and the event was about to start. I asked Mairéad what it was about and she leaned in to me and whispered, Mental health.

What, like suicide and all?

Aye, all that. She looked down into her glass, swirled it. There's some Outsider art too, she said.

Outsider art?

Art by people who aren't part of the art world.

Is anybody part of the art world? I said, trying to sound smart.

Mairéad gave me a look. Very good, she said. Now shoosh.

The woman who had curated the whole thing got up and said a few words about how a mental health crisis had affected communities across the North, except she said 'Northern Ireland', and that told me everything I needed to know about where she was coming from. It was interesting though, she had a lot to say about how it was no coincidence that the rates of suicide were much higher in areas that were most affected by The Troubles: West Belfast, North Belfast, Creggan, Strabane, South Tyrone, South Armagh. Those were the places that had suffered the most, and they just so happened to be the areas that were poorer than everywhere else, even now, twenty years into the peace process. People were still skint as fuck, and all their kids were killing themselves.

I glanced at the crowd around me, stroking their chins, listening as their eyes roved around the room. It didn't sit right with me, the way they stood with their wine and their canapés, nodding along to everything that elegant woman said about underprivileged communities and trans-generational trauma, whatever the fuck that is. And that was the thing, they weren't from the places they were talking about, you could tell by just looking at them, the way they dressed, the way they carried themselves. Their voices. They sounded like those uppity fuckers on the news. It made me self-conscious about the way I spoke, the sound I made when I opened my mouth. I said to Mairéad, This isn't for me, and she slipped her arm through my arm and squeezed.

You'll be grand, she said. You're a big boy.

Inside, the walls were lined with drawings that looked like they had been done by people who had never looked at a piece of art in their lives, but had the maddest dreams. I followed Mairéad, she followed whoever was in front of her, and whoever was behind me followed me, and everybody was so patient and respectful with how long the person ahead of them took over each picture that I began to slow down and really look. There was a lot of blackness; the detail was insane. I stopped at one that looked like a map but was also a cityscape, with landmarks and everything. But they weren't the kind of landmarks you would see anywhere else. They were like nightmares. I tried to show Mairéad, but she was standing in front of a sculpture that had been set up in the middle of the room.

What about your woman saying Northern Ireland? I said.

Mairéad grinned. I knew you'd have something to say about that, she said.

Is that their craic then, aye?

That's her craic. I can't speak for anybody else though.

What about him with the fancy coat? You reckon he says Northern Ireland?

I reckon you need to take a day off.

She turned away from the sculpture and headed towards the far wall, where they had a series of collages made from what looked like papier mâché and came right out of the frame. I recognized a dreary-looking couple Mairéad had introduced me to on the way in. They were standing in the corner, drinking glasses of red wine. Talking quietly about the painting in front of them.

Mairéad's whole demeanour changed. It was like a switch had been flipped and suddenly she was saying things like *astonishing! Beautifully curated*, and *those collages!* I had to drop my head and bite the inside of my cheeks to stop myself from laughing.

Have you seen the video installation? It's overwhelming. I almost walked out.

It was the lad who said this, and he was serious. He ran his hand through his hair and shook his head, staggered. The girl he was with nodded along excitedly. I felt like I was inhabiting the artist's body, she said. Like I was moving through it. But not in a good way. More like a bad trip. I wanted to get out of there. I wanted to run out the door, but I stayed. I stuck through it, didn't I?

You did. You did really well.

The girl smiled. She was genuinely proud of herself.

I could tell by the way they were looking at me that they were waiting for me to say something, to make some sort of observation, and I wasn't cut out for that kind of thing, so I told Mairéad I'd be back in a minute, I'm just gonna look at this painting . . . and got the fuck out of there, to the other side of the room, where I stood in front of a picture of two floating heads in the dark. Then I moved towards the back of the gallery, thinking there must be somewhere to sit down. My feet hadn't recovered from Milltown; all that staggering between graves in steel toe-capped boots had given me blisters. The only place I could find was a small empty room in the far corner of the gallery. The walls were bare and completely white. There was a table, four chairs, and four sets of noise-cancelling headphones. I put the headphones on for a bit of craic and it was like I was sitting in a busy restaurant. People were having conversations all around me, and you could hear the noises from the kitchen, the sound of plates being stacked. Then the sounds receded and a voice came through the babble; a man spoke very calmly about conversations he'd had with Jim Morrison's ghost: *He said I was from hell and that I was Hellex, and that when I was in hell I taught people, I was a valuable member and they wanted me to kill myself.*

I took the headphones off and sat there for a second, taken aback. Then I glanced at the doorway, saw people milling around outside, in the gallery, and put them back on. The man who called himself Hellex told a story about standing in the corner of a car park when he was a child, watching his older brothers playing football. The voices in his head told him to pull his hair out by the root, down to the white jelly, and made him eat it:

That's when I first realized something wasn't right.

I closed my eyes and saw Anthony standing with his hands on the rim of the bathroom sink, his shaved head dotted with blood. He was laughing. His laughter became a high-pitched ringing that faded into the voice of a man with a Dublin accent, who spoke about how the boundaries between the voices in his head and the actual physical world were blurred.

That's how people with schizophrenia get confused and find it difficult to follow actual conversations – they're constantly being distracted by what's going on 'inside'. I call it 'inside', it's there, it's this inner world, which is ever present, which is all around me, layered on top of the physical world . . .

I'm still here, I'm still here –

I pulled the headphones off and looked behind me. There was nobody there.

Mairéad was gone. The couple she had been with were gone too. I did a lap of the gallery to make sure, and when I stepped into the main hall, two lads in white shirts tidied away the empty glasses. I asked where the video installation was and the woman watching over them told me it was on the third floor. I was halfway up the stairs when I saw Mairéad coming down with the lad. The other girl had vanished. Mairéad apologized. She told me Conor wanted to see it again, the first ten minutes especially; he'd missed them the first time round. Conor smiled and told me it was nice to see me again. We're going to the reading if you'd like to join us? he said.

Straight off the bat, I didn't like him. The way he jaunted down those stairs in front of me, smiling, making quips. It was like I was tagging along with the lead singer of a band I'd never heard of. He had a guitar strapped to his back and everything, and everybody knew him. From the bottom of the stairs to the doors, he must've stopped to say hello to about fifteen people, and they all wanted to know where he was going. We're going to hear some poems, he told them, and he wasn't ashamed to say it. In fact, it was as if going to a poetry reading was a completely normal thing to do, and people fell into line. They set their empty glasses on the closest table and followed him out the door.

The sun had dipped behind the library, casting one side of the road in shade, while the other, the side we walked along, was divided by strips of sunlight that gleamed along the empty streets. We turned down one of those streets and walked along a road where all the boarded-up buildings were being knocked down. On the corner, there was a bar I didn't know existed, but which was exactly the kind of place Mairéad and her mates would go. All the punters had piercings, or beards, or hair dyed in a way no self-respecting barber would take responsibility for. They wore denim jackets and green army coats with German flags stitched on the upper arm, and they sat around tables in the upstairs bar, waiting with their legs crossed for the readings to start. Mairéad tried her best. She introduced me as her friend who had studied English in Liverpool. People smiled and said things like, Hey, how's it going? Chairs were pushed back, orders taken. The few people still on their feet moved hesitantly around the room, looking for a place to go. A hand rested on my shoulder: Can I get you another one?

Mairéad answered for me. Please, she said. Two stouts. Sean loves his Guinness, don't you, Sean?

They don't do Guinness. Only Yardsman.

That'll do.

Conor disappeared and came back, squeezed into the seat next to me. Sláinte, he said.

I raised my pint, tried to split the A on the Yardsman glass, and failed.

What do you do with yourself then? I said to Conor. You working or?

I guess you could say I am, yes, but not on anything worth mentioning.

So, you're a student?

I'm a student at Queen's, yes.

What're you studying? English?

More a sub-category of English. At least, it falls under the same school, but doesn't quite have the same theoretical rigour as your straightforward Literature degree: Creative Writing. I'm studying Creative Writing, if that's something one ought to admit to.

I think you just did, mate.

A girl with a fringe stepped up to the microphone. The audience went quiet, and the girl, staring tentatively around the room, explained that the work we were about to hear was a series of responses written by seven writers who had spent the last few weeks thinking about and engaging with the work on show at the exhibition we had just been to. She thanked everybody for coming, then she introduced the first reader, a young fella whose pages shook as he read an essay about a famous ballet dancer who had a psychotic breakdown at the height of his career and spent the rest of his life in a mental institution in Switzerland. I could hear the nerves in his voice, and I could tell that the people around me heard them too, the way they glanced at each other. The better readers leaned in to it. They made jokes, told anecdotes. Punctuated the silence following each of their poems with patter. I glanced at Mairéad. She knew I was looking at her. I could tell by the way her face was set. Only a few years before, I had watched her trail Debbie Porter by the hair across the pavement and punch her over and over again until she screamed for Mairéad to stop. Now she was smiling along to the poems being read by a woman who had translated Catullus. There was a round of applause, a huge thank you to everybody for coming, and for the readers, who had gone back to their seats and were smiling modestly.

I think that calls for another one, Conor said.

Mairéad grabbed her purse from her bag and said, No, it's my round. Same again?

Aye, why not?

Conor went with her to the bar. He leaned with his elbow on the counter and said things that made Mairéad laugh and look away. There was nobody in the vicinity who didn't know him, and they went out of their way to say hello. When they came back to the table, Conor slipped into the seat next to Mairéad. He rested his hands on his knees and said, Again, and I can't stress this enough, I take no responsibility.

What for? I said, and he waved his hands in the air.

For, well. Anything. Anything at all.

I sat at the corner of the table in the beer garden, across from Mairéad, who was squeezed between that girl who had introduced the readings upstairs, the one with the fringe, and another girl I had been introduced to, but whose name I couldn't remember. There were about twenty students from Queen's spread across three tables. They drank craft beer and smoked rollies, talked about the poems that had been submitted to workshop that week, and slabbered about how they had been rejected from magazines who had published people I'd never heard of before, but whose poems were shite.

I drank my stout and sat there quietly, nodding along, laughing when I had to, acting like I understood their quips and jokes, their weird cultural references. It got to the point where I was afraid to say anything. The few times I worked myself up to it, people set their drinks down, looked at me, and then carried on with the conversation as if nothing had happened. I tried to catch Mairéad's eye, but she was too distracted by all the craic she was having at the other side of the table. She was right in the middle of it, her voice pitched, her speech sharp and clear and full of the kind of witticisms that seemed to go down a treat with people who got a tickle out of posing questions like, What would you rather have, hands for feet or feet for hands?

It's gotta be hands for feet, she said. I want to be able to drink my pint with my hand-foot. Or smoke a cigarette. She glanced playfully around the table. I could smoke a feg with my feet, no sweat, she said.

Could you really?

Mairéad pulled her sock off and slapped her foot on the table. Somebody roll a feg for my foot, she said.

Conor took the rollie he was smoking and placed it between her toes.

Not that way, the other way. Turn it round.

Mairéad leaned forward and used her hands to bring her foot up to her mouth. She did this so easily and without effort that her foot seemed to function as a third hand she rested on her chin with the feg poking out at just the right angle for her to smoke casually, as if it was second nature to her. Her mates cheered. I could tell they liked having her around. She added a bit of an edge to what was a fairly bookish crowd. They were all studying for PhDs. The few that weren't were either Masters students who had made a name for themselves, or gifted undergrads who had been brought into the fold. Mairéad fell somewhere between. She had proved herself at undergrad but couldn't afford to do a Masters. Her mates sympathized because she was good, she deserved to have the option to do a Masters if she wanted to. But they couldn't get their heads around why she was moving to Berlin. They thought she was taking a year out to travel like they did when they went Interrailing, or backpacking across Vietnam, which a long-haired fella wearing a beanie hat had done the year before. He wouldn't fuck up about it.

We trekked through Cao Bang, he drawled, in his North Down accent. There were these incredible waterfalls, they looked like something from another planet, and we picnicked there, by the stream . . .

Have you done any travelling yourself? I said to Conor.

Not like this crowd of ex-pats, he said.

What about your degree? Did you do that at Queen's as well?

Undergrad, Masters and PhD, all in one swoop.

No gap years for you then?

No gap years. Hardly a summer.

He glanced at Mairéad, who was showing everybody how she could squirt beer through that hole in her lip. He sighed, shook his hair out of his face, and looked at me as if he had forgotten what we were talking about.

So you've never lived anywhere else? I said.

I keep meaning to, he said, smiling now. But I can't seem to be able to find my way out of the Duty Free.

You must be sick of it.

Sick of what? The Duty Free? He chuckled, spat tobacco out from between his teeth. What was it your man said, I've no reason to go away? Although when I finish my PhD, I might find one.

Mairéad overheard what he had said and laughed.

Don't listen to a word he says, Sean, she said. He won't go anywhere. He hasn't the temperament.

Yeah, another girl said, the one with the fringe. I can't see you leaving Belfast even after you submit. He's stuck to this place, isn't he?

Like a mouse to a glue trap, he'll wriggle around Belfast till he dies.

Conor raised his eyebrows, taken aback, but smiling.

We'll see about that, he said.

The girl with the fringe was called Julia. She had an accent I couldn't place, then I realized she was from Dublin, but from the side of the river where everybody has that proper nasally accent, the one that makes them sound American. She was good mates with Mairéad. I could tell by how she went out of her way to talk to me, even though we didn't have anything to say to each other. She kept bringing the conversation back round to Mairéad.

I hear she's living with you now, she said.

Aye, I'd a spare room there so. Makes sense.

Totally, yeah. She speaks very highly of you.

I'm sure she does, I said, trying to sound ironic. It went clean over Julia's head.

How do you feel about her moving to Berlin? she said.

Aye, grand. She'll do well.

She will do well. She'll do great, won't she?

Aye, definitely.

She glanced at Mairéad, who was having a competition with this other lad to see who could flip and catch the most beer mats. It was getting tense. People leaned across the table to watch. What made you move to Belfast then? I said, thinking that was something we could talk about. But Julia's eyes were locked on Mairéad, and she had this smile on her face, as if she was seeing something else. Belfast? I don't know. I just . . . She gave herself a shake and sighed, almost embarrassed. I didn't want to live in Dublin any more, she said. And they have a decent Creative Writing course up here so . . .

You do Creative Writing as well then?

For my sins.

Listen to her, Conor said, leaning over my shoulder. She could've gone anywhere, she was a star student at Trinity, a real prodigy, and her parents would've been happy to send her wherever she wanted to go. But she chose here. She chose Belfast. Bet you they were delighted when you broke the news. Bet you they were over the moon.

They were actually. They were happy as long as I was happy.

I'm sure they were, Conor said, dropping back on to his stool.

Clio, an American girl, leaned in to the conversation and said, What is it with you and your weird obsession with that question? Can't people from Belfast understand why anybody would want to live here?

I certainly can't, Conor said. Can you?

I agreed, I couldn't.

Clio rolled her eyes. You guys are so preoccupied with your own shit, she said.

Mairéad raised her hands, peaceably. I have to agree with the lads here, it's hard to get your head around it, and that's not to say this place isn't a good place to come to, but when you're from New York –

What's being from New York have to do with anything? Clio said.

The three of us looked at each other, and laughed.

It has everything to do with it, Conor said. Absolutely everything.

13

Talk of a party at Conor's circulated the beer garden that night in whispers and glances. There were the logistics, of course, but also the clandestine task of making sure the right people knew about what was happening without the word spreading too widely – Conor was happy enough to have people back but didn't want a mad one full of randomers he didn't know wrecking the place. The taxis that were ordered were taken by the select few who had got the message but were forced to cover their tracks by saying goodnight and see you soon to the very same people they would meet back at Conor's gaff in fifteen minutes' time. On the way, we stopped at the Hatfield, a bar where licensing laws don't seem to apply, and grabbed two cases of Carlsberg, two bottles of wine, and four bags of cheese and onion crisps. Conor opened a bag of those crisps in the passenger seat. The driver opened the window, and when he pulled up outside Conor's gaff, he charged us eight quid and said, Smell them fucking crisps.

Conor looked at the empty packet he had crunched up in his hand.

Shit, he said. My apologies.

The people who had got into the other taxis had arrived before us. They were waiting in Conor's kitchen, about a dozen of them huddled around the countertops pinching each other's tobacco. They cheered when we stepped through the door, and when we set the cases of beer down, they went into their pockets to pay the cash that was owed. Conor raised a can: Sláinte. The phrase was repeated hesitantly by a few people who were either unsure about saying it, or unused to hearing it. Some slipped out the back for a smoke while others went into the living room and put music on. I leaned with my back against the kitchen counter. I wasn't drunk, but I'd had enough to not care too much about making an effort to talk to people unless they wanted to talk to me, which at this stage of the game, they were more than happy to do. This one girl in particular, who pottered around the kitchen in her bare feet, asked me about Liverpool and whether or not I had thought about going back to university to do a Masters. I admitted that part of the reason I left Liverpool was that I thought that if I moved back home and saved a few quid, maybe I could wing it. Anna – her name was Anna – understood this predicament. She had applied to do a Masters in Fine Art in London. She had done her undergrad there, but she didn't get the bursary she needed to be able to pay for it. I asked if she was raging about having to move back home. She looked at me with surprise and said, No, not at all. Coming back home was the best decision I've made.

Seriously?

I had never met anybody who had gone away and come back and was happier with the life they had here than elsewhere. I said this to her and she said, Hold on, and introduced me to a lad called Francis, a big quiet fella with a gentle face who smiled harmlessly at everything that was going on around him. He had studied in Dublin and had some horror stories about living in house-shares owned by landlords who threatened to evict him every few months for not being able to afford the rent they kept putting up. He leaned with his back against the fridge and talked to me about how he was forced to move from one place to another, and not always with a deposit to carry over. Damp and mould that had already been on the walls when he moved in was used as an excuse to keep his money from him, and when he finally found a place he was able to afford, it always came with some sort of caveat – either it was miles away from where he needed to be, or he was sharing a bedroom with two or three other people. Even then the chances of living there any longer than a few months without the landlord threatening to up the rent, or sell the property, were slim.

Is it like that up here as well? I said.

Nah, it's okay up here. Rent's still affordable enough.

Give it a few years though, Anna said.

Yeah, few years and we'll be right up there with them.

I wanted to ask what was going to happen in a few years, but I had the feeling this was something I was supposed to know. I made a mental note to read up on it some other time and followed them out the back. Conor was there. He was standing on his own in the corner of the yard with one hand in the pocket of his black skinny jeans, the other holding a joint he smoked with his fingers right around the roach. He nodded me over to smoke with him, but I was distracted by the crowd huddled around the garden table. They were talking about how they would vote if a border poll was called tomorrow, and they were all dead sensible about it, weighing up the positives and negatives, in a way I had never heard anybody talk about politics before, like they had no skin in the game. Conor saw me backing towards the door and straightened up. Waved for me to come over.

I know people from your neck of the woods, he said to me.

Do you, aye?

My auntie used to take me to Beechmount Leisure Centre when I was a kid.

I didn't know what Beechmount Leisure Centre had to do with where I was from, they were at opposite ends of the road. I said this to Conor and he chuckled and said, I know, I know, as if I had mis-understood him. My auntie lived at the bottom of the Springfield Road, he said. I practically grew up around Blackstaff. I know a fair few people from around there, and I still see my cousins every once in a while. Mad bastards. Swear to God, I have some stories.

I knew what he was trying to do, and it was weird because this was his house and all the people around us were his mates. He didn't have to pretend he was somebody he wasn't. The only way I could think to check him on it was to ask where he was from; the shame that came over his face when he said Lisburn Road made me feel sorry for him.

Your ma and da must've done all right for themselves, I said.

He smiled and said, They did, to be fair, but didn't say anything else about it.

We were standing next to the window by the back door, which looked into the living room, and I could see Mairéad and Julia dancing to a Joni Mitchell song they had put on the record player. It was the first time I had seen Mairéad dance since we were kids. She would line up with the rest of the girls from about the estate in Bronagh Massey's front garden and do the Steps routine. She didn't have the form Julia had, her movements weren't as natural, or as loose, and when she followed Julia's lead and closed her eyes, she looked less relaxed than she would if she was blindfolded and spun around. It was nice though, she looked like she was having a good time.

They've fallen out with me, Conor said.

Why's that?

He shrugged, took a draw of his joint. He liked to talk with the smoke still in his lungs. It made him sound like he was being choked.

Julia and I used to live with each other, now we don't, he said.

And Mairéad?

Mairéad – well, if she hasn't said anything, I better not.

She's moving to Berlin, I said.

Aye, I know. I was supposed to be going with her.

To Berlin? Serious? What happened?

Conor stared at the smoke he had blown into the air. His eyes were red as fuck.

She changed her mind, he said.

I smiled. I said something like, Sounds just like her, and breathed through the hole that had opened like a wound in the middle of my chest.

Later in the night, I bumped into Mairéad on my way upstairs for a piss. I told her about what Conor had said and asked if it was true. She said, Yeah, it is, and turned as if to go back into the living room. I stopped her.

Is there something going on between yous two?

She came at me so fast I almost tripped over the bottom stair.

Fuck sake, Sean. Don't complicate things any more than they already are.

What's complicated about it? You don't tell me fuck all.

But Mairéad had already pushed past me and rejoined the party in the living room. More people had moved inside and were dancing along to a Paul Simon song. It was awkward, I didn't know how to dance to that kind of music, and everybody knew the words; they were giving it stacks. Not having anywhere else to go, I followed Mairéad into the kitchen. She saw me coming and slipped out the back, and when I went out after her, she somehow managed to skirt around me and duck into the living room. I took the hint and stayed out there, on my own, lingering around the margins of a conversation about Paul Muldoon, his early work in particular, which everyone agreed was his best. And while I stood there pretending to know what they were on about, I caught glimpses of Mairéad through the living-room window. She was dancing with her arms around Julia, the two of them swaying in the middle of the room, staring into each other's eyes, and then collapsing into a fit of giggles. I gave it a minute, then I went in to see if she wanted to leave any time soon, but she was gone. Conor was too. I asked that girl Anna if she had seen either of them and she said no, she hadn't seen Mairéad since earlier on.

What about Conor? I said, stupidly.

He's passed out in the front room.

Anna brought me through to show me. Conor was curled up on the single chair with his hands tucked between his thighs. She took a packet of tobacco from the inside pocket of her black leather jacket and rolled a feg. She had long skinny fingers that were decked out with silver rings, two on each finger, and a rope bracelet that slid down her arm as she licked the skin.

Is Mairéad still here then? I said.

Anna glared at me, and there was irony in her voice when she said, Yes, she's still here.

Where is she then? Is she upstairs?

She's with Julia.

What're they doing? Is she okay? She's been dodging me all night.

Has she? I just thought she was having a good time.

I felt my face go red and looked at the floor. Aye, suppose she is, I said.

Are you not?

I am, aye. I just don't know anybody.

Anna tucked her feg behind her ear. Would you like me to order you a taxi?

Nah, it's sweet. I should probably wait on Mairéad.

You'll be waiting a while.

Why? Is she upset?

Anna laughed. Doubt it, she said. She's with Julia.

Oh, right. Okay. What're they doing?

Do you not know?

I shrugged. I was that slow on the uptake, and when the penny finally dropped, Anna looked at me as if to say, really? Can you not put two and two together? I laughed. I said, No fucking way, only now it was less a defence mechanism than genuine shock. It was Julia. Mairéad was seeing Julia.

Has she been living here? Is this where she's been staying?

Well, no. The Julia thing is a recent development.

Did she actually come out, or is this just –

Just what?

Anna fixed me with a look that made me think very carefully about what I said next.

Like, is she actually gay or?

She's bi. And she came out months ago. Like last year.

Oh, right.

I looked at Conor slumped with his head hanging over the edge of the chair, his mouth wide as a net, and thought, who the fuck are these people? They weren't just some crowd from university Mairéad knocked about with every once in a while. They were her actual mates. People who had become part of her life, who had been there for her since she moved down to the Holylands all those years ago, when she started university, who brought her to literary readings and exhibition launches, and then back to house parties where they talked about politics and poetry and danced along to 'Graceland'.

Does her ma know? Is that why she doesn't live with her any more? I said.

No, it's not that.

I must've looked to Anna like I was missing something, because she said, Her mother's an addict, isn't she? She was so matter-of-fact about the way she said it that I was like, What're you on about, an addict? Not because I didn't know or hadn't seen it for myself; one day I was walking down the street, at about six o'clock, and saw Mairéad standing outside her house in her school uniform. She was locked out and had been standing there so long that I had to climb up the drainpipe and through her bedroom window to let her in. Her ma was lying unconscious on the bathroom floor. The shit was running down the inside of her leg, and all around her, a puddle of piss had spread out over the tiles. I had seen this, but I never would've said a word about it to anyone even if they knew and had seen it for themselves. Because if you're talking about one person's ma or da and the troubles they carry around with them, you're talking about all of them, including, in most cases, your own, and the only thing worse than seeing someone's da standing round the corner from the off-licence trying to get someone to go in for him because he's barred, or someone's ma climbing into the back seat of a souped-up Supra at three o'clock in the afternoon only to reappear a few hours later, barely able to stand, is to acknowledge it for what it is and not as something you catch out of the corner of your eye every once in a while and pretend to ignore.

I tried to explain this to Anna, and she was as understanding as she could be, given she wasn't from where we were from, but then I realized: Anna wouldn't know these things about Mairéad's ma unless Mairéad had sat her down and told her. I asked if that had been the case and she said, Yeah, she's spoken about it a few times, but not often, and only when she needs to. The last few months have been hard for her so . . . Her voice trailed off. The skin around her nose ring had reddened and was flaking. She looked sorry for me.

I'm sure Mairéad would've told you at some point, she said.

I said, Aye, she probably would've, and drank my wine.

Back in the living room, people were flailing about the place with their hands in the air, doing their best Kate Bush impressions. The kitchen was as bad; a group of lads were taking turns on a guitar, singing Bob Dylan. Out the back, things got heated when two people started arguing about the NHS and how important a thing it was to consider when it came to voting in a border poll. It's something I would really have to take into consideration, one of them said, drearily, in a voice that made me want to put my fist through a wall.

I slipped out the door without telling anybody I was away and walked down a street that was wide and lined with trees. On the main road, the only places still open were the Chinese takeaways. I saw lights spilling out on to the pavement and thought, what a life it would be if I could waltz into one of those places right now and grab myself a Styrofoam box filled with rice and curry and bounce into a taxi back up to the flat. No such luck; I had no money, and the only way I could think to get back up the road without getting lost in some street filled with flags I didn't like the look of was to ring a taxi from the depot and hope the driver didn't suspect anything when I told him where I was going.

He didn't. He hardly said a word to me, and when we parked

outside the next block up, I told him I would be two seconds: I just need to run into the flat and grab some cash. I made a real show of pretending to press the buzzer and glancing through the window to the left of the main doors. Then I told the driver I was going to run round the back and knock the living-room window: My flatmate's asleep! The driver didn't mind. He could see where I lived, and if a trick was pulled, he knew where I was and would be coming to knock the door. I scarpered along the entry to the next block down, which was my block, and ducked along the side of the building. It was dead quiet round there, there were no lights on or anything. I peeked around the wall to make sure the driver hadn't got out of his car before slipping the key into the lock and strolling casually through. There was some leftover pizza on the kitchen counter. I sat on the settee and wondered how long it had taken the driver to realize he had been done over. Was it when he got out of his car and went over to the window of the ground-floor flat I had been pretending to look into? Or was it when he rapped the window, gently at first, waking a woman who thought the worst and screamed? He could've been waiting for a fare to come his way for hours. Week nights were always quiet, and when he took the call from the depot on the Ormeau, he might've done so at the price of missing out on that thirty-quid airport run every taxi driver was chewing at the bit to catch.

Lying on my bed fully clothed, with the ceiling tilting dizzily away from me, I felt bad about it only because I was dipping into somebody else's livelihood, and I knew how hard it was to get by.

14

It was always late at night, when I couldn't sleep, when my head started going and going. One thing after another, and before long I would be back on Facebook, scrolling through Aoife's timeline.

She was popular. She got hundreds of Likes, and I could tell from the photos she'd been tagged in that she had loads of mates. Wee girls who looked just like her, who liked to put on make-up and wear nice clothes, who hung around coffee shops drinking iced lattes in the summer. They'd go to Newcastle and walk along the beach, take pictures of the Mournes. Stand in the shallows and watch the sea roll out. Every once in a while, they'd jump on the train to Belfast. They'd walk along the streets I walk through, and for Aoife it was just a jaunt, a wee day trip with her mates. But I had lived for so long without knowing anything about her, and then to see her suddenly sixteen years old and sitting on the grass out the front of the City Hall, the same spot where I had sat a few days before, reading my book, was like watching an actor break the fourth wall.

I wasn't supposed to know anything about her. That's the luxury of estrangement. And it was grand until I started picking at the seal, first my da and now my sister, peeling back just an inch to look. That's when it started messing with my head; the incompleteness of the picture I was getting and the desperate urge to make it clear. To understand the kind of life she's had, and to know for sure that she's okay.

*

I got a phone call from my probation officer the next day telling me that the Fine Collection and Enforcement Service had been in contact with her about my six-hundred-quid fine. She said I would have to ring the Customer Service team and work out a payment scheme, otherwise I would be in breach and brought back to court. The thought of being dragged in front of that judge was enough to get me pleading with the fella on the phone. Unimpressed, he told me five quid would be deducted from my Jobseeker's Allowance every week, which was twenty quid out of the hundred and eighty a month I was getting. That was before my twenty-quid phone bill came out, and the thirty quid I was charged at the end of every month for the overdraft I had been given like a present when I opened my university account.

The only way I was able to get by was to pull tricks at the self-checkouts. It was scary now in a way it hadn't been before, because it wasn't just a piss-take any more, I really needed the food, and if I got caught the cunts would have their eyes on me every time I set foot in the shop. If they wanted to be proper bastards they'd phone the peelers, I'd be reported for breaching my probation, and that would land me in all sorts of shit. I rang my ma for a lend of money only when I really needed it. She was struggling enough as it was without worrying about me. One of the people whose house she cleaned down the Malone Road had found a company who charged half as much for the same amount of work. My ma was told she had to go, after ten years. Just like that.

I had applied for every job on every website and recruitment agency I could find. Call centres weren't out of the question any more, and all those hopes and dreams I'd had of working anywhere that wasn't a nightclub died with every conciliatory email I got telling me that the volume of applications was high and the competition strong. I was starting to think there was some kind of agenda against me; the bookshop said no, and that was okay, I knew it was a long shot. But Asda wouldn't even give me an interview, and I spent days on that application, with help from the stuff Mairéad had sent me before. The fella in the dole was pleased with the effort I was putting into my Job Search booklet though. He told me to keep at it, You're doing well, but he was perturbed by how many jobs I had applied for without getting any bites. The best advice he could give me was to dumb down my CV so that employers wouldn't think I was over-qualified for the job.

Don't tell them you have a degree, he said.

I wondered how much he was getting an hour.

Things were finally looking up when I got emails from two different places telling me they were impressed with my application and would love to have me in for an interview. The first was an internship with a non-profit art organization that had set up shop in an abandoned building at the bottom of Bedford Street. Fully paid for six months, with the prospect of full employment, they were looking for someone to help with exhibitions, organizing events, and to take charge of their social media. The pay was good too, £7.50 an hour, which was more than any job I'd ever had.

I texted Mairéad and told her the news. She hadn't come back to the flat since that night we ended up in Conor's gaff; three days and I hadn't heard anything from her. I messaged her once asking what the craic was and she just said she'd let me know when she was coming back.

Your bags still here
Do you not need it?

Nah its grand
I'll pick it up later in the week
what about this job?

it's for that arty farty place I told you about
They want me in for an interview

Unreal
U buzzin?

                              aye
                    beats the bar like
              Not getting my hopes up tho

Mairéad's advice was to spend the next few days reading about the kind of exhibitions the organization put on and the artists who worked there, and to really ham up my interest in working in the arts: Tell them about the magazine you edited in Liverpool, and tell them you did all the fundraising for it, they love that kind of thing. She sent me a list of questions I might be asked, and she told me to make sure I knew what I was going to say, but warned against sounding like I had rehearsed. I took her advice onboard, and in the meantime, I sailed through my first interview, in a nightclub in the Cathedral Quarter called Ollie's. The manager brought me into the VIP area, where she sat on a stool with a clipboard on her knee and said, So how soon can you start?

I was buzzing, and the buzz stayed with me right up until I stepped into the art studios a couple of days later. It was dark, there were no lights, and there was a strange smell, like turps. A stylish man in a grey turtleneck told me it was nice to meet me and brought me into a gallery room. Three chairs had been placed neatly in a row in the middle of the room and, facing those chairs, one solitary chair I was told to sit on. I was wearing the grey trousers and shirt I wore to my graduation the year before. I thought I looked all right, Primark clothes weren't the worst. Then these three intimidatingly dressed middle-aged people entered the room from somewhere behind me and introduced themselves: Philippa, James and Richard. They shook my hand and swooped on to the chairs in front of me.

It's lovely to meet you, Sean, Philippa said. Shall we get started?
She was wearing a scarf that hung all the way down to the floor,

and there was a real elegance about how she eased me into the interview, with compliments about my CV and how impressed she was with it. The men sitting at either side of her agreed, with little inclinations of their heads.

Tell us about the magazine you edited in Liverpool, she said.

It was like I had stepped out of myself. What I saw was another person with another voice explaining how he had used the funds he had raised through events he had organized, and the advertising he had acquired from local businesses around Liverpool, to pay for a print run of a thousand copies of the magazine, which were distributed for free. When it came to the question about how the skills I had acquired during that experience were transferable to the work environment at the arts organization, the person sitting on the chair I was sitting on spoke about how editing a magazine with a team of people required a degree of resourcefulness that was essential to the day-to-day running of an arts organization, particularly when it came to working with the public, whether that was through exhibitions, collaborations, or open studio days. Philippa smiled. Richard, the man to her left, stared into the space above my head, as if the question he was about to ask was being beamed to him from some presence deep inside the gallery wall.

Tell us about your experience with social media, he said.

I remembered reading something on the internet about how important it was for arts organizations using social media to make their online presence more interactive. I also remembered reading an article about increasing audience participation through media engagement. I dropped these phrases into a couple of sentences about how I would use social media not only as a way to publicize events and exhibitions, but as a means of connecting people with the artists the studios had working there. I know some artists would be more comfortable with this than others, I said. But you could have them doing collaborations with other artists to produce online content. There's this gallery in London whose name escapes me – that's what I said, 'escapes me', in that absent-minded way posh people do, as if through no fault of their own – and they've been doing some interesting collaborative projects with writers. They write responses to whatever work they're exhibiting, then they produce online publications for people to read and engage with.

Have you taken into consideration the cost of these kinds of collaborations?

I haven't. I just thought it was an interesting idea.

Well, luckily for us, we aren't short of interesting ideas.

There was laughter, mostly from Richard, who looked at me like I had broken into his house. Aside from taking responsibility for our social media accounts, there are more practical aspects of the job, he said. We insist on the gallery floors being mopped twice a day. Once in the morning, and once before we close. The hallways and stairs will need to be vacuumed, and the communal kitchen cleaned up. I assume you have no issue with taking the bins out?

No. No issues at all.

And these nightclubs you've worked for, El Divino, Thompson's Garage, Eivissa –

He said each of the names with the lofty tone of somebody who was tremendously amused.

Was table service part of your duties?

In the VIP lounge, aye.

The VIP lounge. The very place.

He glanced at James, and James chewed his bottom lip.

We tend to hire catering for exhibition launches, and often with our open studio days, we like to provide refreshments. Simply put, it would be useful to have somebody around who can attend to those duties. It could save us an awful lot of hassle, couldn't it, James?

It most certainly could.

I told them I could be that person, no bother. If that's what they needed. I'd put on a shirt and trousers like I had that morning and swan around the room with a tray, asking people if they fancied a canapé.

Do you have any questions you would like to ask us? Philippa said.

I had read somewhere about how asking questions at the end of a job interview was an opportunity to show your enthusiasm for the role. The three I had prepared were good questions about opportunities for progression, the work culture, and what the employers themselves enjoyed about their jobs. I was convinced they would go down well right up until it came to asking them, then it was awkward, there was a tricky silence. Not for the first time, the two men glanced at each other. I bit my tongue and kept my eyes locked on Philippa. She was the only one who took me seriously. I appreciated that, she was dead nice to me. But I saw how the other two were carrying on and knew that no matter what I said, it wouldn't make a difference. Their minds were made up.

The thing I like most about this job is the people you meet, Philippa said. We get artists from all over the world coming here to work, we get to know them, their stories, and it can be very fulfilling, I must say.

What about people from where I'm from? I said, and she smiled.

Those people too, she said.

I got the rejection email on my way home from community service. It had been a long shift, we must've cut about a hundred acres of grass, and although the rain had held off through the afternoon, Joe had us working down the back again, where the ground was wet and marshy, and I was covered in mud.

The email was the same as it always was: the people on the panel were impressed by the standard of my interview and hoped I was encouraged by how far I had gotten in the process. It wouldn't have been so bad if I hadn't got carried away thinking about what it would be like to work in a place like that, to be surrounded by artists, to make friends with them even, somewhere that wasn't a nightclub, where I felt like I was part of something. It was daft, but I had begun to think that working in a place like that would open my life up in some way, that I might be able to have something like Mairéad had with her mates from Queen's. A group of people who were into the things I was into, who went to events and knew how that world worked. Turns out, no. That wasn't going to happen. The doors into those worlds were bolted shut.

I took my keys out of my pocket and was walking up the stairs slowly, footsteps echoing through the block, when two men came down from the fourth floor. They were dressed like peelers in black vests and white shirts, and they had earpieces, like bouncers. Bald, brooding, with tattooed arms and bullish necks, they stopped in the hallway behind me and watched.

I came out on to the fourth floor and kept on going, to the top. The lights were broken up there. It was dark, but their voices carried. They were coming back up the stairs. I panicked and tried the maintenance cupboard, saw there was no space even for me, and slammed it closed. The men must've thought I had gone into one of the flats up there because all of a sudden their footsteps stopped. The block was quiet, and then one of them said something and they traipsed back down the stairs, their big boots thumping like bricks on the ground.

I crossed the hall quietly, on tiptoes, and looked out the window to make sure they were gone. Five minutes passed that way, then I went down to the flat. There was a notice on the door:

NOTICE OF REPOSSESSION

TO ALL WHOM IT MAY CONCERN

TAKE NOTICE that these premises have been repossessed today by order of the owner J M McClean Group Limited.

AND TAKE FURTHER NOTICE that any attempt to enter the premises is prohibited without written permission of the owner or its solicitors or agents, effective from 18th October 2013.

I rang my ma and told her what was happening, then I rang our Anthony, who said he would be over later on, with the van. My clothes went into the suitcase I dragged from the cupboard in the hall, then I emptied my bedside drawers and chucked all the empty paracetamol strips and broken phone chargers into the black bin bag I had hung from the bottom of the bed. There was space in the suitcase for some books, the rest went into boxes and Bags for Life I had bought from Asda and never used again. I pulled everything I needed out to the hallway and looked down at how little of my life was made up of things I owned. The only thing left to sort out was Mairéad's bag. I messaged her and asked what I should do with it and she messaged back saying she could call up to the flat that night and grab it, if that suited? I said no, I would be gone by then, and she said, No sweat, will I call up to your ma's?

The thought of her seeing me holed up in that wee house filled me with dread. I told her I could drop it in to her next time she was in work and she said, No, I need it before then, I have to sell shots. I didn't know what that had to do with her bag until I opened it and saw the dress she wore those nights she worked in Mono. It was short and black and smelled like cinnamon. I held it up to my face, and for a while I just sat there, on the floor in the middle of the living room, holding Mairéad's dress in front of me.

15

Our Anthony turned up to the flat in a ten-year-old Berlingo he had bought a few months ago, when he was deep into another four-week stint of being his best self, eating clean and working hard, staying off the drink. Posting motivational quotes on Facebook with updates about his diet plan for the week, the session he had just done. It was a lifestyle choice that consumed him for as long as he could resist the pull of those Friday night phone calls. And then, usually after a long week on the job, when the fumes from the paint he had been inhaling since he was a teenager began to prickle his itchy skin, he would find an excuse to call into the local, and that was it: three days later he would be sitting in a house somewhere in Twinbrook, broke, trying to rustle together enough cash for another bag of toot.

He parked his van out the front of the block and opened the back doors. There were a bunch of paint cans in there, some rollers and extension poles, a pile of dust sheets that needed to be taken out and folded to make space. Running up and down the stairs wrecked me; the lift was broke and we were both breathing heavily. When everything was packed and cleared away, I went up for one last look around the flat. Through the living-room window, the mountain had nothing written on it that day. Even if there was, I wouldn't be able to see it; the clouds had come down over the hill, and the houses had disappeared in the fog.

I walked back down the stairs. Anthony was standing in the middle of the road with his hand shading his eyes, staring up at the sky.

What's wrong? I said.

Nothing. Get in.

He drove slowly, cautiously, with one eye on the road, the other on the clouds he leaned forward to look at. It had started raining. Big eighteen-wheelers whooshed by.

See that helicopter? he said. Up there. Look.

What about it?

Everywhere I go. All day. Fucking everywhere. See it?

I could. It was hovering away up there, a little speck of red light flashing so high above that neither of us could hear it. Anthony rolled his window down and flicked the ash from his menthol.

Cunts have been all over me, he said. Last few weeks – He looked at me out the corner of his eye. They had you in for an interview, didn't they?

Aye, ages ago.

Did they say anything about me?

Nah, nothing.

Well, somebody's talking, he said, as if he suspected me.

I looked at him. You serious? I said.

Anthony was deadly serious. That's where his head was at.

He pulled over outside my ma's house, climbed out of the driver's seat and walked round to the back of the van without the slightest dip of his head even though it was pissing down. He lifted a box of books and shoved it into my chest. My hands worked the edges for grip. I struggled, almost dropped it.

You need to get to the gym, he said. You're looking weak.

We took some stuff up to the room above the barbers next door, which my ma's landlord owned and let her use for storage. There was already a pile of boxes and black bin bags in there from years ago. I tried to look through it, but the woman downstairs was waiting to close up shop. We ducked under the shutters and grabbed my suitcase from the back of the van. Our ma was waiting for us at the door. She gave me a hug and a kiss. My wee son, back with his mummy, she said.

My wee son, Anthony repeated, in a whiny voice.

He's delighted, aren't you, son?

Aye, best day ever.

Did you get that magnet? she said to Anthony.

Aye. Come here till I show you.

Anthony dragged a stool from the breakfast counter over to the electric box and showed her how to stick the magnet on the side of the meter. He pressed some buttons, moved the magnet up and down, and watched as the numbers on the display dropped right down to one. My ma closed the blinds. She stood with her arms crossed in the middle of the room, chewing the inside of her lip.

I'm too old to go to jail, she said.

You're not going to jail, ya rocket.

What if the electric man comes?

Pull the magnet off before you let him in. It won't show up anyway.

My ma blessed herself. God forgive me, she said.

I showed her the fan heaters she had asked me to bring from the flat, and the oil heater Ryan's da gave us when we moved in. She plugged it into the socket next to the settee and flicked the switch. I didn't realize how dark it was until the lamp came on. Suddenly the living room and the kitchen became two separate rooms, with the breakfast counter acting as a partition in the middle. At the other side of the counter, my ma checked the fish fingers she had under the grill. I can throw a couple on for you, if you want? she said to me.

I'm all right, I'll get something later.

Anthony sniggered. Will you not have a wee fish finger? Give him a wee fishy finger, mother.

Leave him alone, you. He's having a hard time.

Hard time? What would he know about a hard time? He dipped

his head as if to throw a punch and pulled me into a headlock. What would you know about a hard time?

He was laughing. I laughed too, but it was awkward. He smelled like sick.

Telling you what, it's not a bad wee gaff, he said, looking around. It's small, but sure if it's only the two of you.

It'll do the job, I agreed.

My ma ran her hand under the tap. She had burned her finger.

Sure it's only temporary, isn't it? she said.

I agreed, it was. Anthony glanced between us.

He needs a place to live, fuck sake. Don't be saying that.

What?

It's only temporary. He's your son.

Oh, God. No. I didn't mean it like that. She raised her finger to her mouth and sucked it. He knows he can stay as long as he wants, don't you, son? I meant for him. It's only temporary for him. I'm here on my own sure, aren't I?

But Anthony was annoyed. He went to the bread bin and pulled out the packet of Wagon Wheels my ma had stashed in there, behind the loaf. He munched four in a row, each one down the hatch in three bites. What's the plan then? he said to me. You gonna find somewhere else to live or wha?

I'm gonna find a job then go from there, aye.

Can you not get him some work? my ma said.

No chance, mother. I've had to lay people off. It's only me and Gerard left, and Johnzy. Johnzy comes in one day a week.

My ma took her hand out from under the tap and dabbed it with kitchen roll.

What about your degree? she said to me. Why don't you teach?

I'm not qualified to teach, I said.

Can you not become a journalist or something?

I did English Lit, mother. Not journalism.

For God's sake, what use is that bloody degree then?

It's no use at all, I said.

Anthony slapped his hand on my shoulder and squeezed. Sure we're gonna write a screenplay together, aren't we? We're gonna write a blockbuster.

Is that right?

Aye, well. Sean's gonna write it. He's got the education, he knows all the right words. I'll give him my ideas and we'll write them down in script form, won't we?

I don't know, Anto. I've never written a screenplay.

It's easy. You just lay it all out. I've got a book in the house that shows you.

He pulled a stool out from under the breakfast counter and sat down, all business now, and started expounding on these ideas he had. I've got this one for a TV series set in the eighties, in America, he said. It's gonna be proper eighties, like with the cars and the music and all. What's gonna happen is that there's these creatures that have been living underground for years and years, secretly, and they only come out at night. They're superhuman. Night Hunters, I call them. They can run like fuck, and they can climb buildings and all. Basically, the main character, he's a Navy Seal, and he has to get his family out of there, out of the city, because the city's all destroyed now, the Night Hunters have wrecked it, and they have to get to this compound in the country where it's safe. It'll be like the first season of *Walking Dead*, you know? Except instead of zombies you'll have these creatures that only come out at night, and they're far scarier. They run on their hands and feet, all crouched over, and they scream. Like them cunts who chase Frodo in *Lord of the Rings*. They scream like that, all loud and screechy. Wouldn't that be class? I've got the whole story planned out. Ten episodes. Telling you. They'll be throwing money at us.

Don't be getting your hopes up now, my ma said. It's hard to make films.

Trust me, I know what I'm doing. I've been watching films since

169

I was a child. I can see where they go wrong every time. Like *The Sopranos*. That ending. Worst ending I've ever seen. I would've had Tony taking on New York. I would've had him wiping them all clean out. You telling me that wouldn't have been a hundred times better?

He looked at me expectantly. I didn't want to hurt his feelings.

Aye, you're right, I said. Sounds brilliant.

We'll organize a weekend, will we? We'll sit down and write it all out.

I did what I always do and pretended I was up for it, that I was excited by the prospect even, knowing that the chances of it actually happening were slim. The way Anthony had been carrying on the last few months – he couldn't commit to a full shift of work, never mind an entire script. He didn't just go on the rip for a day or two either, he kept going and going until there was nobody left to party with. And then there were the comedowns, the cold sweats, the panic attacks every time he looked into the bucket next to his bed and saw blood. The only way he had of coping with it was to lock himself in his bedroom, in the dark, and eat an obscene amount of food – crisps and chocolate and takeaways, sometimes three or four a day. He would lie there from morning until night, watching conspiracy theory documentaries about alien abductions and Area 51. Bernice couldn't say anything to him. She couldn't even mention the possibility of him going back to work. He'd go nuts. Even when they'd no money, when the cupboards were empty and mortgage payments were missed. Bernice would ring my ma and cry down the phone. She couldn't take it any more, she was going to leave him, and my ma would tell her to grab the kids and get out of there. But she never did. She had been with Anthony since she was thirteen, they had their first baby when they were fifteen, and they were married at twenty-three. She didn't know anything else.

One of these days, she'll do it, my ma warned him. She'll not think twice about it. She'll pack her bags and go.

Anthony crossed his fingers. Please, God, he said.

Stop getting on like that now. She's the mother of your children.

She drinks every night, mother.

She does not.

She does. She drinks a bottle of wine and goes to bed blocked.

God love her. She must be depressed.

Depressed? She's a fucking nutjob.

You're a nutjob.

Anthony laughed. I haven't touched a drop in three weeks. Three weeks, he said, and held his fingers up to show. I need to get out. I need to clear my head. One weekend with the boys and I get dog's abuse.

I know, son, my ma said, softly now. But them drugs. I can't sleep with the thought of you taking them drugs.

Jesus Christ. I've a wife and kids and she's sitting here lecturing me.

I don't care if you're fifty. I'm still going to be lecturing you. I'm still going to worry.

Anthony moved past her, sheepish now, and tried to turn the attention back on me. What about this criminal? he said. Give him a bit of stick for once, will you?

He gets his fair share.

He's gay is what he is.

There was another dig on the shoulder, another feint.

Fruitcake, he said.

When Anthony left, my ma took her fish fingers out from under the grill. She set them on a plate with a round of toast she had buttered, took her plate over to the settee and set it on her knee. There was a forty-inch TV mounted on the wall at the bottom of the stairs. It was showing one of those housewife reality shows she liked to watch, the ones where rich women get into arguments and throw drink in each other's faces. I told her about what Anthony had said, about the helicopters and how he thought they were following him, and she looked down at her plate.

He's getting worse, isn't he? she said.

I don't know, is he?

My ma nodded. I think so, she said.

I went upstairs to unpack. There was a mattress on the floor, next to a set of drawers. I put my clothes into the drawers and set my books on top. The only source of light came from the window at the top of the stairs, and only with the door open as far as it went before it hit the bottom of the mattress, meaning that no matter what time of day it was, the room would be in darkness. I lay down to see what it was like and had the feeling that I was looking up from the bottom of a well. It was that small, about half the size of the bedroom I grew up in, and that room was the box room. I spent so much time there when I was a kid, playing video games, reading books, talking to wee girls on MSN Messenger. It was where I took myself off to when I wanted to be alone. Now, there was no alone. There was me and my ma on top of each other in that wee house.

I must've drifted off. When I woke up, I heard my ma talking to somebody downstairs. I sat up and listened, then I lifted Mairéad's big leather bag and brought it down with me. My ma had taken her by the arm and was walking her around the living room, showing her the paintings she had hung up on the walls. The first was Madonna from the *True Blue* album cover with her head thrown all the way back. It was supposed to be a present for my uncle, but my ma had made a mistake she couldn't fix, so she painted another one for him and kept the first for herself. Next to Madonna was a more recent painting of the lakes in Killarney, which was actually pretty good, and provoked a more enthusiastic response from Mairéad, who said, Fucking hell, that's class, and had to check herself for sounding surprised.

My ma was too excited to notice. She dragged Mairéad over to the big one she had hung on the wall between the living room and the kitchen. She described it as that painting of Jesus on the cross looking down at the world she copied from your man: What's his name? I said, Dali, and she said, Yes, Dali. What do you reckon? Mairéad's mouth fell open. My ma, thinking she was awed by it, said, I know.

The last was the least painful. My ma had painted seven individual portraits of the seven signatories on little 6 x 9 canvases and placed them along the kitchen counter, under her framed print of the Irish Proclamation. She was donating them to be auctioned at a fundraiser the Shinners had organized for the family of an old volunteer who had died a few weeks before.

Hope somebody bids for them, she said. God, imagine they didn't?

Mairéad opened her bag and checked everything was there. This is awkward, she said. But do you mind if I run upstairs and get changed? I've to be in work at ten o'clock, and by the time the train gets me down there . . .

Go you on, frig sake. Sean, ring her a taxi.

It's grand, I'll get the train.

Well, you walk her over to the station then, my ma said, fussily.

She knew she was embarrassing me, and she begrudged me for it.

Get your shoes on and walk her over, she said.

Her eyes lit up when Mairéad came down the stairs all dressed up in that black cocktail dress she had. Oh my God, look at this, she said, and wolf-whistled. She actually wolf-whistled. Look at the body on her, and those legs, where did they come from? She's gorgeous, isn't she, Sean?

I agreed, she was. Mairéad rolled her eyes.

Your heads are lit, she said.

My ma gave her a hug before she left. If I don't see you before you go, have a brilliant time, and don't be a stranger. Send me a message on Facebook and let me know how you're getting on, she said.

On the way over to the station, I told Mairéad I was sorry about the flat. I thought we'd have another few weeks at least.

Don't worry about it, she said. I've a place to stay anyway.

Where's that?

With a friend. Over on the Ormeau.

She didn't tell me who that friend was, and I didn't ask.

The rain was more of a drizzle now, but the wind blew it sideways, forcing us into the corner of the station platform, between the fence and the wall, where we hid under Mairéad's umbrella and waited. She was wearing a faux fur coat over her dress and a pair of white Converse. Her legs were goose-pimpled, and as we stood there, she shivered with her shoulders bunched up, protecting herself from the raindrops dripping down the back of her neck.

I'm leaving in two weeks, she said.

Jesus Christ, so you are.

I'm nervous. Look at me, I'm a state.

She made a face like she was scared. I put my arm around her and squeezed. I felt like I could do that, we were comfortable with each other in that way. She put her head on my shoulder.

Do you reckon you'll come back? I said.

If it goes tits up, aye. I'll be straight back.

It won't though. You'll be sweet.

Hope so. Knowing my luck.

I couldn't see her face because of how we were standing, the angle of her head against me, but I could tell that she was smiling. I ran my fingers through the fur and she leaned in to me, with her head on my chest now, and one arm around my waist.

I'll see you before you go though, won't I? I said.

Aye, we'll do something.

Another trip to Holywood.

That'd be nice.

You can teach me how to swim.

The wind was going for it now. It battered the top of the umbrella and sent raindrops spraying everywhere. We huddled in closer to the fence. People had written their names there, in paint and permanent marker. I took my keys out and scratched our initials into the panel, with the year underneath: 2k13. Mairéad took a picture on her phone.

You gonna put that up on Instagram as well? I said.

Nah, that's just for me, she said, but she was scundered. I could tell.

Go on, put it up.

No, fuck off.

I took her phone off her and tried to do it myself, but the screen locked. She typed the pin in for me and watched.

There now, I said. That's nice, isn't it?

Lovely.

Will I take a picture of us as well?

No. That's enough.

She put her phone back in her pocket, and for a while we just stood there, staring at the tracks, listening for that squealing sound they make when the train's coming down the line. When we heard it, Mairéad gave me a hug and a kiss and moved towards the edge of the platform.

Don't be a dick now, she said. Stay in touch.

You stay in touch.

I will.

When I got back to the house, my ma was sitting with her laptop on her knee, scrolling through Google image results, looking for something to paint.

I'll let you have the living room sure, she said.

I told her it was grand, don't worry about it, but she had made up her mind. She took a glass of water upstairs with her, and she told me to make sure to put the burglar alarm on before I went to bed. I promised I would, but I sat up late reading Alice Munro stories and forgot. In the early hours, I heard my ma going downstairs. Instead of a metal bar being dropped across the door like when I was a kid, I heard buttons being pressed, then a buzzing noise, a bleep.

The walls were thin. I heard her bedsprings creak.

*

When I was growing up and we still lived in that house in Twinbrook, there was a phone box on the top road, about ten minutes away from our street. After the morning I came home from my granny's house and my ma told me I could never see my da again, I would walk up to that phone box and ring his house phone. I would hold my hand over the mouth of the receiver and wait for my da to say hello, and then I would hang up. I did this every few weeks, for months. Then one day I looked down at the broken glass at my feet — someone had smashed the windows again — and waited for the dial tone. It didn't come. The line had been disconnected. That's when I knew my da had moved away.

16

From the pitch-black dark of that tiny little room, to the bathroom light that cut the eyes clean off me. A shower. Steam rising upwards. The sandwich in the fridge I had made the night before.

Have you got everything? my ma said, from the top of the stairs.

I got the bus up to Balmoral then walked for twenty-five minutes to the cemetery. In the courtyard, one of the lads was lifting petrol strimmers out of the container and setting them carefully on the ground. No worries about how wet the grass would be, Joe brought us over to the far side of the cemetery where the graves were more densely packed. Through the morning we worked from one row to the next, each of us moving at our own pace, careful as always to work around the effigies that had been set in front of the headstones. Now and then it couldn't be helped; the Virgin Mary lost her head. Fra was beside himself. He scooped up every statue and took them with him back to the hut where he spent his lunch break trying to fix them with Super Glue he had tucked into the front pocket of his rucksack. In the afternoon, the sky darkened. Clouds swallowed up shadows cast by headstones across the grass. I followed Joe and the rest of the men from one side of the cemetery to the other, my hips rotating from side to side with the strimmer almost mechanically now, with no thought about what I was doing beyond the odd rush of pleasure that came over me when the strimmer wire sliced cleanly through the overgrown grass. Cleaving through it like a pendulum, marking the passing seconds, each one falling out from under me, a slow landslide back to that night I looked down and saw a lad lying on the ground in the middle of an empty street. The strangeness of that feeling right after I'd done it. Like it wasn't even me who hit him.

I fingered the muck out of the spool for the millionth time and changed the strimmer wire. Then I refilled the tank with petrol and sat for a while at the edge of the group of men on their break, staring across the cemetery towards the Belfast skyline. The sky hummed with the weight of the clouds, and the breeze stirred through the trees lining the back of the cemetery. It spread out across the longer grass in a wave that gathered more momentum the closer it came to the graves. I shivered and pulled my hood up. Watched the cars moving along the motorway.

What do you reckon? Fra said to me.

About what?

He nodded at the sky and said, How long do you think we've got?

Dunno, about twenty minutes?

He looked away from me, shiftily, and made sure nobody was sitting close by. In his hand was a memorial card he had taken from a grave we walked past earlier that morning. He held it out for me to see. On it was a photograph of a wee lad wearing one of those fake Burberry hats everybody used to run about in, the ones you'd wear with the peak pointing up to the sky so everybody could see your fringe. He looked like every wee lad I knew growing up. He had the gold hooped earring and the thick gold chain, the Berghaus coat and the Fred Perry top with the collar flicked up. The dates under his picture confirmed it: he was born the same year as me, and he died when he was seventeen.

I said the only thing I could think to say: He's a good-looking kid.

Fra sniffed, wiped his nose with the back of his hand, and put the card back in his pocket.

It's gonna rain, he said.

He was right. Within the hour, the rain was coming down heavily and we were soaked. Joe let us off eventually and the men walked with their strimmers tucked under their arms back to the front of the cemetery. Fra hung back. He took the statues he had fixed during the lunch break out of his bag and headed off towards the rows of graves we had worked around that morning. One of the men had taken his strimmer for him, and his harness and face shield, saving him the hassle of having to walk all the way back to the hut before going out again, which was what I did. I hung my strimmer with the rest of them in the tool shed and headed back into the cemetery. It was pissing down, the headstones were getting pelted. In the distance, a figure was on his knees in front of a grave. In his hand, a statue of St Anthony had been cut perfectly in half.

I can't find the other half, Fra said. I've looked everywhere.

His face was specked with muck, and his weatherproofs, from his shins to his belly, were covered. It looked like he had been crawling on all fours through the dirt.

My ma would break her heart, he said.

His bottom lip quivered. He looked away.

Do you wanna talk about it? I said.

Talk about what?

Nothing, I thought . . . You seem upset.

Upset? You're lucky I don't smash this statue over your fucking head.

I told him I was sorry, I didn't mean anything by it.

Are you a fucking faggot or something, is that what it is?

No, I just –

He raised the statue up in the air and smashed it off a headstone. Shards of porcelain flew everywhere. His hand was bleeding. Blood ran over his palm and dripped from his middle finger.

See what happens? See what you made me do?

He looked at his hand and staggered backwards.

Jesus Christ, he said.

I tried to walk with him back to the hut, but he pushed me with the hand that wasn't bleeding and told me to get away from him. Through the rain, I saw the gates at the front of the cemetery, the mountain beyond the gates, and the sky, where the clouds had started to thin and the sun gleamed weakly through. Joe was standing at his office door. He watched as Fra went into the hut and came out again with his bag over his shoulder.

Keep that cunt away from me, that's all I'm saying, he said.

The rest of the men were standing around the doorway of the hut. I could see their faces through the windows, the rain running down. They told me Fra was the kind of man who could have you dragged down an alleyway and shot through the backs of your knees. I couldn't tell if they were serious; they kept egging each other on. When the shift was over, Joe called me into his office. He wanted to know what happened. I told him Fra picked up a broken statue and cut his hand.

Why was he annoyed at you then? he said.

I shrugged. I had no idea.

I had my first shift in Ollie's that night, at seven o'clock. I had brought a change of clothes with me to Milltown, thinking I could bounce into a black taxi as soon as I finished my shift and head on down. But I was stinking. I had to go round to the Kennedy Centre and wash myself over the sink in the disabled toilet. I wasn't nervous. I had been the new start enough times to know there was nothing to it as long as I didn't get in anybody else's way. Donna, the manager, seemed to sense this in me and stuck me at the end of the bar, next to the VIP area. The only thing I struggled with was the cocktails, which were two for one until eleven o'clock. The girl working next to me kept me sweet though. She had just come home from Australia, she told me, and she was doing everything she could to get back out.

This place is breaking my heart, she said.

Whatever tips I thought I'd make didn't come. The few that did were given obnoxiously, as a way of getting rid of shrapnel. I had one man who handed me 32p change from his seventy-quid round, and another who swapped his order three times before settling on four double Morgan's and two white wine spritzers. He counted the change I gave him then asked how much it was for a double Morgan's. I told him £9.50 and he did the maths on his phone. The next fella pushed the same button in a different way; he told me not to be shy with my measures. I poured and he watched me pour, and when it came to the rim of the measure, he said it again, Don't be shy. I said, Is that enough, mate? and he said, Perfect, and gave me a thumbs up. Then there were these three women who tried to coax me into giving them two for one cocktails even though it was after eleven. I tried to tell them, I said, I can't, it's my first shift. What started out as a few friends chancing their arms turned suddenly hostile. They told me there was too much ice in their glasses. Then there was a problem with the lime. Then one of them lifted her glass up to the light and said, Is this clean? I'd like a new glass, please. I made the drink again. I set it in front of her, for the third time, and she looked me dead in the eye.

See? That wasn't so difficult, was it?

The lights came on ten minutes before the club closed, at two o'clock. Donna came up to me when the clean-up was done and asked if I could come in on Monday night. The rest of the staff had moved towards the VIP area and were waiting to be told they could go. I was introduced as the new lad on the bar. The lads standing closest to me shook my hand and said things like, Welcome to the mad house, and, Hope you last longer than the last one. Donna told them to shut up. They think they have it hard, she said. I followed them out the fire escape where a few stragglers hung around outside The Merchant with their hands held out for cars that wouldn't stop. The hotel sorted us out with staff discount for taxis home. I rang my ma to make sure she was still up, I needed a few quid to cover my end of the fare. When I got back, she was sitting with her best mate, Mary, at the breakfast counter, smoking a big joint.

What's going on here? I said.

My ma glared at me shamelessly through the smoke.

We're smoking dope. Why? What's the problem?

Mary told me to sit down, have a drink. She poured a glass of wine right up to the rim and said, Get that into you, kid. Then she came at me as she always did with a big smacker right on the lips. It was worse because her teeth were bad, and she didn't look well even when she was done up. Not in an ugly way, she was just thin, and drawn. She held the joint out to me and said, Do you wanna wee puff?

No, he doesn't. He's not allowed.

I took the joint from Mary and said, Aye, why not?

My ma watched, petulant, as I blew smoke up into the air.

You wee shit, she said. That's it, go to bed.

Shut up, you, he's having a drink with his Auntie Mary.

He's smoking drugs in front of me. He's not allowed to smoke drugs.

Listen to her, Mary said. Smoking drugs.

I took two draws and handed it back to Mary, who passed it to my ma. My ma smoked like she was showing off in front of her mates. Watch you don't whitey now, I said.

Me? I've never whitied in my life.

What about that time in London?

That doesn't count, I hadn't ate anything, and that stuff we had wasn't weed, it was something else.

Mary rolled her eyes. She thinks she's Pablo Escobar, she said.

I asked them how their night had been and they told me they had gone to the Devenish for a dance and ended up spending half the night in the toilets, as they always did, fixing their make-up and telling the young ones how beautiful they were. There was this one girl my ma got talking to, she was about my age, and she had this aunt who did ten years in Armagh Gaol – she was in Cumann na mBan. My ma grabbed the girl by the hand and trailed her over to Mary. She was in Cumann na mBan too, my ma said. Mary was in Cumann na mBan, weren't you, Mary?

I had nothing to do with anything, Mary said.

My arse you didn't. Mary was high up, weren't you, Mary? Tell Sean about passing notes over to the men in the H-Blocks. Go on, Mary. Tell us about how you used to pass the notes.

Mary stuck her chest out, sexily, and flicked her hair out of her face.

I kissed every man in Long Kesh, she said.

She hid the notes under her tongue, didn't you, Mary?

Aye, wee rolled-up pieces of paper.

What else, Mary? Tell us more.

There's nothing else to tell, love. I had nothing to do with it.

She did, my ma said. She's only saying that. She never says anything.

Mary leaned with her chin in her hand, amused. You did your bit as well sure, didn't you? she said.

I only hid a few guns.

You did more than that.

I didn't. I had my kids. I didn't wanna lose my kids.

My ma glanced at me, anxiously. You have to understand, son, the Brits were torturing us. They were turning our houses inside out, they were shooting us in the street, and they were interning everybody we knew – your granda's brother, Paul, he was interned, and your Uncle Joe. They were trailed out of bed in the middle of the night and sent up to Castlereagh. God, we hated them, didn't we, Mary? But sure, Sean knows this, don't you, son? I've told him all this before.

My ma batted a hand, wearily, and drank some wine.

I don't know how it went from talking about this stuff to my ma and Mary dancing around the kitchen to 'Rhythm Is A Dancer', but that's what happened, and it was some craic watching them, the way they carried on with each other, bopping it out like ravers in a field.

This is our music, Mary said. This is what we listened to.

She was on the coffee table in the middle of the living room, giving it stacks.

I need to sit down, my ma said. I'm getting old.

You are? I'm near sixty, love. I'm on my way out.

That's enough of that talk, you are not.

I am. I can feel it.

Mary winked at me. She knew saying things like that wound my ma up in a very particular way. My ma raised her hand as if to hit her. Mary cowered and said, Look at this, she's trying to beat me, she's trying to beat me, and cackled. Have I not been beaten enough? she said.

Not by me, my ma said.

No, not by you. Never you.

The life you've had though, my ma said.

Some life. Both of us.

Sean could write a book, couldn't you, son?

I could, but it would be too long, I said.

Too depressing, you mean.

Wise up, Mary said. There's more good than bad and you know it.

That's why I love you, Mary. You're always positive.

What? You can't let all that stuff hang over you, love. You have to keep going.

I know, but the things you've been through.

The things you've been through too, so what? We're here now, aren't we?

My ma agreed, they were.

It's hard to forget though, isn't it? I find it very hard.

My da owned his own shooting ground – I learned that from the interview he did, the one in the country sports magazine. That night when I got into bed, I looked it up on maps. It turned out that the clay ground was registered to the same address as the people who owned it: my da and his wife. After a moment, I dragged and dropped the little yellow man on to a lane in the middle of the countryside. In front of me, there was a dirt track leading up to some sheds and outhouses. No people. No cars even, only the buildings and the fences and the cold country quiet.

This was where he lived. The company information and registered address all pointed to this exact location. And the chicken coop. There was a chicken coop in the field at the bottom of the lane. My da kept chickens when he lived in that house where I used to stay at the weekends, before he moved away. I wondered if they were the same ones. I dropped on to the road outside that old house next, and stared from the top of the driveway. There was a Fiat 500 parked up outside, and there were flower boxes on the window ledges, filled with red and yellow blossoms. I could see the stables over the wall, they were a part of a new extension that had been built on to the back of the house. The house itself looked cosier now, there was more brightness and colour. I zoomed in and tried to see through the living-room window. Those Sunday mornings my da fucked off to the clay ground, I would sit in there with Aoife and his wife, and all Aoife did was cry, and you couldn't watch TV because she had to have CBeebies on and would go nuts if you turned it over. It melted my head, those stupid jingles, and the silly voices the characters put on, like they were babies too. The only way to get away from it was to go out the back and play football against the garage wall. There were conker trees there, and in the autumn the ground would be covered with broken shells. I would fill bags with them to bring home to my mates, and when the weather was good, I would climb up on to the garage roof and watch the cows in the next field. My da's wife would shout at me to get down, it wasn't safe, but I liked it up there. I liked being able to see.

Back at the place where he lived now, I clicked along the driveway leading up to his house, but I couldn't go any further. The Street View car wasn't allowed: Private Property. The house was right there too. I could see it on the satellite imagery, tucked behind the outhouses at the bottom of the lane. The only thing I could think to do was drag and drop the yellow man on to every road around the house, but there was no getting at it, the camera wasn't powerful enough to zoom in from so far away. I dropped myself back on to the lane and started heading towards the main road, stopping every so often to look at the rusted farm equipment that had been ditched in the fields, the empty sheds, the desolate-looking house on the corner. I paused, looked both directions along the main road, and spotted a sign at the top of the lane. It had the name of the clay ground on it, a picture of a bird, and two contact numbers: a landline, and a mobile.

I sat stunned in front of the screen. All I had to do was dial the number into my phone. The simplicity of it scared me. To imagine myself actually pressing the Call button filled me with the kind of terror I had felt, sometimes, when I thought I saw somebody who had died walking down the street. I took a screenshot, closed my laptop, and pulled the blanket up over me. It was five o'clock in the morning. I could hear my ma and Mary singing in the kitchen: 'Killing Me Softly' by the Fugees. It was their favourite song.

17

I didn't have to go back to Milltown again until the following week. The peelers had set up a roadblock out the front of the cemetery; a meat wagon had been hit with a pipe bomb the night before. I stood out the front of the huts with the other men and watched them redirect traffic back down Andytown and up the Glen Road. There was a helicopter out, it had been hovering over the houses till the early hours. One of the men on community service said he had been up all night. The helicopter had flown so low over his house that he thought the windows would break.

This is what they do, he said to me. Fucking bastards. Look at this. Look at the state of that traffic.

The rest of the men watched quietly, with solemn expressions.

I recognized the two lads standing closest to me from the last time I was there, when Fra smashed the statue. I asked if they had heard anything from him, about his hand, and they laughed and said, Oh aye, we've heard plenty. I thought they were trying to wind me up, then a man I didn't recognize said, Is there something wrong with your head? Move out of the way. He said this at the exact moment I dropped my litter pick on the ground in front of him and had to bend down and pick it up. I couldn't tell if he was having a go at me for getting in his way, or if it had something to do with what the other lads had said, about Fra.

In the hut that afternoon, when we were on our lunch, Joe called me into his office. My probation officer was sitting there. I must've looked like I didn't know what was happening because she said, No need to be worried, Sean. I'm just here to check your progress. She told me how many hours I had done and how many I had left, then made me sign a form to confirm that I had been supplied with all the appropriate gear. When that was done, she asked how I was getting on and if there were any issues I would like to bring up with her. I thought about what those lads had said earlier in the morning, about Fra. Nah, I said. I'm all right. She scribbled something on her clipboard, then she said, Would you be interested in moving to another site?

There was a place going up at Holy Trinity, in Turf Lodge. It was farther away than Milltown, but the late afternoon shifts would suit me better, and it was all indoors. I wouldn't have to work in the freezing cold any more, and I wouldn't have to be locked in the hut every time we were rained off site. My probation officer told me about these things like I needed to be persuaded. I listened as if I was debating it. The deal was sealed when she mentioned that if Holy Trinity didn't suit, she would try and get me sorted with a charity shop somewhere closer to my ma's gaff. I thanked her. She followed me back into the yard. Joe was standing by the gates, watching the road.

All sorted? he said.

Aye, all sorted.

The roadblock was still there at the end of the shift. Five peeler jeeps, four cars and a bomb squad, all kitted out with automatic rifles. I saw one man drive right up to the barricade and scream that he had to get down the road, he had to pick up his child from school. The peelers stayed where they were with their rifles pointed upwards, watching the traffic steadily build, the roundabout becoming a bottleneck, with cars heading in all the wrong directions. I saw on Facebook later that night that the road didn't open again until six o'clock. There were dozens of comments. I scrolled through them while my ma fried an onion with some diced-up peppers, bacon and Denny sausages she had bought for £1.99 in the Spar across the way. Then she added red pesto with some cooking water, tipped in the pasta as soon as it was ready, and stirred it through.

I should be cooking for you, I said.

That'll be the day.

Later that night, when we had eaten our dinner and were sitting on the settee, watching TV, I asked my ma about that time she hid guns. She had her feet up on the coffee table, and her pyjama bottoms were tucked into her socks. Her socks were pink with pink pompoms at the front. They looked like something a wee girl would wear, and sometimes, when I looked at my ma, that's what I saw.

What do you wanna know about that for? she said.

Dunno. You've never really talked about it so.

I talk to you about everything.

I know.

She drank her tea, kept her eyes locked on the TV. What do you wanna know? she said.

Just like, how'd it come about?

Well, they called to my door and asked me, son.

And you just went, aye, fuck it?

Pretty much.

She told me she was living on her own at the time, in a flat in Twinbrook, and she had two kids – Anthony had just turned three. Things were hard. Gerard and Anthony's da was taking nothing to do with them, he wasn't paying any child support, and the dole was just about enough to get her through the week. She was lonely and young, and in her darker moments, when days had gone by without her seeing anybody, she imagined what her life would be like if she hadn't fallen pregnant that first time, and was raked with guilt. Then she got this knock on the door one morning she was making breakfast for the kids. It was a proper hard knock, the kind you'd hear before a squad of Brits pushed their way into your house, randomly, with no warning, and started tearing the place apart. She lifted Anthony up into her arms, partly to protect herself, and was relieved when she answered the door to two fellas she knew from about the estate: Jackie Short and Conor McGreavey. They had been in her class in school.

Jackie's dead now, she told me. He hijacked a bus and the Brits shot him.

For stealing a bus?

He was using it for a roadblock, we used to have to build roadblocks at the top of our streets to keep the Brits and the loyalists out. They caught him. They pointed their guns at him and told him to get off the bus. Jackie got out with his hands up and they shot him in the back of the head.

Jesus. Did you know him well?

Since I was a child, she said. He used to walk me home from school.

She went quiet for a second, remembering. Then she told me about how Jackie and his mate came back early the next morning with guns and bullets they hid under the floorboards, and in pillowcases and cupboards around her flat. They told her not to worry, it was only for a few days, then they'd come back and move them somewhere else. My ma put on a brave face, but her nerves were shattered; all she could think about were the things she'd heard about Armagh Gaol, the abuse women suffered there, the terrible conditions. Then it started to dawn on her, as the afternoon went on, that if she were to get caught, they would take her children off her. They'd be sent into care homes run by priests and Christian Brothers, and everybody knew what went on in those places. It was an open secret. I had to put it out of my head, my ma said. I had to tell myself that I was prepared to face whatever came my way. I'm a republican, and I had to support the struggle.

Later that afternoon, while she was helping Gerard with his homework, she heard something coming from the entrance of the estate, a quiet rumble. At first, she didn't think anything of it, those big lorries were always going back and forth along the top road. But the rumble got louder, and she heard voices. People were shouting. She went to the bedroom window and peeked through the blinds. It was the Brits. The Brits were coming. They were driving down the road towards her, a whole convoy of them, with soldiers that ran alongside them peeling off in every direction; they smashed front doors in, dragged people out into their gardens, and raided every house on the street. It was like a storm, she could hear everything, and the storm was coming to get her.

She ran into the living room, grabbed Gerard, and tried to remember where all the guns were, the bullets and the cartridges; she wanted to throw them out the back window. Then she looked out, saw soldiers moving along the entry, their heads ducked low, and staggered backwards across the room.

God protect us and keep us safe, she said.

She had Gerard and Anthony in her arms now, they were clinging with their wee hands around her neck. In that moment, with the entire flat shaking around her, when she could hear voices on the steps outside her front door, young and panicked, filled with adrenaline, she went somewhere else. She left her body and was looking down at herself from the ceiling. Anthony looked up at her, it was like he could see her, his big eyes staring right through her, and then she felt this pull. It dragged her downwards back into her body, and that was it. The soldiers were gone.

The next day, Jackie and his mate showed up at my ma's door again, this time with Semtex, and an RPG. They told her they could plaster them into the walls and nobody would know any different. She couldn't do it. They tried to coax her, but she said, No, get them guns out of my flat right now, and they did. My ma was like that, she wasn't afraid of anybody, and she had her children. Nobody was going to put her children at risk. I'd die for my children, she said. I'd die before I let them be taken away from me.

She finished her cup of tea and set it on the table. Her hands were shaking.

They shouldn't have even asked you in the first place, I said.

I know, you're right. They shouldn't have.

Then she thought about it, and she frowned.

Why not? she said.

Because you were on your own, you'd two kids.

But that was part of the struggle, son. That's the way it was.

Still, they took advantage —

They didn't take advantage of anyone. It was my choice.

She jumped out of her seat and went over to the sink. There was a pile of plates in there that needed washing. She turned the tap on and let it run. If I didn't have my sons, I would've been out there with them, she said. I would've volunteered.

Seriously?

Aye, she said. Wouldn't you?

I tried to have a nap before I went to work that night but I couldn't sleep. I carried the tiredness with me through the crowds of well-dressed people leaning over the countertop, tapping cards, entering pins, asking which brands of gin were available and if there was any cucumber. Mistakes were made, orders confused. I dropped a bottle of vodka that smashed all over the floor. The girl working next to me, who was called Maria, squeezed my shoulder and said, Don't worry, we've all been there, and helped me clean up the broken glass. I turned to take the next order and saw Ryan and Finty hovering at the back of the crowd. They grinned at me, and when they got to the front of the queue, they stared around in disbelief, as if they couldn't believe they had got this far.

What're you doing here? I said.

We called in to see you, dickhead.

Ryan had lost weight. I could see it in his face. He had those big white teeth people get when they've been taking too much gear. He handed me a score note and said, You gonna sort the boys out or what? I poured four double vodkas like I would for anybody and charged them for a single. Ryan glanced towards the till, then at Maria, and clocked that we were the only people working on our section of the bar.

You could make a fortune in this place, he said.

They came back later in the night with two girls with big hair and big eyelashes. They staggered to the bar in heels they struggled to walk in, and necked the shots I had lined up for them. Ryan ordered vodkas. I overcompensated and gave him doubles. He slung his arm around the more heavily tanned girl, with mad eyebrows, and winked at me. I asked what their plans were for the rest of the night and he told me they were partying: Why? You up for it? I said I might be, and Finty, knowing that managers watch more closely when they know your mates are at the bar, plucked a baggie from his shirt pocket and mouthed the words, This is for you.

I laughed. Come back when the bar quietens down, I said, but they were heading back up the road now. They told me to give them a shout. I said I would even though I knew I wouldn't, and turned to ring the next order into the till. My manager was standing there, checking transactions.

You didn't charge for those vodkas, she said.

What vodkas?

She pointed at the screen and showed me. You served those lads four vodkas, I saw you.

I must've forgot to charge them, I said.

You forgot?

I'll get them back, two seconds.

I moved as if to run after them, but Donna stopped me.

Just keep serving, she said.

I worked mechanically, one punter at a time, pouring drinks and taking money, ringing it into the till. Time passed. Worries receded. I thought I'd get away with a warning to never do it again. Then Donna told me to follow her out the back of the club, to the loading area, where two kitchen porters were sitting on crates next to the fire escape, having a smoke.

I'm gonna have to send you home, she said.

I tried to plead with her, tried to make her see that this was a stupid mistake. The bar was rammed. I had been working that day and the night before and was really tired, ask Maria. I've been messing up orders all night, I said. I dropped a bottle and everything. But Donna had been in this game long enough to know fine rightly, and she had caught me red-handed.

I'll check the cameras at the end of the night, she said. Then I can bring it up with HR and see where we stand, okay?

That was it. One look at the cameras and I was beat.

I messaged Mairéad. She usually finished selling shots around this time, and I thought that talking to her might help. She told me she had got off early and was at Julia's. That's all she said: *I'm at Julia's.* I thought, fuck it, fair enough, and walked round to get a taxi outside McDonald's. It was mad, people were running about the place like lunatics, singing Celtic songs, jumping on each other's backs. I got into the first taxi I saw and told the driver to fire me up to Lenadoon. Then I messaged Ryan and told him I was on my way. He replied with a photograph of him with his arm round Finty, the two of them pumping their fists in celebration. It made me laugh.

There was a line waiting for me on a plate in Finty's kitchen. The room was small and grubby. The tiles had yellowed, the paint on the wall was flaking, and there were no blinds on the window. I could see my reflection. I kept looking at it while I told Ryan and Finty and the two girls who had come back with them about how my manager was standing right there watching me pouring those drinks, and I really hammed it up, telling it like a funny story, like I was having a laugh.

One of the girls, whose name was Laura, said she felt terrible.

You were giving us free drink, she said.

We went through to the living room, where the walls had been papered and the paper had been painted white. There were feg burns and spill stains all over the carpet, and a tatty old white mat lay like a carcass in the middle of the floor. I sat next to Laura. She was still feeling bad about me losing my job, and she was in one of those moods where she couldn't let it go. She told me she was sorry, and when the conversation moved on, she repeated that she was sorry again. Then she shuffled across the settee and stared at me guiltily, with her bottom lip sticking out. I told her not to worry about it, seriously, and she glanced at her mate, who had curled up on the two-seater next to Ryan. He had taken the plate from the kitchen into the living room and was sitting with it on his knee, bank card in hand, the corners of his chapped lips sticky with saliva.

Laura took the plate off him and stopped, hesitating.

I don't do this all the time, do I, Ciara?

Ciara shook her head vigorously. She really doesn't, she said.

The last time I had a drink was my birthday three months ago, and the last time I did this was —

She tried to count the months in her head, but couldn't.

I'm not judging, I said.

I know you're not, but I'm just letting you know. I have a wee boy.

That's okay, I said. I don't care.

Laura stared, then she became serious again. What're you gonna do now? she said.

About what?

Work, you maniac. What're you gonna do for work?

Ryan cupped his hands around his mouth and shouted, He's going to Australia with me.

Are you? Oh my God, I wanna go.

Where? I said. Australia?

Me and you, wee son, Ryan said. I'll pay for your ticket.

Hold on. What's this about Australia?

Ryan had got his visa, he had booked his flight. His da had sorted him out with a few quid to get him on his feet, and he had a scheme going in the phone shop he had started working in a few weeks before, which would keep him flush. I asked him what the scheme was and he shimmied to the edge of the two-seater. He had this big grin on his face as he told me about how he was taking contract phones out under fake names and getting them unlocked, then selling them across the border for four, five hundred euros a pop.

Will they not catch on? I said.

Fucking right they will, but I'll be gone. I'll be at the other side of the world.

His cousin was already over there. He had a job lined up for Ryan and all, with a construction company. His plan was to live in hostels for the first few months, then go to Melbourne, stay with Jamesy and Gavy and those other lads we knew over there, then who knows?

We could head out to Bali, or Thailand. Go see the world, he said.

I told him to hold on, slow down. I could hardly afford to move out of my ma's never mind Australia, but he wouldn't leave it alone. He talked about hostels. He talked about parties. He talked about girls and nightclubs and beaches. Imagine what it would be like in the airport, before we left, he said, sitting at the bar with our bags at our feet, waiting for our flight.

He spoke dreamily, with a faraway look in his eyes. Then his eyes widened.

Let's do it, let's fucking go, he said.

Mate, I'm skint, I said, laughing.

I'll give you the two grand. Seriously. I'll give you two grand to book your flights.

Where are you gonna get two grand from, ya maniac?

I could get two grand, no sweat. Do you want it or not?

I shook my head, no, and he threw his hands up in the air.

See? He doesn't even wanna go, do you?

I looked around the room, stunned. What is this? You trying to peer-pressure me into moving to Australia? I nudged Laura and said, Can you believe this cunt?

Laura sighed and said, No, I actually can't.

I'm just saying, there's two grand there —

Where? Where is it?

I could get it.

I glanced at Laura and rolled my eyes. I'm sure you could, I said.

I could.

All right, mate, I said, laughing at him now, shaking my head at the shite he was talking. Because the only way to get Ryan off your back was to make a dick out of him — he had as much of a chance of pulling two grand out of his hole as I had, and he was getting on like he had it there, cash in hand. I also had a feeling that he was more interested in Laura than Ciara, and it was clear to everyone in the room that Laura and I were getting on well. He kept looking at us. Then I went for a piss, and when I came back, Ryan had swiped my seat. Finty had taken the seat next to Ciara, and the only place left for me to go was the floor. Laura saw that I was sitting on my own and said, You look awful lonely over there, and crossed the room to sit beside me. She waited until Ryan went into the kitchen and lowered her voice.

Ryan tried it on with me in Ollie's, she said.

Oh aye? What happened?

Nothing. I knocked him back.

I was surprised. Most girls went for Ryan; he was a good-looking bastard, and when he was on form, there was nobody better to be around.

He just came on a bit strong, Laura said, hesitantly.

I asked her if he was getting on like a dick and was relieved when she shook her head and said, No, it's not that.

What was it then? I said.

She sparked up a feg and took a draw, and the way she blew the smoke through her lips, with the smoke coming out slowly, in little wisps, made me want to kiss her.

He kept asking me where I work, she said.

Where do you work, right enough?

Laura levelled me with a look. I don't tell people where I work, she said. Not a lot of girls working in retail do.

Why not?

Because men are creeps. They like to 'drop by'.

Does that happen a lot?

All the time.

She told me about how she used to work on the make-up stands in Debenhams. Men would show up out of the blue to say hello to women they had been on a date with once. They'd bring flowers, chocolates. They'd hover around the doors, staring in. It was worse because the women weren't allowed to leave their stations, so if a fella did corner them, there was no escape. It's a nightmare now with dating apps, she said. I've seen girls who've matched with lads and spoken to them a few times, then those same lads show up halfway through their shift, all smiles, asking them if they wanna do something later. Swear to God. They see where we work from our Facebook bios and just show up. That's why girls who work in retail never say a word to any lad they're going with until they know for sure he won't.

I don't blame them, I said. I mean, I don't blame you.

The whole time she had been talking I had been thinking about that day I stood across the road from Mairéad's work and watched her fold clothes over the table at the front of the shop. I told Laura about it, thinking it was a funny misunderstanding – it really was a coincidence, Mairéad just happened to be at the front of the shop when I was walking past – but I was the only one laughing. Laura had moved away from me, she was looking at me like she couldn't believe me. I tried to tell her. I said, I was only after getting interviewed by the peelers, and I was dandering about the town, trying to clear my head. The next thing I knew I was standing across the road from Mairéad's work, watching her fold clothes. I didn't know she'd be working, and I only stood there for a couple of minutes. It wasn't like I was watching for ages, you know?

Then I thought maybe I did go there, unconsciously, with the intention of seeing her. Not because I was trying to creep on her or anything like that; I just wanted to talk. I wanted to tell her about what had happened.

Laura took this as an admission of guilt.

I'd have washed my hands of you there and then, she said. But if she's still your mate, who am I to say?

I looked at my phone; it was too late to ring her.

I think she's still my mate, I said.

I landed at my ma's door at four o'clock in the afternoon, stinking of drink, and still wiped from the gear. Bernice was there. She was sitting with my ma on the settee. There had been some crying. I could see the tissues on the coffee table. Bernice had another one scrunched up in her hand.

What happened? I said, and my ma looked at me.

Anthony wrecked the house. He smashed everything.

Bernice sniffed. She had bags under her eyes, and her face was drawn, pale, like she hadn't slept in days.

Did he hit you? I said, but it was my ma who answered.

No, he didn't. He just wrecked the place.

What happened?

He went nuts, Bernice said. Smashed the TV, put his fist through a wall.

Where are the kids?

They're with Bernice's mummy, my ma said. They're okay.

Bernice dabbed the corners of her eyes with the tissue. I can't do it any more, she said. Swear to God, that's it. I'm not taking him back this time. I'm done.

My ma put her arm around her and held her.

Where is he now? I said.

He's over in Gerard's. He's gonna stay there.

My ma glared at me from over Bernice's shoulder. Look at the state of you, she said. Are you on something? Jesus Christ, look at his eyes. I should bloody put you out, you're a disgrace.

It's okay. Don't worry. I just need —

I moved towards the kitchen sink, changed my mind, and staggered upstairs to bed.

PART THREE

My feeling is that nothing follows it [. . .]
Only a great darkness, a great closing down of the light.
László Krasznahorkai

18

Christmas snuck up on me out of nowhere that year, and it wasn't like I was working flat out or anything like that. I couldn't get a job. The man in the dole was threatening to send me to River Island to do forty-hour weeks, unpaid, to gain retail experience. He had it in his head that that was where I wanted to be. Twelve weeks of signing on was the cut-off point and then it was this Steps to Work programme they were trying to get me on to, or no Jobseeker's Allowance. You'd think I'd be using all the free time I had to get my hours done, but it was such a pain in the hole to get up to Turf Lodge from Dunmurry that I did the bare minimum, one shift a week.

The first night I was there, the supervisor was waiting for us outside the chapel. He told us there were three christenings that weekend and he wanted the place spotless. There was a storeroom at the far side of the vestibule, and in there were these thirty-foot-long hoses we trailed out and plugged into holes that were dotted around the room, for suction. I stretched mine down the back and hoovered along the kneelers, then the aisles between the pews and at either side of them. The beige carpet streaked with every sweep, the fibres flattening one way, then the other. I worked right down to the front of the chapel and up the steps to the altar, then across the marble tiles around the tabernacle. Nobody spoke. There was something about moving through that space that made me feel like we shouldn't, and I guess the others felt it too.

The shifts up there were four hours long, from five o'clock until nine o'clock at night; it took me two months to get forty hours done. I still had a hundred-odd to go. My ma was sound about it though. She didn't go on at me or anything like that. But she did expect me to take the bins out, and she had me doing chores around the house, which was fair enough. She wasn't taking any rent. She couldn't have even if she wanted to; I was skint. I was back to pulling tricks at the self-checkouts, in the Tesco up the road.

I showed my ma how to do it one day we went together. I talked her through it while I was actually doing it, blatantly, in front of the man who came with his card and swiped every time the machine said, *unexpected item in the bagging area.* She grabbed me by the arm and said, Don't you ever do that again, you hear me? It's a sin, you'll end up in jail, which was a geg because she had stopped going to Mass ages ago, after years of being made to sit on her own in the middle of the chapel and watch while everybody else went up for Communion. And that priest who tried to get five hundred quid out of her for an annulment, she would never forget how he spoke to her that day. She was wiser to it now though. She wouldn't have got her electric chipped if she wasn't. She would've stood firm, the way she did when we were growing up and every meter in the street had magnets stuck to the side of them. I asked if she regretted that decision now and she admitted she did. It would've made life a bit easier for us, she said. But that was who she was back then, those were her beliefs, and we got through it all right, didn't we?

I didn't have to get her a Christmas present that year. But seeing my niece and nephews and not having anything to give them made me feel wick. My ma saw this and called me upstairs to her bedroom. Here, give them this, she said, and handed me three fivers. I was shaking, I didn't know how to give kids money, and I was worried in case they thought a fiver was tight and judged me. My brothers would, no matter what, that was the way they were. I waited until the kids were leaving and slipped the fivers into their pockets so nobody could see how much they were getting. My niece looked sorry for me. She tried to give me the money back.

It's okay, you don't have to, she said.

Anthony and Gerard near fell off their stools laughing.

The big lad's tightening the purse strings this year, Gerard said.

Anthony and I were both shorter than Gerard, but we were stockier around the shoulders, whereas Gerard had the kind of metabolism that made him self-conscious. He had taken to the sunbeds and was going to the gym all the time, trying to bulk up. All three of us got the vanity from our ma, she had always taken her time in front of the mirror, but Gerard took the piss. When he still had hair, he used to carry a tub of wet-look hair gel around with him everywhere he went. People called him Danny Zuko. Gerard leaned in to it and bought himself a leather jacket. He was the first out of the three of us to go bald, his head was bicked right down to the scalp now, but he had that head shape that made it look good. He was built like a string of spaghetti though, and Anthony loved taking the piss out of him about his gym membership. Gerard raised his arms up over his head and flexed.

Give it six months and we'll see, he said.

We opened our presents before dinner; there was the usual Lynx set, the box of Quality Street, the Calvin Klein boxers my ma bought on the cheap from China, and a bottle of aftershave. We took turns in front of the mirror and sprayed our necks. My ma didn't have any presents to open. She had done that thing she always does and bought herself a pair of earrings the week before and made Anthony and Gerard pay for them. She pulled her hair back to show me. I had never looked at her earlobes before. They surprised me.

Are they not nice? she said, seeing my reaction.

No, they are. They're lovely.

She pinched the skin around her neck. I'm getting old, she said.

The four of us squeezed around the breakfast counter. We pulled crackers and put paper hats on. Gerard talked about going to his ex's house that morning to watch his son opening his presents. He said it was worth the money just to see my nephew's face when he came downstairs. Anthony agreed, there was nothing better. He had gone over the top like he always does with bikes and tablets and video games – he had spent a grand on each of his kids, and his wife, Bernice, who was still his wife because they weren't divorced yet, got a two-week holiday in Vegas. Anthony's excuse was that he wanted to give his kids everything he didn't have growing up. The reality was that Bernice came from a family who had money and he was always trying to keep up with them. It had never occurred to him that his kids would be happy with whatever they got. He was too far along the path laid down by his da, who had fuck all to do with Gerard and Anthony growing up, but lavished them with hundreds of pounds' worth of presents. They played cards with him every year, on Christmas night. It was a big game with big stakes and the same six or seven men every year.

Why don't you go with them? my ma said to me.

I'd only take them to the cleaners.

Anthony ooh'd. That's the attitude I like to see. Big talk.

Very big talk, Gerard said.

How much would he need to play?

A lot.

I could lend you money, my ma said.

I don't want a lend of money, mother. I'm all right here.

How much would he need, Gerard?

Few sheets, I'd say. Few ton.

I'm bringing four, Anthony said.

Four? Is that all?

Listen to big buck over here.

You'll need more than four, way more than four.

Six?

Gerard laughed, but he wouldn't say anything; knowing what your opponent has going into a card school means something. My ma was scandalized.

Six hundred? Where do you get all that money from?

Selling drugs. Robbing people.

Gerard's a male prostitute.

Strictly S&M. Gimp masks and nipple tassels.

You see him every Friday night round the back of the City Hall, six-inch heels and thigh-high suspenders.

Bumped into our Sean there last week.

That's enough. I don't like this talk, our ma said.

What talk?

All that drugs and robbing people talk. It's not funny.

We don't rob people, mother. Only drug dealers.

Stop now. I'm not joking.

Neither are we.

When they left that night, it was just me and my ma sitting at the breakfast counter. She was still wearing her paper hat. It sat lopsided on top of her head. You'd think they'd stay with us for once, she said. You'd think they'd stay for you, or bring you up –

I told you I don't wanna go. Why would I go?

I can tell it annoys you.

It doesn't annoy me in the slightest.

It does. I can see it in your face. They leave you here every year.

Word spread as it usually does, through rumours circulating online. Somebody had died at a house party in Twinbrook. There was talk of a bad batch of pills, people being rushed to hospital. More deaths. I messaged Ryan to see if he had heard anything. He told me a wee lad from Ardoyne had dropped dead in the middle of the street, in front of his mates. He was sixteen. There was a woman in Andytown as well, and three people in East Belfast. It was all over the news. A reporter stood at the top of Summer Hill and described delirious men running out of a ground-floor flat, stripping their clothes off in the middle of the street, and screaming that their insides were boiling. Anthony was one of them. Gerard rang my ma and told her. He had dodged the worst symptoms and was sent home from hospital after being kept in overnight. His mate was dead though. One minute he was dancing around the living room, bopping it out, the next he was on the floor, having a seizure.

That could've been Anthony, my ma said. We could've been burying Anthony.

When Anthony finally rang her back, my ma went up to her bedroom and didn't come down again for over an hour.

Is he all right? I said.

He's okay, he's back in Gerard's.

Well, it's good he's somewhere.

It's not good, son, she said. He has to stop taking them drugs or he'll be dead. I said that to him and he told me to stop going on at him. How can I not go on at him?

She hardly slept the next few days. I heard her going downstairs in the middle of the night and turning the TV on. Anthony had stopped answering his phone. My ma had asked if she could call over and see him, she was worried sick about him. He said no. Then she said she would see him at the funeral and he told her he didn't want her to go.

Why can't I go? she said. What have I done?

You haven't done anything, I said. Anthony just needs his own space. His head's all over the place, and seeing you might make him feel worse.

But I'm his mummy, she said.

I came downstairs on New Year's Eve morning and found her sitting at the breakfast counter in her housecoat. The blinds were closed, the TV was turned off. There was an empty glass in front of her and a bottle of wine that hadn't been opened. I lifted the bottle and put it back in the cupboard, set the glass in the sink. Black rings darkened the skin around her eyes. She looked like she was ill.

Was I bad? she said. Was I not a good mother?

You were perfect, mother. We had brilliant childhoods.

I started talking about how she used to take us to Bundoran for our holidays, when we were kids. She would get a budget loan from the bru and use it to put us up in a bungalow she'd rent with my auntie at the edge of the town; about a dozen of us would stay there for the week, cousins and all. We would spend whole days at the amusements, playing on the bumper cars, and we'd go to the beach and climb the rocks and walk across the fairy bridges. Remember Anthony jumping off the diving boards into the sea? I said, and she shook her head and looked out the window. It was snowing. The snow wasn't landing, but it fell in great swirls across the road.

I feel like it's my fault, she said.

What is?

She looked at me. I could see her eyes going back.

How did I not know? she said.

She was talking about Anthony. She was talking about what my da did to him when he was a wee boy. I tried to stay calm. I tried to be the voice of reason, but it was like trying to swim to somebody who had been dragged out to sea. She was already gone.

Oh, God. I'm sorry, son. I'm so sorry.

She tore off a strip of kitchen roll and held it with both hands in front of her.

I didn't know. I swear to God, I didn't know.

I moved round the counter and tried to put my arm around her. She panicked and said, Don't, I'll cry. But she was already crying. She covered her face with her hands and wept.

I went upstairs to check on my ma that night. She had her jumper pulled down over her hands and was lying with her back propped up against the headboard, watching TV. She looked better than she did that morning, she must've had some sleep, and she was calmer, more subdued. I told her to move over and she fixed the pillows next to her and shuffled across. We were used to lying next to each other like this, we had no choice during those weeks I came home from Liverpool, when my ma lived in my granny's spare room. We ate our dinner in that room, watched films, and at night, I slept on cushions on the floor. Then one morning my ma tried to step over me to get to the bathroom and fell arse-first on to my face. I asked if she remembered that and she grinned.

Thank God I was wearing pyjamas, she said.

There was an empty crisp packet on the bed beside her, and there were crumbs all over her woolly jumper. She tried to brush them away, but the crumbs had got tangled up in the wool and she couldn't get them off. She slapped at them with both hands, violently, she was really hitting herself. I grabbed her by the wrist and told her to stop. She looked at me, confused, then slumped back against the headboard.

I still dream about him, she said.

Who? I said, but I knew exactly who she was talking about.

She told me about this dream she'd had where they were driving down the road together, in my da's car. He was wearing that white vest top he used to wear in the summer, with the red shorts, and he was lovely and tan – he'd been working outside, on a building site, and you could see the muscles on his arms. 'It's Raining Men' was playing on the radio, the old version, The Weather Girls one, and my da had turned it all the way up. The windows were open, the breeze was blowing through the car, and when he stopped at the lights on the Falls, everyone could see him, they were all laughing at him. My da couldn't give a fiddler's. He was just driving along, singing away at the top of his voice. Then they were in bed together, they were making love – that's what my ma said, 'making love' – and it was just like it used to be, back when they first started going with each other, when they would talk about getting married, having children. Getting out of this place and starting a new life together. She knew she was dreaming too, and that was the thing about it. In the dream she was herself from back then, so happy and in love she couldn't do anything, she couldn't function, but also at the same time she was the person she was now, and she kept thinking, no, you can't do this, you need to stop.

What if Anthony finds out? she said, in the dream.

My da just smiled and said, It's okay, don't worry, nobody's gonna know, and led her back to bed.

I'm a terrible mother, aren't I? she said.

I put my arm around her and held her.

It's okay, I said. I dream about him too.

19

I should've thought about what I was doing before I started doing it, but sometimes these things take on a momentum of their own. Suddenly it was two o'clock in the morning and I was sitting at my ma's breakfast counter, reading over what I had written.

There was a character waking up the day after Boxing Day, coming down hard. There was a scene with a mother standing at the top of the stairs: *That could've been you, we could've been burying you.* There was a brother who leaned over the steering wheel to look up at the sky. There were rumours, there was suspicion. There was a death hanging over everybody's head, and there was love; two characters whose lives had gone in different directions, it was what it was, and that was what it had to be.

I brought it with me into the town the next day, desperate to get out of the house. I went to a coffee shop and sat like I had seen people do, at a table by the window, and watched a woman feed pigeons with a loaf of bread she carried around with her, in her handbag. Instead of paying for something to eat, I had brought a tuna sandwich with me and kept it under the table in case the manager saw what I was at and kicked me out. I threw it into me on the sly, while I read over the work I had done that afternoon, and noticed a girl sitting across from me reading Emily Dickinson. I picked up my copy of Clarice Lispector's stories and angled the book so she could see the cover. Nothing came of it. It never does.

At five o'clock, I got the train back up to my ma's and watched the mountain disappear behind the trees. It was January, the sky was one big cloud, and on the mountain, another sign had appeared:

FREE MARIAN PRICE ♀

I messaged Mairéad and asked if she would have a look at my story. She replied straightaway and told me to wing it over. I didn't know if she was working fewer hours or if she was low on mates over there, but I was hearing from her more often than I did before she moved away. She was doing well, although it was touch and go for the first few weeks, a lot of the jobs she went for wanted a German speaker, but then she landed this sweet gig as an editorial assistant for a feminist film magazine she had been a fan of since uni. It was a six-month internship, and if all went well and the right funding came through there was a good chance she'd be made permanent. On Instagram, there were pictures of her wearing scarfs and woolly hats, mooching around Berlin in the snow. She had gone to the Berlin State Library and got someone to take a picture of her wearing a long black coat, standing at the corner of the stairs looking down at the floor, forlorn, like your man in that film she loved, *Wings of Desire*. She posted the picture with the caption, *longing for mortality*. It got seventy-four Likes.

When I was done writing the email, I looked up and saw a girl who looked like Aoife sitting at a table further down the carriage. She was in the aisle seat facing away from the direction the train was going, and she was sharing a set of earphones with the wee girl sitting next to her. At one point, she leaned her head against her mate's shoulder and closed her eyes. It wasn't her. It couldn't possibly have been her, but still the feeling was there, in my chest; I wanted to know who she was.

I found a clip of Aoife dancing that night, when my ma went to bed. Her dance academy had made a video montage of all the performances they had done at their winter showcase and uploaded it to YouTube. It started with the youngest ones first, they were only four or five, and they pranced around the stage in little pink tutus, melting hearts. Then there were the older girls, the teenagers. They moved like they had been doing this their whole lives, calmly, patiently, with their necks held in that way only dancers can, like they were swans. I skipped forward because I didn't feel right about watching them, it felt a bit creepy, and found Aoife on her own in the middle of the stage with the light shining down on her. She was beautiful. The way she turned and smiled and raised her arms up in the air, with an unbelievable confidence, like this was where she was supposed to be, and then she was gone. I skipped back and watched it again and again, and each time I watched it I noticed different things about her expression, the way she stared out into the crowd. The light, the stillness. The talent she clearly had. The way her face changed when she locked eyes with someone in the audience and her smile softened. It could have been one of her mates she'd spotted, or her dance instructor, or her ma, but I didn't think so. I was convinced she was looking at my da.

Mairéad and I planned to have a phone call that week, but I landed an interview in a coffee shop and had to cancel. The interview went okay though, the manager seemed to like me well enough. Then he rang me the next day and asked if I could start the following Monday. I told my ma when she got home from work and she sighed, dropped her shopping bags on the floor and said, That's great, son. Does that mean you can help me out a wee bit?

Aye, as soon as I get paid.

Thank God.

The coffee shop was across the road from the City Hall. It was still dark at half six in the morning; the light from inside spilled out on to the pavement. I was given a red trainee T-shirt, a black apron, and a forty-odd-page booklet with all the rules and regulations laid out. In a few weeks, there would be a test. I had to pass this test to get a black

T-shirt. A black T-shirt meant you were an official barista. I asked the manager what happened if I didn't pass the T-shirt test.

We might have to let you go, he said, frowning.

I stuffed the booklet into my bag and left it in the stockroom, which was also the staffroom. Out the front it was like being on the bar again for the first time, only instead of drunken punters screaming orders at me, a steady stream of retail workers surged continuously through the store. Frothing milk was the tricky part, and there were standards that had to be met for each drink: a latte had to have a thin line of froth, a cappuccino had to be three-quarters froth, but the froth needed to be silky so that when you spooned it back, you could see where the milk had mixed in with the shot. There was a whole thing about adjusting the grinder, tamping the handle, timing each shot so that when you sprinkled brown sugar on top of the crema, it showed. I tried my best but I could only take in so much, and we hadn't even got round to the iced drinks yet. At ten o'clock, the store quietened down. There was a break at eleven, and for the rest of the day, I washed dishes, cleared the floor, and served every customer that came through the door. When the shift was over, I felt like I'd done a session in the gym, and I still had community service to go.

I went to the Linen Hall Library and nabbed the desk at the back of the biography section, with the window looking down on Donegall Square, and read the latest email from Mairéad. She said she liked my story, she thought it was great, and in the next paragraph, after she had given me some feedback, she told me there was a magazine down south looking for submissions. I went on their website and read their guidelines. They looked like they knew what they were doing, they had published some writers I had heard of, and Mairéad told me they were good.

Reputable, she said. Well regarded.

It was a miserable day outside; the rain was coming down the window. I watched umbrellas bob between the buses and thought, maybe they'll like it. Maybe I'll get published.

I left the Linen Hall and grabbed a meal deal I ate on the 81 bus up the Springfield, to Turf Lodge. Paddy, the supervisor, was there as usual at the door. He handed us cloths and wood polish and told us to clean the pews. A girl called Róisín was doing the row across from me. Instead of bending over to spray and wipe like I did, she sat on the pew and slid backwards as she worked. I spotted two lads doing the same thing and copied them. The rhythm of it was almost like the strimming, wiping back and forth, only it was more peaceful. It gave me time to think, to go over the things that had happened, the shit that seemed to follow me around everywhere I went. Ryan, Mairéad, Anthony and my ma. Daniel Jackson. What it must've been like for the people who were there that night, what went through their heads as they watched me run about the street like a lunatic, screaming at everybody, telling them I was going to kill them. I had seen it for myself plenty of times, when lads kicked off over nothing and their mates struggled to hold them back. It's always ridiculous. It's always stupid, and right up to the moment I hit Daniel Jackson, people must've been nudging their mates and saying, Look at the state of this cunt. Then I threw the punch and it was like, What a fucking scumbag. Because it had all calmed down. I had stopped trying to fight everyone, and when Daniel Jackson held his hand out to me, thinking it was over and done with, I punched him. I knocked him clean out. What kind of person does that?

It took an hour to get the place sorted, then Paddy brought us down to the meeting room round the back of the chapel. We waited out the rest of the shift in there, drinking tea and eating Hobnobs, listening to Paddy tell us about his plans to go to the Gaeltacht for a week at the end of the month. He had a pre-fab up there, in Donegal. He and his wife went every chance they could get, right down to the odd weekend, when the two-hour drive there and back was as much a part of their escape as the time they spent walking along the beach in Gweedore, sipping whiskey from canteens they carried along the strand.

What actually is the Gaeltacht? Cricky said.

What do you mean, what's the Gaeltacht?

Cricky's eyes dropped. He was sitting in his usual corner of the room, separate from the rest of us, with his hood up. He chewed the string and pulled his jumper up over his mouth. Like, what do you do there? he said.

You stay there. You speak Irish. You daft or what?

I've never been either, Róisín said. Is it good?

Paddy closed his eyes and took a deep breath.

Yes, it's good. It's very good.

Can you go there if you can't speak Irish?

You can, but you wouldn't get far.

I can say the Hail Mary, is that enough?

Go ahead then.

Sé do bheath' a Mhuire, atá lán de ghrásta, tá an Tiarna leat . . .

She stood up and did a celebratory dance at the end, as if she had won.

I may book a wee weekend myself, she said. Show off my skills.

Paddy rolled his eyes. He looked like a pug. There was something cuddly about him, the woolly jumper he never bate off him, and that way he had of sipping his tea, like he was an old man sitting by the fire. He told us he was going upstairs to check something and we knew fine rightly he was away to light a candle.

Who do you reckon he's praying for? Róisín said.

God, who do you think? Jamesy said.

You don't light a candle for God, ya balloon.

Who do you light it for then?

Somebody you love, Cricky said, and everybody looked at him.

When the shift was over, me and Cricky were heading in the same direction, down the Monagh Bypass. The weather wasn't as bad as it had been, the random snowfalls had given over, but it was dark, cold. Cricky was shaking. Apart from the hood that was stuck to his head, he didn't wear a lot of layers, and he was a skinny kid. His shoulder bones stuck out. I asked him how he had ended up doing community service. He told me the peelers stopped and searched him one night he was out on his bike. They found weed in his pocket. It was nothing, a bit for a joint, but the peelers carried on like it was a big bust.

Why'd they stop you in the first place? I said.

Dunno, mate. I was just out on the bike, flying about.

He squirted spit through his teeth and made a sucky sound.

Sometimes I go for a wee jaunt, he said. I get on the bike and see where I end up. Bring a bit of dope with me, have a smoke. Gets me out of my head. Best place is Cave Hill. I go up there and look down at the whole city. It's unbelievable, do you ever go up?

Not since I was a kid.

You should, it's lethal. Best view in the city.

Is that where you were when the peelers stopped you?

Nah, I was just cycling up the Boucher. I was coming back from the towpath, know down Belvoir? There's a field down there. Nobody bothers you. You can just sit there and watch the ducks on the river, it's great. But aye, they saw me coming up the Boucher and pulled me over, asked me where I was from and where I was going. I said I was from the Falls. Next thing I know, they'd me pushed up against the meat wagon, patting me down.

He laughed, but I could tell he didn't think it was funny.

Worst thing is, I got laid off a few months ago, I'm a qualified spark, but see trying to get a bit of work? You need a degree to get a job in a bar these days, he said.

What'd they do you with? Possession?

Possession, aye. Hundred hours. What about you?

Assault, I said. They hit me with two hundred.

Two hundred hours? Fuck me.

And a six-hundred-quid fine as well.

Cricky stopped. What the fuck, for assault? Did you plead guilty?

I didn't answer. I turned away from him so he couldn't see my face, but he knew. He understood.

Dopey bastard, he said, laughing.

When I got back up to Dunmurry that night, I saw Anthony's van parked up outside our ma's gaff. Both windows were open even though it was freezing. It was the middle of February and he was sitting there in a T-shirt and a pair of sweats. I asked him what the craic was and he said, Not much, bounce in. I got in and closed the door. The window was still open though. I tried to roll it up, but Anthony said, No. I'm acclimatizing myself to the cold, he said, and he wasn't joking. He blew into his hands and gave me the usual patter about how he hadn't touched a drink in weeks. He was back at the gym, he was bench-pressing, and although the weight he carried hadn't shifted an inch as far as I could see, he swore he was stronger, faster, lighter on his feet.

I've been writing as well, he said. Started that screenplay.

It was the same screenplay he told me about before, the one with the Night Hunters, only now it sounded more like *Independence Day*. He was obsessed with films about the end of the world, anything with a zombie apocalypse, but also aliens, space invasions – any film that tapped into the conspiracy theories he was up to his eyeballs in since he fell down that same YouTube hole Ryan had with the Bob Lazar stuff, only Anthony was buying into it wholesale. He talked about Roswell and he talked about Area 51. He talked about how the moon wasn't the moon but an alien outpost. He pointed up at the sky and said, See? They've been up there this whole time, keeping tabs on everyone. The government were hiding it from us because they wanted to keep us under control. It's all about control, he said. Because let's be honest, if people knew what they were up to, if the truth came out . . .

He made a face like I didn't want to know.

What're you at now then? I said.

I asked this question in that way people do, in the hope that when the person tells you the answer, you can say, I better not keep you then, and leave them to it. Anthony wasn't playing ball though. He said, Fuck all, and carried on with the conversation like he hadn't been interrupted. Now he was making plans. He wanted me to spend a whole weekend with him on the laptop, writing up these ideas he had. No amount of writing down ideas would make us a film, but I didn't want to let him down.

When it finally got to the point where he was happy enough to head on, he stopped me, one more time, and leaned with his elbow on the open window.

Tell me this, he said, very casually. Do you know where your da is?

The first thing that went through my head was that Anthony was going to kill him. Anybody who knew him would think the same. What didn't sit well with me was how he had been waiting on me coming home from community service, outside our ma's house, in his van, to ask me this question. Things hadn't been good between him and my ma since Christmas, and that sort of explained why he wouldn't want to go into the house. But at the same time, he could've rung me. He could've taken me for a drive.

I'm not gonna go after him or anything like that, he said. I just wanna know where the cunt is, you know?

Aye, I know what you mean. I do too.

So you don't know, nah?

Nah, haven't a clue, I said.

That's all right, I didn't think you would. It was just on the off chance . . .

His voice trailed off. He started up the van.

I went straight into my ma's and told her what Anthony had said. She was drinking a cup of boiling water with lemon. She took these kidney infections, usually when she was stressed or run-down. It had been bad for a few days now. She had to take Monday off work. Then she had to work the rest of the week while she was still in pain because she couldn't afford to stay at home – there was no sick pay with her cleaning jobs, no holidays either. She showed up or she didn't get paid. It wasn't the best time then, to spring this on her, but I had to. There was no one else.

Do you know where he is? my ma said, meaning my da.

Nah. Even if I did, I wouldn't tell him.

Good. Don't.

She took her feet down off the coffee table, winced and held her back with one hand behind her as she sat forward.

He's been parking up outside your aunt's house, she said.

What for? I said, but I already knew.

He's been waiting to see if your da will call in to see her.

Jesus Christ.

I know.

He's not gonna do anything, is he?

My ma looked at me. Her eyes were completely white.

Don't say anything –

I won't.

She lowered her voice. She was almost whispering.

One night we were in here, having a drink. Anthony told me he regretted stopping the IRA from executing your da.

The Ra were going to execute him?

When it all came out, aye. They were going to shoot him.

What happened?

We got a phone call, a couple of men called to the door.

Who were the men?

Dunno, IRA men. You wouldn't know them.

She was at her nails now. The skin around her thumb and index finger.

I didn't want them to do it, she said. I said to Anthony, If you get him shot dead tomorrow, that would be the easy way out for him, but not for us. We would have to live with it for the rest of our lives. It would be on our conscience. Then Anthony told me he didn't want it done either. He didn't want them to kill your da.

He stopped it?

We both did.

I sank back into the settee. Jesus Christ, I said.

I know. I should've told you.

No, it's not that. It's just – I thought I knew everything.

My ma sighed. There's a lot you don't know, son, she said.

20

I got my first wage at the end of the month, on the Tuesday. I went straight to the cash machine and took it all out because I knew I'd be getting hit with that thirty-quid overdraft charge any day now and I didn't want to get stung. My ma told me not to worry about the gas and internet bill. Keep it towards finding somewhere to live, she said. She had seen me sitting at the breakfast bar at night, scrolling through property listings. There wasn't much going about the road. The few one-beds I found were too expensive, and all the house-shares were in North and South Belfast, in areas I didn't know. Then I found this place near Queen's, on University Street. It was one of those three-storey town houses you see around that side of the city, where all the students live, and it was a fifteen-minute walk from the town, which was perfect for work. I emailed the landlord. She got back to me the next day, and on Friday, I went for a look.

It was the first time I had gone to view a place on my own. My strategy was to act like it wasn't. The landlord brought me into what should've been the living room and it was an office instead, with filing cabinets and everything, and explained how she had registered the charity organization she was involved with to this address, years ago, before she retired. She didn't use the office any more, nobody did, and she was very clear about this; everything was legit and above board. She locked the office door behind her, then she led me down the hall and introduced me to a Vietnamese lad called Tung. There was a gaming computer on the desk at the bottom of his bed, and all along the windowsill, empty cans of Monster had been stacked like a pyramid. I shook his hand and he smiled and looked at the floor.

They're good boys, the landlord said. Never any hassle out of them. Lovely quiet students. You're a student too, aren't you? What're you studying?

English, I said.

Queen's? My niece is at Queen's. Medicine. She's going to be a doctor.

She brought me upstairs and showed me the room I was there to see. There was a double bed, a wardrobe, and what she said were two south-facing windows. I pulled the curtains open and the sun peeped out from behind a chimney stack across the way.

It comes with office space too, the landlord said.

Office space?

Between the bedroom and the landing, there was a room with a desk and a bookcase. I turned to the landlord and said, Both these rooms? She smiled and said, Yes, both. They come together. I laughed. I said something like, Holy fuck, and went back into the bedroom for a proper look. There was no damp as far as I could see, no mould, and the carpet was clean, the mattress brand new. I sat at the bottom of the bed and stared around.

£220 a month? I said.

Yes, £220. But that doesn't include bills.

I met Tuan, another Vietnamese lad, on the landing. His bedroom was a belter. It was big enough for a settee and a double bed, and there were two big windows looking out on to University Street. Buckets of light. I thanked him for letting me have a look and he said, It's okay, and followed us upstairs. There was another bathroom, another two bedrooms, and the kitchen, which was on the top floor. I had a cursory look around and did the whole, Aye, looks class, thing, without really taking anything in. I was too excited. Tuan leaned over a pot of broth he had simmering on the hob. He dipped a spoon and held it out for me to taste.

That's unreal, I said. Cheers.

On the way back downstairs, the landlord told me she had another two viewings lined up that afternoon, so if I was interested, I would need to move fast. I have the contract here, she said, and right enough, she did. She took it out of the folder she had tucked under her arm and showed me. The only problem was that the room I would be moving into wasn't available for another two weeks. She was happy enough to take the deposit from me now, and the first month's rent on the day I moved in, if that suited me. It actually did. It was better than paying the full whack now. Then I would still have a few quid to get me through the rest of the month.

I had one more look around the bedroom and office space, and while I was looking, I was going over in my head how much I'd be getting paid from the coffee shop and how I could stretch that money to get me through each month. It would be tight, but doable, and there was no way I'd find a better place for the money I was paying. I said, Right, okay, I'll take it, and the landlord brought me downstairs to sign the contract. I put my granny down as guarantor, and I took a copy of the contract with me so I could get her to sign it. The move-in date was set for the 27th March. I shook the landlord's hand, and I shook Tuan and Tung's hands. They had come downstairs to see me out.

I couldn't believe how easy it was, the first room I had looked at, and it couldn't have been in a better spot. Botanic Avenue was at the top of the street, the university was round the corner, and at the bottom of the road, you're at Shaftesbury Square. The cinema was a ten-minute walk away. I could dander down whenever I wanted and watch a film. There was a second-hand bookshop as well, next to the falafel shop. I spent a good hour in there, searching through the fiction section, and the classics, where I found a copy of *The Unbearable Lightness of Being*. I opened it at a random page and read a paragraph, and then I flicked back to the title page and saw an inscription some-one had written there: *Vivienne, I hope this book touches you and fills a void, until I learn to give you what you need. I love you, John.* I bought it for two quid and took it with me to the coffee shop down the street.

Outside, the sky was red and the road looked like it was being held up under a heat lamp. It was all students too. They came down from Queen's and gave the bars and coffee shops a good turn; Maggie Mays and Boojum had queues out the doors, and they were all dressed the same, in tracksuit bottoms and GAA tops. Those poor bastards sitting on the ground outside the Spar didn't get a look-in. Neither did the woman selling *The Big Issue* outside the chippy. She was old, she could hardly stand, and she shuffled back and forth across the pave-ment, pleading for people to stop. I walked past her on my way to the coffee shop. There was a table by the window with my name on it, and I sat there with a coffee and a caramel square and tried to imagine what it would be like to live there. My mind kept going back to Mairéad. I thought about how this was the kind of thing she would've got up to – passing some time before heading round to watch a film in the QFT. She was always going on about the QFT. She said it was her favourite place to go. I went on their website to see if there was anything on. It was all foreign language films, I'd never heard of any of them, but there was one that sounded like something I might be into. It was called *La Haine*, and it was on that night, at nine o'clock. I thought about messaging Mairéad and asking if it was worth waiting around for. She would know. And then out of nowhere I spotted that girl she was seeing walking across the road. Julia. She was heading towards a place called No Alibis. Another bookshop. I waited ten minutes before heading across, then I stood for a while out the front of the shop, afraid she wouldn't recognize me, or that she would and pretend not to.

I pushed the door open; it was rigged with a bell.

Julia was at the counter with Conor, who was sitting on a stool behind the till. They smiled and said, Hey, how's it going? I dipped my head and waved stupidly, with my hand sort of flicking out, and went down to the back of the room, to the fiction section. After about ten minutes of being stuck there, in front of the same shelf, Conor straightened up and said, Are you looking for anything in particular? I asked if he had Kundera's first book, *The Joke*, and he came out from behind the counter. The only Kundera book he had was the one I had just bought. He could order *The Joke* into the shop for me though, if I wanted. I said, Aye, sounds good, and followed him back to the till. Julia was leaning with her shoulder against the wall, drinking a can of craft beer.

What's your number? Conor said.

My number?

For letting you know when the book comes in. We'll send you a text.

I went into my contacts, but I couldn't remember if I had saved it under Me, or Sean. Or New Number. Julia saw that I was struggling and told me to take her number and message her. I sent her a Whats-App saying *hello*. She called my number out to Conor and Conor typed it into the computer.

That's it ordered, he said.

I thanked him, but I didn't leave. I stayed where I was at the counter and stared around the shop. There's a lot of crime, I said, meaning crime novels.

Conor couldn't help himself. It's a bad area, he said.

Julia pulled a can from her bag and held it out to me, tentatively, like she didn't want to scare me away. Conor took one too.

Are you allowed? I said.

I am now.

He came out from behind the counter and flipped the door sign round to CLOSED. He had Paul Simon playing, and on the way back to his seat, he did a wee dance. I found my feet with some talk about Mairéad and how she was getting on in Berlin. Julia was sure she was doing well – it was Mairéad, she couldn't not be – and that made me think she hadn't heard anything from her. Julia admitted as much when she said, She'll reach out in her own time, and looked at me, searchingly, as if to see how I would react. I smiled. I knew what Mairéad was like. Whole years could go by without hearing a word from her, then she would appear out of nowhere and slip back into your life like no time had passed at all. I said this to them, but they didn't recognize that Mairéad. They hadn't known her long enough to have seen her go.

Later, when we were standing on the street outside, watching Conor pull the shutters closed, Julia invited me round to Bookfinders. Conor wiped his hands on his jeans and said, Yes, come to Bookfinders. I didn't know what Bookfinders was, and when I asked Conor and Julia, they said things like, You'll see, it's just a place we go, and grinned excitedly.

It didn't look like much from outside. There was a red door, a window with a rusted grill, and a sign above the window that read: BOOKFINDERS BOOKSHOP & CAFÉ. Conor nudged the door open with his shoulder and led the way through a room filled with old, battered-looking books. It smelled like dust and mould, and in the corners of the ceiling massive spider webs hung limply with dozens of dead flies weighing them down. He moved one of the chairs blocking the entrance to the café out of the way and said, Hello, it's only us. It was dark back there, and cramped; tables lined each side of the passageway. Sitting around the big table down the back was a group of people I recognized from Conor's gaff that night. They were drinking wine and smoking rollies. I sat next to a drip of a fella who spoke about cycling around France during the summer. Behind me, an old woman with bushy grey hair sat at the table next to the radiator. She had a glass of rosé in one hand, a cigarillo in the other, and she smoked extravagantly, with her chin tilted upwards. She was called Mary, and she ran the shop. She made the ham and cheese toasties and the vegetable soup, and when it came to about four o'clock in the afternoon, give or take, she would approach whatever customers were still hanging around the shop and tell them they had to leave, she was about to have a business meeting. That's what I had been invited into now. It was like an inner sanctum.

This is Sean, Conor said, introducing me.

Mary shook my hand hesitantly, like she wasn't sure about me, and then Conor told her I was mates with Mairéad and her whole demeanour changed.

Oh, Mairéad. We miss her, don't we?

We do, aye.

How's she keeping? Have you heard from her?

She's doing well, she's working for a magazine.

Oh, that's wonderful. We always knew she would land on her feet, didn't we?

I agreed. We did.

I took another one of those craft beers Julia was handing out and spoke to a fella called Paul, who read poems that night after the exhibition. I told him I liked the patter between his poems and he thanked me. Have you tried your hand yourself? he said.

A wee bit, aye.

Poems?

Nah, the other one.

He looked at me curiously and said, you're not on the MA, are you?

The MA?

At Queen's.

Oh, no. Jesus. I work in a coffee shop.

Paul didn't hold that against me. He asked me how it was. I told him the six a.m. starts weren't the best and he grimaced. I know that pain, he said. I used to work in a call centre.

The Kundera book was a nice segue. I took it out and showed him the inscription. His eyes lit up. He asked if he could show everybody else and I said, Aye, whack away. The book was passed around the room. People laughed. Others looked horrified. It came round to

Mary and she put her glasses on, but it was too dark for her to see; there weren't enough candles. Conor read it out for her. She was scandalized.

Has anybody here read *The Unbearable Lightness of Being*?

Nobody had. Mary pointed with her cigarillo. Then you don't understand what this inscription means, she said, cryptically, and handed the book back to me. As I was putting it away, Paul asked if he could take a picture. I watched as he held his phone up over the open page.

I must get a copy, he said.

Take that one sure.

Oh no, I couldn't do that.

You could. I've got one in the house. Take that one.

I didn't actually have a copy in the house, I just said that so he would take it. Paul was awkward and grateful.

That's very kind of you, he said.

The people in Bookfinders were all students from Queen's. Literature was their bag. Poetry in particular, but their interests weren't limited by any stretch. During the hour I was there they spoke about quantum physics, tennis, Yugoslavia, Butlin's, and that one time Anna got off with an Australian fella in Madrid, who asked if they could listen to Justin Bieber while they dry-humped on the settee. What's this dry humping? Mary said, in a voice that could've been inherited straight from the aristocracy. In my experience, there's nothing dry about it.

There was an explosion of laughter.

Oh, Mary, people said, dabbing tears from their cheeks.

Mary had to get the train at seven o'clock, she had to close up shop. Moves were made towards Lavery's. Conor asked if I fancied it. I thought I may as well kill some time before the film started. On the way down the road, I heard somebody say, Who's that? Then Paul noticed I was on my own and waited for me to catch up. He wore a tweed jacket with elbow patches, and brown shoes with heels that clacked as we walked along.

Would you play a game of pool? he said.

I would, but not very well, and not for cash, I said, joking.

No, no money. Just a bit of sport.

No hustling?

Goodness no. You're among friends here.

I watched as he unbuttoned his cuffs and rolled his shirt sleeves up to his elbows. He was the same age as me but could've passed for ten years older. That gentle way he had of talking, his antiquated manners. I don't frequent the old pool halls quite as much as I used to, I heard myself say, which would've sounded weird to anybody who knew me. In fact, my mates would've hit me a slap on the head if they heard me, but that was the effect Paul had on you. Without being conscious of it, he forced you to operate in his register, and it made you come off with all sorts of shite you otherwise wouldn't. Finely cued, I said, when he took on a long pot into the corner pocket. Bravo!

He beat me fair and square, with three balls left on the table. I shook his hand.

Good game, I said, and he agreed. Good game.

The people who weren't interested in that kind of thing were huddled under a heat lamp in the smoking area. Julia was there. She was staring into nowhere between two lads talking across her. They had their phones out and were watching a video that was going around showing some priest that had been caught taking gear. He was sitting at the kitchen table in his parochial house, having a smoke, talking in that way people do at that stage of the game, like he didn't want the night to end. One of the fellas he was drinking with offered him a rolled-up tenner and the priest leaned over to snort. Whoever was taking the video let the camera linger on his face as he choked and coughed, making sure they got him, and then the video ended. This is the best thing I've ever seen, Conor said, and I agreed, it was funny as fuck, but I actually felt bad for the priest; he had been done over something shocking. Then somebody found an article that said there was Nazi memorabilia all over his house. It didn't look good. The priest said they were historical artefacts he had been collecting for years, there was no harm in them, but that didn't change the fact that he had a SS Stormtrooper hat displayed alongside a folded-up Nazi flag on the table at the bottom of his bed. Conor thought it was hilarious.

I might start going to Mass, he said.

I bought him a pint. He had been sound to me that day, and I was starting to think he was all right. Julia was a different story. She hardly spoke to me the whole time I was there, and when we somehow ended up sitting next to each other, she stared down into her glass and smoked. Again, it was Conor who broke the ice. He asked if I wanted to go to the Menagerie that night, there was some DJ over from England playing drum and bass, but I had already booked my ticket for the QFT.

Julia leaned forward. Are you going to watch *La Haine*?

Aye, at nine o'clock.

She looked at me like I was winding her up, then she laughed. The fella sitting next to her joined in and I was about to say, What the fuck are you laughing at? Then Julia explained that she had booked tickets for the same screening.

Will we go together? she said.

Sounds good, aye.

The film didn't start for another hour so we went to the falafel place I had spotted earlier on Botanic. Julia knew it already. She watched as I picked the tomatoes and the onions out of my wrap and set them on the plate. She was a vegan. At least, she ordered a vegan meal, and I didn't know why anybody would do that to themselves if they weren't. She ordered two beers for us as well. I didn't realize how drunk she was until she started eating. It was like she was at the end of the night. She kept missing her mouth.

Mairéad spoke highly of you, you know, she said.

Did she?

All the time. She said you were her best friend.

She must've had a few swalls, I said.

Julia shook her head. There was sauce on her chin. I had to tell her. She grabbed a napkin and smudged it in.

She hasn't spoken to me since she left, she said.

Has she not?

No. Not at all.

I looked down at my plate. I had taken three bites out of my wrap. There were too many things in it that I was afraid of. When I looked up again, Julia's eyes were wet. She batted her hand over her face, then she picked up the napkin she had used to wipe the sauce off her chin and dabbed the corners of her eyes.

I didn't know yous two were a thing, I said.

She never said anything about it?

Not really, no.

Julia took this the wrong way. What I had meant to say was that Mairéad had never told me she was bi. I explained this to Julia and she looked surprised.

Why wouldn't she tell you?

No idea, I said.

I picked a bit of chicken out of my wrap and ate it. Julia wasn't touching her food at all now. Her nose was blocked up.

I'm not sure I can sit through a film, she said.

She didn't have to apologize – it was better for her to go back to her mates – but she did anyway. She gave me a hug too, outside. It was one of those hugs that asks a lot of the other person. Instead of leaving it at that, she looked at me and said, We're both suffering without her, aren't we?

It was a bit much.

There was a bar in the foyer at the QFT, but they only served craft beer and I didn't know what to be at. The girl at the till kept me right though. She knew where I was coming from and handed me an IPA she said was good. It tasted a bit fruity, like that beer people go mad for at the continental market, but it was strong; a few cans of this gear and you'd be lit. Five minutes before the film started, I went for a piss. When I came out, people were queuing up to go in. I handed my ticket to the girl who served me, she was doing the door as well. She smiled and said, What do you think?

Class, I said, showing her the can. Cheers.

I sat in the middle row and watched the seats fill up around me. It sounds stupid, but I was proud of myself. I had crossed some threshold. Like that time I went to the exhibition launch with Mairéad, then the poetry reading after. I would never have done that on my own. I would never have done this.

21

My probation officer got me sorted with a few shifts in a charity shop in Finaghy. The aul doll running the show had me and this fella called Gary locked away in the back room all day, tagging things and marking prices. There were clothes on rails all around us, shelves filled with books, DVDs, board games, and gaudy little statues Gary picked up and laughed at as if they were funny. He was into his heavy metal, he wore a Metallica T-shirt every day he was in, and he had sideburns that came right down to his chin and made him look like an overweight Wolverine. He had done community service in that charity shop the year before and stayed on volunteering after he had finished his hours. He didn't say a word about what he'd done to end up there, but he was all talk about how far he'd come from the place he'd been before.

I was in a dark, dark place, he told me, just like that. Now he had a job, he was part of the night security team in Victoria Square, where all the shops were, and his fiancée was pregnant. They were going to have a wee girl.

Just goes to show, you can really turn your life around, he said.

I went from the charity shop up to Holy Trinity and put in a shift with Paddy, who was in a bad mood for some reason, and sent us out with litter picks around the chapel grounds. I didn't get back to my ma's until ten o'clock that night. It had been a long week. I had knocked out thirty-odd hours of community service and worked twenty hours in the coffee shop. The plan was to finish community service before I moved out of my ma's; I didn't want it hanging over me any more, and I didn't want to move to the other side of the city only to come back every week and sit in that chapel with Paddy, talking shite. I could've finished them handily enough if my manager let me cut my hours down. But the rotas had been up for two weeks, and although they weren't written in stone, it wasn't easy to get shifts covered on such short notice. I was the only member of staff on a part-time contract – everybody else was working forty-hour weeks, and I couldn't bring myself to ask.

I could've slept as soon as I'd thrown a bit of food into me that night but I hadn't had any time to myself all week and I wanted to chill out in front of the TV. I flicked through the channels and landed on one that was showing *The Shawshank Redemption*. It was at that part when they're sorting through piles of books for the library and your man pronounces Alexander Dumas as Alexander Dumb Ass. I took a picture and sent it to Ryan. He told me he was going to Australia next weekend and was looking a few pints before he went. I said I'd be there with the wind in my hair and he replied with a thumbs up emoji. Then I looked down at my work T-shirt. It smelled like milk.

At twelve o'clock, I went to bed. I was out for the count as soon as my head hit the pillow, then my ma came wailing home at two o'clock in the morning. There was somebody with her. I could hear voices.

Never mind work. Get him up. Get him on the beer.

It was Anthony. She had brought Anthony back.

Stop it now you. It's late.

Get the tunes on.

Keep it low, for God's sake.

Keep what low? What kind of party is this?

I squeezed my earplugs into my ears and pulled the pillow round my head, but every shout and laugh came through, and it wasn't like they were trying to keep it down – they had the music blasting, and they were drunk as fuck, talking at the top of their voices. I got dressed and went down, thinking I could make them feel bad for keeping me up, but they were too far gone. Anthony especially, who saw me coming downstairs and erupted.

Go on, my son, he shouted. The king himself.

He grabbed me into a headlock, kissed me on the side of the face, and dragged me over to the fella he had brought with him. This is the biggest legend you'll ever meet in your life, he told me. Terry Brennan.

Terry had spent too much time on the sunbeds. He had the top three buttons of his shirt undone, and he was wearing a gold chain that hung like tinsel around his neck. He was my ma's age, but could've passed for ten years older; that leathery look had aged him, and dyeing your hair will only take you so far when you look like a handbag. He shook my hand. Your brother hasn't fucked up about you all night, he said.

What's he been saying?

That you're gay as get-out, Anthony said, and jabbed me on the arm.

My ma looked pained. I had to bring him back here, she said, when Anthony went upstairs for a piss. I didn't want him to disappear and not come home again, and sure if he's here with me, I know he's safe. I know he isn't getting into any trouble.

She chewed her bottom lip. Her eyes were filled with guilt.

Anthony came back and it was Terry's turn to go for a piss. They crossed paths in the middle of the living room, behind my ma, and as they passed each other, Anthony slipped a baggie into Terry's cupped hand. My ma wasn't stupid. She knew what was happening, but as long as they weren't racking lines up in front of her, she could turn a blind eye. She had to. If she said anything, there would be an argument, and she couldn't cope with Anthony's temper. Not when he was like this.

What day are we on now, Terry? he said.

Day two, Terry said.

It's only day two, mother. We've another two or three to go.

You're not staying here three days, no bloody way.

I've work in the morning, I said, and Anthony laughed.

Hard luck for you then, isn't it?

Terry staggered across the room and leaned with both hands on the kitchen sink. He was blowing hard, and he made this smacking sound with his lips, like he was going to boke. There was a wedding ring on his finger, and I could tell from the tattoo on his arm that he had four kids: he had their names written on a scroll that was decorated with flowers. Anthony tousled his hair. I've been telling him all night, he's too old, he needs to slow down, he said.

Terry took this to heart. He turned as if to throw a dig.

Oh fuck, here he comes, Anthony said, skipping back, laughing, holding his hands up like he was ready to go. This man would murder you in your sleep, he said to me. He's got more notches on his belt than Scappaticci, don't you, Terry? Scary man. Back in the day, people crossed the street to get away from him. They still do, isn't that right? You're talking about one of the hardest men from about the road here.

This went on for a while, the flattery and the adulation, the mad stories about unspeakable things Terry had done to people in the past. Like the fella he pistol-whipped for talking about him behind his back. You got him in Beckett's, didn't you, Terry? The cunt was just sitting there, enjoying his pint, and Terry tapped him on the shoulder. His arse must've fell out of his hole, did it?

Terry chuckled and said, Aye, it did all right, but his face had gone red. He glanced at my ma. It's not like that now, he said. That was back then, there was a war on. People had to do things.

And what'd you do, Terry?

My ma was glaring at him from across the breakfast counter. Terry's blush deepened. He tried to mutter something about operations and my ma laughed.

Operations? They kicked you out, Terry, remember?

They didn't kick me out of anywhere. I stepped down.

You tarred and feathered Bronagh Convery.

That wasn't me.

It was you, Terry. Everyone in Twinbrook knows it was you.

Terry looked at Anthony as if for help, but my ma had stood up off her stool and was pointing across the breakfast counter.

What about Joe Sloan? she said. He was fifteen years of age. He was a child, and you trailed him down an entry and shot him through the knees. Fifteen. Big brave man, aren't you, Terry? Big brave man shooting children on the street.

Somebody needs to police our districts.

Oh aye. Robbing drug dealers. Taking drugs off them and selling them to wee lads on the estate. You're no republican. I know republicans, and you're not one of them.

That was Anthony's cue to step in. All right, take it easy, he said, laughing now, charming them into thinking they were both right, in their own ways, without telling them what they were right about. Yous have seen it all, he said, from the beginning to the end. Yous were born into it. We can only imagine what that must've been like, isn't that right, Sean?

I agreed, we could. Anthony looked at the beer I had hardly touched.

You gonna ring in sick or wha? he said.

He's not ringing in sick, my ma said. He only started that job.

Where is it? A coffee shop? You need to get the head down and write more stories. Did I tell you about our Sean writing a story?

Aye, you did all right, Terry said. That's class, kid. What's it about?

It's about a wee lad whose mate drops dead at a house party, my ma said.

Sounds familiar, Anthony said, laughing.

That's because it is.

I saw where this was going and tried to tell my ma it wasn't the right time, but she had got it into her head that it was something Anthony would want to hear, he'd be flattered by it, and she thundered on without me, telling him the whole story and how it was about his mate that dropped dead at that house party over Christmas. The brother character is just like you, she said, excited now, as if she was breaking the best news. He's based on you.

What do you mean? Anthony said. In what way?

He's all protective and tough, and he says things the way you would say them. Just the way he's described. You can tell it's you, the same way you can tell the mother is me.

Hold on a second, what's going on here?

Anthony glanced at Terry and sort of laughed, but not really. He looked trapped.

What've you said about me, Sean?

I haven't said anything, she's making it sound worse than it is, I said.

He turned to our ma. Is there any of that stuff in it?

What stuff?

He gave her a look. Oh, God. No, my ma said. It's not about any of that.

I'd never write about that, Anto. I wouldn't write anything about you without talking to you about it first.

You haven't said anything to me about this though, have you?

I've been meaning to. I just haven't had the chance. I wouldn't do that.

Anthony heard the panic in my voice and softened.

I know you wouldn't, he said. He slung his arm round my neck and squeezed me. I don't care what you write about, as long as you're writing.

Swear to God, Anthony. You can read it yourself. I'll send you a copy.

Don't be stupid. You write what you have to. If it's about me, it's about me. If it's about all that stuff with your da, I don't give a fuck. He's your da. I'm still going to love you to death.

My ma teared up watching this. Anthony saw and got emotional.

Nothing comes between us, isn't that right, kid?

That's right.

I've looked after you your whole life, haven't I?

You have, aye.

Remember I bought you that laptop so you could write? His computer was riddled with viruses, so I got a few quid together and bought him the best laptop you can get. Took him right through university, didn't it?

I still use it, I said.

He still uses it. He wrote that story on it and everything. That's why I bought him it, so he could write his books.

You're a good brother, Terry said.

I'm not his brother. I'm his da, aren't I, kid? I've always been more of a da than a brother.

You have been.

My ma made this weird noise, like a hiccup. She was trying to cry, but the drink had blocked the reuptake of her serotonin, or dopamine, or whatever it was she needed more of, and she just couldn't do it. I'm so happy to have you here, she said. My sons. All we need is Gerard and it would be perfect.

Where is that cunt, right enough? Give him a bell, Terry, see where he's at.

Something wasn't right with my ma. The whole time your man Terry was there, she had her eyes locked on him, watching him. Usually, she would've gone to bed. She would've just left them to their own devices and worried about the state of the place when she woke up. But she stayed where she was on that stool at the breakfast counter right through to seven o'clock in the morning, when they finally left.

I had slept for two hours and was back up again, getting ready for work, when I heard her staggering upstairs.

Who was that fella? I said.

Terry Brennan.

Aye, but who is he?

Do you really wanna know?

She had collapsed on to her bed, fully clothed, and was lying star-shaped across the covers.

That was the man who was gonna shoot your da, she said.

That was him? Seriously?

She nodded with her eyes closed. Her legs twitched.

Who was the other man? I said.

What other man?

The other man. You said there were two men.

My ma moved her head from side to side. Can't remember, she said. Fra something.

Fra?

From down the road.

I could barely open my mouth.

Fra McCullough?

That was your man in Milltown, that was his name. Fra McCullough.

Something like that, my ma said. Fra McSomething.

Mother, was it Fra McCullough?

I had raised my voice. I had to. She was falling asleep.

I don't know, son, she said. I can't remember.

I went back to Milltown as soon as I could. Outside the cemetery gates, I tried to see into the yard. There was a small digger parked up outside the hut. The wheelbarrow had been left over to the side. A man I didn't know leaned with his hand against the railing and looked out on to the road. Behind him, the headstones at the top of the bank were black against the sky.

I thought about turning back. I checked the time and everything.

Then Joe came round the side of the hut with two strimmers tucked under his arm. He stopped, looked at me, and frowned.

Didn't think I'd see you again, he said.

I was just walking past. Thought I'd call in.

As soon as I poked my head into the hut, I knew Fra wasn't there. Somebody had taken his seat in the corner, a young lad who bent down to tie his laces. I pulled my hood up and went outside to make sure. The rest of the men had chosen their strimmers and were standing around the yard, smoking, waiting to put in a shift. None of them was Fra.

Right, let's go, Joe said.

They headed off to work at the Republican Plot. Easter was coming up and Joe wanted it looking well for the commemoration parade. I kept my distance and watched them work. There wasn't much to do, the site had been maintained immaculately, with fresh flowers and wreaths that had been placed along each side of the walkway. I ventured into the memorial and saw men with bags and litter picks following along behind me. Some of them blessed themselves. Others stayed on the outside looking in. I stopped at Bobby Sands' marker and read the names of the men he had been buried with: Terence O'Neill and Joe McDonnell. There was no epitaph. No lines from poems, no quotes. Nothing to distinguish them from the people who had been buried alongside them. It was better that way, I thought. This was a man who had sacrificed his life for the cause, kind of thing, but also, here was a man who was from where I was from, who ran about the same streets I ran about. I felt that deeper than I had ever felt anything, but it was fleeting, and by the time I stepped away from the memorial, the feeling had already receded.

The men had stopped for a smoke break. They sat on the graves and took their phones out. I hovered at the edge of them, then sat down too. I used to be down here, I said to the lad next to me. Two hundred hours.

He rubbed the back of his neck. Where are you now? he said.

Holy Trinity. The chapel.

I leaned against a headstone and stared at the graves across the way. Have you been here long? I said.

Few weeks just. Not long.

What'd you do?

I didn't do fuck all. Assault.

Brutal. How many hours?

Hundred and twenty.

He took a draw of his feg. It was a short draw, an angry draw. The kind of draw you take when you're thinking bad thoughts.

What about your man, Fra, is he still here? I said.

Fra?

Aye, the aul fella. The scary one.

Fra McCullough? You wouldn't have to go far to find him.

Is he here?

No, fuck. He's across the road.

He said across the road like it was a specific place. Turns out it was McEnaney's. If you're looking for that crazy bastard, that's where you'll find him, he said.

In the bar, Fra was sitting on his own, drinking a pint of Guinness. I noticed that he had about forty quid in coins stacked neatly in front of him, in piles of five. He bought his pints from those stacks, and he made new stacks with the coins that were left over. I stayed for about an hour, watching him. He didn't speak to anybody. He didn't even look at his phone. He just sat there, drinking, reaching for his pint like he had one eye closed and was trying to gauge the distance. Eventually I went over and slid on to the stool next to him. He looked at me as if from across a busy road.

What school did you go to? he said.

La Salle.

My son went there. Did you know him?

He took the memorial card out of his pocket and showed me. I knew exactly who he was. He was in the year below me.

He killed himself, Fra said.

I know. I remember.

He touched his son's picture with his thumb, gently, and stroked it.

You need to go now, he said.

I got a black taxi back up the road. It was just me and a wee lad with his hood up sitting in front of me, on the flip-down seat. He knocked the window and got out at the Poleglass roundabout. I looked at the driver, the size of him in the front seat, and wondered if he was a volunteer. It was always a possibility; prisoners that had been released at the start of the peace process still carried criminal records, they couldn't get jobs anywhere, and the black taxi depot was one of the few places that would take them on. You could never ask him though. You could never be like, Here, mate, were you in the Ra? It was one of those things. Like my great-aunt. Nobody in our family knew anything until she died. Couple of fellas called to my granny's door and told her she was to have a republican funeral, with the flag over the coffin and the guard of honour. She hadn't a clue. That's the mad thing about it. You could be in a taxi driven by someone who's put a bullet in someone's head and you wouldn't even know.

The driver's eyes were in the rear-view mirror. You going to Summer Hill?

Nah, just on round to Cherry, mate. Cheers.

We were back in Twinbrook, following the road around the pitches. The sun was only starting to come down, the clouds had opened up, and the yellowy light tinged the leaves of the trees running along the River Path. There was a group of wee girls down there, at the big stone, drinking bottles of blue WKD. They wore tracksuit bottoms with vest tops and gold earrings that glinted as they danced. Not like Aoife. She was all dolled up in jeans and crop tops, and she took selfies in front of her wardrobe-door mirror. I was scrolling through her posts, admiring how tirelessly she had documented her favourite outfits, when I got a message from Anthony.

Help me, it said.

I rang him. What's the matter? You all right?

Please, Sean. Quickly.

Where are you?

I'm in the flat. Gerard's flat. Don't leave me.

I'm not. Hold on.

I got out of the taxi at the bottom of Aspen and tried to pay the driver through the passenger-seat window, but I couldn't get into my pocket, my hands were full, and I dropped a load of change that clattered across the ground. Behind me, a squad of fellas I recognized from about the estate watched as I slung my bag over my shoulder and ran like fuck up the hill, to the flats on the corner, where I could see Gerard's front door lying open. I still had my phone out, talking to Anthony, asking him where he was, but he had already hung up.

I'm here, he said from the other room. In here.

He was on his knees in the middle of the living-room floor. He'd no shirt on, his jeans had fallen down below his waist, and his belly was bigger than I had ever seen it. The way it hung over his waistline, with the stretch marks, those long purple gashes that went right up his back. He clutched his hands to his chest and whimpered.

I can't breathe, he said. I can't breathe.

I tried to give him water and he told me, No. I need a beer. Grab me a beer.

I handed him one from the case and he opened it with his teeth.

I can't stop thinking about it, he said.

Thinking about what? What is it?

Oh, Jesus. Jesus Christ.

He closed his eyes and tried to breathe in through his nose and out through his mouth, like our ma showed us when we were kids, but he was shaking. Not just his hands, his entire body, and he kept tensing up, as if trying to push through it. Then he jumped to his feet and paced up and down the room. For a second, he was okay, it seemed to pass, and then he buckled. He fell to the floor, curled up into a ball, and groaned. I thought he was going to die. You need to go to hospital, I said, but he said, No, it's just a panic attack.

It'll pass, he said.

I counted the days since that night he came back to our ma's. I remembered him saying he'd been on it for two days before that, which meant he'd now been drinking and taking gear for nearly a week.

A week? Is that all? he said, chuckling.

The beer helped. I gave him another one and he necked it. Then he pulled himself round and sat with his back against the settee. I moved towards the window and he said, Don't, but I was only opening it, I didn't touch the blinds. He closed his eyes and leaned with his head against the cushion. I let him sit there for a minute, then I got down on the floor beside him.

I can't stop thinking about it, he said again.

He drank his beer, breathed. Drank some more. Looked away.

I had wee Anthony down here with me, he said. He was on the floor, playing with that keyboard he has, and he was just sitting there, hitting the keys. Then he turned round and looked at me, his wee face, and it all came back to me. I could see it clear as day, but I wasn't seeing it through my eyes any more. I was seeing it through his eyes, your da's eyes. I was him, Sean. I was looking at myself when I was that age, and all I could think was, how could anybody do that to him? How could anybody do that to a wee boy?

He turned away from me, and for a while we just sat there and listened to the sounds from the street coming through the open window: a woman shouting, a child laughing, and somewhere far away, a scrambler tore across the fields.

He never did anything to you, did he? Anthony said.

No. Nothing.

He looked at me. It was hard. His face was swollen. His eyes were

247

completely red. If he did anything to you, I'll hunt him down and kill him, he said.

He didn't, I said. I don't know why he didn't, but he didn't.

Swear to me. Swear to me right now.

I swear over our ma's life, Anto. He never touched me.

He dropped his head. The sweat ran down the back of his neck.

I wouldn't have said a word, he said. I wouldn't have said anything, only I thought it was happening to you. He shook his head, cursed himself. I shouldn't have said anything, he said. I should've just kept it down. I'm the reason you lost your da.

You're not —

I am. I fucking am.

He grabbed his chest as he said this. His face twisted in agony.

It's back. It's coming back.

He held his knees to his chest and rocked back and forth.

I can't breathe, he said. I can't breathe.

22

The regional manager turned up at the coffee shop on Thursday – he wanted to oversee my black T-shirt test. He asked me to make him an espresso. The run-time was twelve seconds on the dot, the temperature was just right, and when he sprinkled brown sugar on top of the crema, it didn't dissolve, which was good. Then he asked me to make a cappuccino. It didn't go as well as it could have; it was a bit frothy. The regional manager spooned it back and said, Yeah, you can do better than that, and made me make another one. He asked for a latte next, then a flat white. Then he brought me over to a table in the corner and tested my knowledge of the things I was supposed to have read up on in the forty-page booklet. I hadn't. I got six questions wrong. The regional manager sucked air between his teeth.

I'm sorry, Sean, but this isn't good enough.

He failed me, and my heart sank.

We can try again in a few weeks, he said.

Am I not sacked?

No. But you have to pass it then, okay?

Aye, okay. Cheers.

They had sprung the test on me. If they had let me know I could've sat down the night before and studied up. Now I had to do it all over again, and this time I had to pass, otherwise that was it. Unemployed again. Signing on. Stuck in my ma's gaff because there's no way I could afford to rent somewhere without money coming in, and I'd lose that deposit on the flat in Botanic as well. It really got me down because I was trying. I hadn't gone on the rip in ages, I hadn't seen my mates in weeks, and I had been flat out working every hour I could, in Holy Trinity and the charity shop, trying to get my hours done. It didn't make a difference. I couldn't do anything right.

When I walked out of work at the end of my shift, part of me was like, fuck it, I'm gonna get wiped off my nut. I'm gonna take a load of gear and let it all go. That's where my head was at. Standing in line at the black taxi depot, waiting for the next car to take me up to Andytown to meet Ryan and Finty for Ryan's leaving do, it was the only thing I could think about: getting completely fucked. Then I looked at my phone and saw the photo Aoife had posted on her story. I nearly had a stroke. She was standing with her mate by the escalators in Victoria Square, literally round the corner from where I was now, and the photo had been uploaded less than an hour before. She could've still been there.

I ran like a maniac down Castle Lane. By the time I got to Arthur Square, I was sweating pints. Aoife was nowhere to be seen, and me like a dick standing at that exact spot next to the escalators in the middle of the shopping centre like she might come back. She didn't, but I kept refreshing my feed just in case she posted another picture, and finally I got a black taxi up to Andytown at seven o'clock that night, after walking along the streets for hours and hours, in and out of shops, until they had all closed. Trying to spot her through the crowd.

I had told Ryan I would meet him and Finty in the Andytown for a few swalls. He was going to Australia the next day. I had no excuse.

The taxi dropped me off outside Biddy Duffy's and I dandered up the entry to the social club. It wasn't the kind of bar you could just walk into. There was a buzzer you had to press to get the attention of the man sitting at the desk at the other side of the doors. He checked the cameras to make sure I wasn't some headcase coming to wreck the place, then he made me sign the guest book. On the wall behind him, there was a mural showing James Connolly wounded on a stretcher. There was a framed Proclamation as well, and the words *Cumann Sóisialta Bhaile Andarsan* had been stencilled across the floor. The man looked up at me.

You meeting somebody?

Aye, my mates are in there, I said.

He looked down at the guest book. Fintan McKenna?

Aye, Finty.

The man nodded. Go ahead, he said.

I found Ryan and Finty down the back of the poolroom. They had put away some amount of drink already, their table was filled with empty glasses, and they were all over the place telling me about how we had to make it a big one for Ryan's last night. Ryan took a baggie out of his pocket and twiddled it in my face. I slapped his hand away.

You nuts? Put that away, I said, glancing round.

This place wasn't like the Laurel Glen, people weren't queuing up at the cubicles for a key, and if you got caught taking gear like that, they'd do more than just throw you out. I said this to Ryan and he told me it was sweet: Don't worry about it. They know Finty's da, don't they, Finty?

Oh aye, they know all right. They know all they need to know.

The chances of Finty's da backing them up were slim on a good day, and they weren't doing themselves any favours. The way they were carrying on, talking about how much gear they had taken, the partying they planned to do. There wasn't a man in the poolroom who didn't stop mid-shot and watch Ryan saunter into the toilets, brazenly, jingling his keys as he went. He wanted everybody to know what he was doing because fuck them, he could do what he wanted, and he wasn't going to let a bunch of aul lads who fancied themselves as pillars of the community tell him any different. When he came back, he slipped the baggie into my back pocket and said, Go ahead, wee son. I told him no, I couldn't. I had work in the morning. He looked at me like I had spat in his face.

Is that what this is? What the fuck is this?

He grabbed my work T-shirt as if to pull it off. I slapped his hand away and he laughed, nudged Finty.

I'm moving to Australia and this cunt won't even take a line, he said.

I don't know what he was thinking, he had forty-odd hours of travel ahead of him, with stopovers in Dubai and Thailand, and he was getting on like he was already there, drinking cocktails on Bondi Beach, having the time of his life.

I tried to talk him out of it, but Ryan's nerves were at him, and he carried on rowdily, with his arm around Finty's neck, singing along to songs they put on the jukebox just to annoy the aul fellas stationed along the bar: Vengaboys, Backstreet Boys, Westlife. They shouted across the room at us, told us to knock it on the head: There's money on the table over here. But Ryan and Finty couldn't help themselves. All right, all right, they said, and then, ten minutes later, just when the men had settled back into their games, 'Uptown Girl' came on and Ryan and Finty were on their feet, dancing, singing along to every word.

In the toilets, a man in a Hunger Strikers T-shirt pulled me into the corner. You may tell your mates to rein it in, he said. They're gonna get themselves hurt.

He wasn't messing about. I told Ryan, and Ryan started getting on like a big lad saying he wasn't afraid of a few wannabe Ra men thinking they had the run of the place. He knew the craic though, he wasn't stupid, and his short temper was short-lived in that way. He settled. Finty did too. They went back to trying to tempt me into a mad one, and they were all talk about these girls they were supposed to meet up with later on, in the Whitefort. Ryan showed me pictures on his phone. Look at the shape of her, he said, and held it up for me to see. She was wearing leggings. Her arse was unreal. Not unreal as in class, but unreal as in it didn't look real. Finty got angry just looking at her.

Fuck sake, look at that like, he said.

Look at what?

Her. Breaks my heart.

Ryan stared at the picture, then at me. Wait'll you see her mates, he said.

I don't know if Finty had a sixth sense about these things, or if he was more observant than the rest of us, but he noticed three men sitting at the bar who weren't there before. The man behind the bar was talking to somebody on the phone. Finty looked at the three men again and said, They don't have any drinks. At the door, the man from the front desk was watching us. These cunts are up to something, he said, but Ryan wouldn't back down.

Fuck them, he said. What're they gonna do?

Then I saw Finty's face, the colour draining out of it.

Daddy, no –

He was trailed off his stool and punched in the face. He tried to protect himself with his hands over his head, but his da was too quick, too strong. He dragged Finty into the corner of the room, to the fire escape, and disappeared with him out the back. Ryan tried to run after him, but he was grabbed by the neck and told to sit down.

What the fuck? What'd we do?

There was panic in his voice. We were surrounded.

Empty your pockets.

What for?

Empty your fucking pockets.

I showed them what I had and Ryan did the same, minus the gear. One of the men had sauntered over to the jukebox and put on a Christy Moore song. I glanced at Ryan. He tried to play it cool and drink his pint like he didn't give a fiddler's, but he wasn't convincing anybody. The glass shook in his hand.

We were only messing about, he said. It's only a bit of music.

Finty's da thought different. He stood over Ryan with a fist cocked behind him. He was massive, bigger than I remembered, and he leaned over Ryan with his face right up close.

Where is it? he said.

Where's what?

He leaned with his hand on the back of Ryan's chair.

I don't have anything, swear to God –

He grabbed Ryan by the scruff and dragged him off his stool towards the fire escape. There was no kicking and screaming, no struggle whatsoever; he was like one of those string figurines that had collapsed, and his legs were completely limp.

It's in my sock, it's in my sock, he said.

We had to take our shoes off – so Finty's da could see we didn't have anything else stashed in there – and our socks, which he didn't let us put on again until we had walked through the bar barefoot, in front of everyone. Outside, the rain had stopped but the ground was wet, there was no way of avoiding it; our socks got soaked. Finty's da watched us hobble from foot to foot, trying to tie our laces. If I see you anywhere near this bar again, you'll be following my son out the back, you hear me? he said.

Ryan walked with his head down, staring at the ground.

That was a two-hundred-quid bag of gear, he said.

We found Finty sitting on the steps outside Fusco's. His mouth was bleeding. Ryan got some tissues from the woman behind the counter. She came out with a medical kit and told him to let her see.

You've lost a tooth, she said.

She gave him a bottle of water from the fridge, and she got him a bag of ice as well, for his eye.

You may get down to A&E, she said.

Is it bad?

His lip's sliced open.

Come here, open your mouth.

Finty was laughing. There was blood all over his shirt.

I can't feel anything, look.

He clenched his teeth. Blood gushed down his chin.

It's the gear, Ryan said. You've had too much gear.

We got a taxi down to the Royal and waited with everybody else to be seen. The woman sitting further along the bench had her wee girl with her and the wee girl was in her pyjamas. There was another woman in her housecoat, reading a magazine, and at the other side of the room, an aul fella leaned with his head against the wall. We thought we'd be in and out, Finty only needed a few stitches. But there were a lot of people in that waiting room, and you could tell they'd been waiting for hours. Finty told us to go on, there was no point sitting there all night, but it didn't feel right leaving him on his own, and I would rather sit with him than get roped in to the White-fort with Ryan. He had those girls messaging him, asking where he was, then his phone died.

Is there a pay phone? he said.

It didn't matter if there was. He didn't know their numbers.

Finty was finally seen at twelve o'clock that night, four hours after we got there. His mouth didn't look good, he could hardly speak, and he was feeling it now that the gear had worn off. Ryan got a lend of a charger from a fella who had the sense to bring one with him. He tried to get through to those girls in the Whitefort, but they didn't reply.

We've missed our shot, he said, but didn't seem too fussed.

I went to the vending machine and bought a bag of crisps. When I came back, Ryan was scrolling through a Facebook group that had been set up for Irish people who were moving to Australia. He showed me pictures. They looked like they were having a good time.

Would you not be up for it? he said.

Going to Australia? Nah, it's not for me.

Ryan laughed. You're sitting there in a barista T-shirt, ya header.

Looks well on me though, doesn't it?

Does it fuck. Take it off and burn it.

He stuck his hand into my bag of crisps and pulled out a massive one that was folded over nicely, like a flower.

Seriously, what're you gonna do? he said.

He wasn't being snarky. He genuinely wanted to know.

I'm gonna move down to this gaff on Botanic and go from there, I said.

I knew this didn't make sense to Ryan, he didn't understand what difference moving down there was going to make, and I wasn't going to explain it to him. I didn't know how to. He slumped into his seat and stared at the nurses' station down the hall.

I'd be as well taking it easy tonight, he said. I've some travelling to do.

What about this cunt? I said.

Finty was shuffling along the hall towards us. His face was out like a bap, but he was smiling.

He's not going anywhere, Ryan said. He's here for life.

I got an email from the magazine I had sent my story to that night, when I was standing at the bus stop outside the Royal. It said what I thought it would, that they weren't going to publish my story. But the editor had written things like, *the sentences are wonderfully weighted and the story runs smoothly*. He even suggested ways of rewriting the story that could make it work better. Then he said, at the end of the email, *I just want to reiterate that I think you have a wonderful ability, and I hope you will submit to the magazine again*. Part of me thought he was blowing smoke. But then again, why would he? He had hundreds of submissions to go through, I was sure, and there was no way he would reply to them all with emails like that.

I took a screenshot and sent it to Mairéad. She rang me.

I fucking told you they'd like it, she said.

I had to remind her that it was a rejection. It's a good rejection though, she said. He wants to read more of your work.

I don't have any other work, I said.

Well, you'll just have to write something else then, won't you?

I hadn't thought that far ahead, but aye, that's what I would have to do.

I was in Bookfinders the other day, I said.

No way, did you meet Mary? I miss her so much.

She misses you too, they all do.

Who was all there?

I named the names I knew, then I got round to Julia. She took me to some falafel place, I said.

Julia did? Wait, hold on. How did you end up with Julia?

I went back to the start, to viewing the room on University Street – Mairéad was buzzing for me, but she also thought the landlord sounded shady. Then I told her about seeing Julia and following her across the street to No Alibis.

You followed her?

I just saw her going that way. I wanted to say hello.

I told her about the inscription in the Kundera book, then I told her about Paul's reaction to that inscription, and she said, That's exactly the kind of thing he'd be into. I left out the part about giving him the book. It made me sound like I wanted to be his mate. Then I told her about Lavery's, the poolroom, and finally, the falafel place. All through this, there was silence from Mairéad's end of the line. I knew she was there though. Even when nobody's talking, you can tell. There's a small sound. It's like having a hand pressed over your ear, but far away.

She wasn't in good form, I said, about Julia.

The sound that broke the silence was a sigh. Mairéad groaned. I didn't want to have to tell you this, she said.

Tell me what?

I'm bi, Sean. I'm fucking bi.

I know you are.

Yes, and I know you know.

Then why didn't you just say?

Because it isn't that easy, is it?

Fuck sake, Mairéad, it's me.

I know, it's just –

She paused. I heard that small sound again. Mairéad took a breath.

I went to Queen's, she said. I met all these people that weren't like the people we grew up with, I had this whole other life, and I wasn't afraid of my sexuality any more, you know? I was out and I didn't have to worry about what anyone would say. Then I bumped into you that night in Mono. Part of me was like, wise up, it's only Sean. He's hardly gonna care. The other part wanted to hide myself away. Because I still feel it. I still have that fear.

You don't need to be afraid of me, I said.

I know.

Where does the stuff with Julia come into it then?

Mairéad sniffed. That's a whole other thing, she said.

I heard a shuffling sound, like she was changing position. Then I heard something being set on a table, a glass, maybe. I tried to imagine her sitting in her apartment in Berlin, but it was too far away.

I stayed in Julia's one night, she said. We had a few drinks. I don't know, it just happened. Then it happened again. I kept going back because it was a place to stay, and every time I went back, we slept together. After a few weeks, it got intense. Julia started talking about moving to Berlin. Her parents were gonna give her money to go, it was a whole thing. Then she told me she loved me. It was all just – I should've nipped it in the bud, after that first night. I should've been straight with her from the start.

You were straight with me, I said.

Exactly, and look at us.

I laughed. We're a shambles, I said.

We really are.

There was another pause. I had left the bus stop and walked up the road towards Beechmount. The Beehive was empty. The few men standing out the front smoked pensively, with their eyes locked on the puddles at their feet. I nodded as I passed them, and then I crossed the road because there was a crowd of young ones standing outside the Chinese and I couldn't be arsed walking through them.

One of the wee girls shouted something. I thought she was shouting at me, but then I saw another crowd walking up Nansen Street. She was just calling for her mates.

Conor told me he was supposed to go to Berlin with you as well, I said.

Aye, for about a day. He was all talk though.

He was getting on like you didn't want him to go.

Mairéad sighed again. He would say that, she said.

I sat on the steps outside Cultúrlann and watched a man walk his dog along Brighton Street. The rain had stopped, but it was cold. I could see my breath.

I think Julia thinks I was using her, Mairéad said.

What like, for a place to stay?

Aye.

Were you?

Mairéad thought about this. The fact that she had to think made me wonder.

She offered me a place to stay and I took it, she said.

But you knew she wanted to be with you, didn't you?

Aye, I did, and I wanted to be with her. It just didn't work out that way.

Because she said she loved you?

You ask more questions than a peeler.

I'm just curious.

No, you're not. You're trying to work out if I was using you.

Were you?

What do you think?

It was my turn to think it over. It didn't take long.

Sorry, I said. I'm being a dick.

Yeah, you are.

She went quiet again. I thought that was it, the conversation was over. Then I heard a can being opened. Beer. She was drinking beer.

How do you feel about moving down to Botanic then? she said.

I could tell she was smiling when she said this. Something about the way she sounded, like she was speaking from the front of her mouth.

It's a different world, isn't it? she said.

I agreed, it was. Students everywhere, I said.

Too many students, unless you're a student. Then it's the best craic ever. You'll get used to it though.

You think so?

Aye, you'll be grand. You'll fit right in.

It didn't feel that way the other day, when I was with her mates. But I didn't say anything about that. I didn't want her to think I didn't like them.

You still enjoying yourself over there then? I said.

It's unbelievable, Sean. Honestly. I was sitting on the grass out of the front of the Reichstag the other day, reading a book, and then I stopped and looked around and was like, what the fuck am I doing here?

It's no City Hall though, is it?

No. Definitely not.

No Cultúrlann either.

Cultúrlann?

That's where I am now. Sitting outside.

Oh, right. Random.

I watched two women saunter down the road towards Beechmount. They wore big coats with their hoods pulled up, and as they walked they swigged from bottles of Diet Coke. Across the way, at the top of Shiels Street, there was a suicide awareness mural showing two hands reaching out to one another, with a caption that read: *Reaching out is a strength not a weakness*. It was one of those murals that had been made by kids from the local youth club, and it had that quality to it, like it had been done in a classroom.

You should come to Berlin sometime, Mairéad said. Even just for a few days. You could stay with me, you'd only have to pay for your flights.

You wouldn't charge me for the room?

Nah, sure you didn't charge me, did you?

Speaking of which —

Don't you fucking dare.

I laughed. The women walking down the road looked over at me.

Maybe in a few months, when I get settled into this gaff, I said.

Yeah, definitely. I'd love to see you.

Aye, you too.

There was another pause. The women in the big coats had stopped outside the bookies. One of them tried to spark up a feg, but it was too windy. I waited until they were gone, then I said, I miss talking to you.

I know. I miss it too.

Seriously though. You're the only person I can talk to.

We can still talk.

I know.

I stared at the tree at the end of the path. The leaves were white in the moonlight shining down. It made the pavement look like it was moving. I waited for the ghosts. They didn't come.

I've been wanting to tell you something, I said. I mean, there's something I wanna talk about.

Okay?

It's about my family. About when my da went away, you know?

Yeah. I know.

You know what?

She was quiet for a second. Do you want me to say? she said.

Aye. If you want.

He was abusive, wasn't he?

I nodded, but Mairéad couldn't see that I was nodding, so I had to say, Aye, he was abusive, and then I had to make sure she didn't get her wires crossed.

Not me though, I said. He didn't abuse me.

Was it Anthony?

261

Aye. Just Anthony.

That's all I could say, and even that felt like too much.

You okay? Mairéad said.

I nodded again. The tears came out of nowhere. I tried to breathe through them, but quietly, so Mairéad couldn't hear.

I need to go, I said.

Okay. But promise me something, Sean.

I'm not gonna do anything stupid.

I know you're not. That's not what I'm saying.

She sighed through her nose. For a second, I thought she was crying too.

What is it? I said.

Promise me we'll keep talking.

I laughed weakly.

Seriously, Sean.

Right hand up to God, I said.

Okay, well. Before you go . . .

Her voice trailed off, there was a strange glitch noise, and then her voice came back solid and clear down the line.

You know I love you to bits, don't you? she said.

I nodded again. I love you too, I said.

23

I got a phone call from my ma one afternoon. She had stopped in
Tesco on the way home from work and was in so much pain she
needed help carrying the messages. Her kidneys were bad again, she
was getting infections every couple of weeks, and every time she told
the cleaning agency she couldn't travel far, she wasn't well, they
ignored her and sent her wherever they needed her, even if it was two
or three bus journeys away. When I got there, she was sitting on a
bench out the front of the shop, on her own, with the handles of the
bags looped through her fingers.

My wee son, she said. You're so good.

She slipped her arm through mine and leaned against me.

People are gonna think I've a toy boy, she said.

At home I unpacked the messages and put them away for her, and
then I sat at the breakfast counter and looked over the notes the editor
from that magazine had given me. They were good notes, but I was
tired. I wasn't in the mood to write, and I kept going on the internet
and scrolling through social media. It was late in the afternoon, my
ma had taken her fish fingers from the freezer and was waiting for the
grill to heat up. She washed her hands with washing-up liquid and
the smell of lemongrass filled the kitchen.

It's the bleach, she said. It irritates the skin.

I typed Aoife's name into the search bar like I did most days now,
to make sure I hadn't missed anything, and nearly dropped my phone.

She was sitting on that onion ring sculpture in the town, the one on Arthur Square, where me and Mairéad had eaten a McDonald's after Mono. She had her hood up, you could see the rain on the ground behind her, that dull sheen, and she was grinning, sleekedly, as if she was somewhere she wasn't supposed to be, then the story ended. I opened it again and held the screen with my thumb to keep it there, to double-check I had seen it right. She was in Belfast again. She was mooching around the town with a group of girls who dressed just like her, in leggings and denim jackets. I took a screenshot. It was easier, and I wasn't crossing any boundaries or anything like that; her profile was open to the public. Anybody could click on to her page and see.

Maybe that was what she wanted. Maybe she knew there was somebody out there looking for her. Then I remembered what happened last time and I wasn't so sure she wanted to be found.

I went back to my Word doc and tried to work through those edits.

My ma had eaten her fish fingers and was having a nap on the settee. She had her fleecy jumper draped over her like a blanket, and she snored so loud she startled herself awake. I laughed. She looked at me, smiled, and drifted off again.

Eventually I finished my writing and let myself take one last look on Aoife's Facebook. She didn't post much there, it was all Twitter and Instagram. I flicked through the photos she had been tagged in, the ones where she was all dressed up in sparkly dance costumes, tutus, and glittery eye make-up. There were dozens of comments under these photos telling her how beautiful she was. She Liked and replied to them, usually with a similar compliment, unless it was a boy trying to get her attention, in which case she said something like, *thank you, Sam, appreciate your input*, and moved on. I loved to see it, the way she stuck up for herself. She didn't take any shit, but she also wasn't afraid to make fun of herself either: *why would I study for my exams when I can look at eyelash extensions and dream about being a dance mom?*

I thought about what would happen if I added her as a friend. If I messaged her and told her who I was. What she would say. How long it would take before we got to the point where the question was asked. And that was what stopped me, knowing she would want to know and I would have to tell her: our da abused my brother when he was a wee boy. He crept into his bedroom at night while my ma was in bed and did terrible things. I couldn't put that on her. I didn't want her to have to carry it around. Chances were, she wouldn't want anything to do with me anyway. Because that's her daddy, and she would believe her daddy over anyone. Unless he'd done something to her too.

I scrolled down. She had been tagged in a post with three other girls at the Lyric Theatre: *we're only four hours early*. It was the same day, at three o'clock. She was here to watch a show. I went on the Lyric's website. The only thing on that night was a dance performance called *Madra Rua*. I didn't read what it was about. I bought a ticket and waited for the email confirmation to come through. At six o'clock, I got ready, and by half six, I was on a bus down the Lisburn Road.

I couldn't see her, there were too many people, and they milled around the theatre bar, drinking wine from plastic cups. I took a stool by the window and scanned the crowd. It was like a dance, the way they disengaged from one conversation and moved on to the next. Nobody lingered too long, there was always somebody else to talk to, and that made it hard to keep track. Ten minutes before the play was due to start, I checked to see what Aoife had been wearing that day, in that photo on the onion ring sculpture. Every time I saw a denim jacket, my heart jumped.

The intercom told us to take our seats. There were two entrances, one at the bottom of the stairs and one at the top. I went towards the top doors slowly, with my hand on the banister, my legs like jelly every time I turned to watch the streams of people move along the hallway below. Eventually, I thought I had made a mistake; she wasn't there, and I felt something like relief. Then I spotted her, at the back of the queue. She was on her tiptoes trying to see over the crowd that had bunched up around her, at the bottom of the stairs. About twenty steps separated us, and she moved with everybody else, expectantly, with an anguished look on her face.

Tickets, please, the woman at the door said.

I went into the auditorium and there was fuss all around me; everybody stood up to let a squad of women squeeze past. Then the fella next to me kept leaning forward. I strained my neck to see, and after a while, when everything had settled down, I finally found Aoife again, a few rows in front and over to the left, sitting with her mates. Four of them giggling and laughing, covering their mouths with their hands. Then the curtains opened and Aoife's mate nudged her to put her phone away, and for the next ninety minutes, I watched her watching the show.

Every so often, she glanced at her mates, and her mates looked at her and nodded as if they had seen it too. That's how I knew she was impressed with something. The way she leaned ever so slightly forward, her attention back on the show. I imagined going up to her afterwards and asking what she thought of it, and then listening to all the things she had to say. Introducing myself as her brother. Giving her a hug. Telling her where I had been all this time and why.

The show ended and the room erupted. A standing ovation.

I kept my eyes on Aoife. I didn't want to lose her, and as I headed back down the stairs I saw her again, walking with her mates towards the bar. There was a well-dressed woman waiting for them. She must've asked them how it was, they were talking excitedly, but I couldn't hear what Aoife said, there were too many people, and they kept blocking my way. Then the crowd parted. She was walking towards me. I couldn't move, and as she passed, she looked right at me. There wasn't a flicker of recognition. No double take. She was gone.

I wasn't going to tell my ma about where I'd been. When I saw her lying on her bed that night, watching TV, I thought, no. Just leave it. But then she patted the space next to her and said, Come on, sit beside me. I climbed on to the bed from the bottom and sat next to her, slumped with my back against the headboard.

Have you started packing? she said. Anthony said he'll give you a hand.

Aye, he was saying.

He's doing well now. He's back at work and all, and he's off the drink.

That's good.

I said to him about getting some help. He just laughed.

What kind of help?

Counselling or something. The waiting lists are terrible though. People are waiting years to be seen to.

What about you? Would you not go?

Nah, I tried it before. Didn't work. They kept making me talk about my past.

I thought that was the point.

She glanced at me out the corner of her eye. She was wearing the fleece now, zipped right up to her chin. The way I see it, the past is the past, she said. I just move on. Get on with life. But Anthony's different. The things that have happened to him. He needs help, doesn't he?

We all do, I said.

You think so?

Aye, I do.

My ma pulled her sleeves down over her hands and crossed her arms. Where were you tonight then? she said.

Just down watching a play.

Where was that?

The Lyric.

Oh, excuse us. The Lyric Theatre, she said, in her best posh voice. What was the play?

It was more like a dance show.

A dance show? Didn't know you were into that.

I'm not. I just went.

Was it good?

It was grand, aye. Aoife was there.

Aoife? Aoife who?

My wee sister.

My ma's eyes widened. Did you speak to her?

Nah. I just saw her. She was at the other side of the room.

How did you know it was her?

I found her online. She posted something about going to the Lyric and I went down. There's pictures.

I took my phone out and showed her.

God, she's gorgeous, isn't she?

I nodded. I didn't know what else to say. My ma looked at me. I can see your da in her, she said. And you. She looks like you.

Nah, she doesn't.

She does. You have the same nose, and the eyes. Very dark. Like your da.

I took the phone off her and locked the screen. I don't know if she knows I exist, I said.

I'm sure she does.

How would she? She was only four.

You wouldn't know with your da. He's probably concocted some story. When we broke up, he told people I was an alcoholic. He tried to get social services on me and everything.

Seriously?

He wouldn't leave me alone. I'd look out the window at night, when I was putting you to bed, and see him standing across the street, watching the house like a stalker. I'd be in the town with your granny doing a bit of shopping. I'd look behind me and see his face in the crowd. That's the way he was.

She glanced at the window, saw that the blinds were open, and got up to close them.

Is he out there? I said, jokingly.

My ma lowered herself on to the edge of the bed.

I wouldn't put it past him, she said. We'll get him though. One of these days. He'll be put away for good.

There had been some talk over the years about taking my da to court. My ma always said it was something Anthony should do, and Anthony had said that he wanted to, but when it came down to it, he never did, and I didn't blame him. There was no guarantee things would go his way. Doesn't matter how strong a case you have, Anthony knew as well as anybody that the courts are the courts, and in the end, it's people who have a few quid in their pocket that win cases.

We can't make him do anything he doesn't want to, my ma said. We have to wait until he's ready.

I don't think he'll ever be ready.

She saw the expression on my face and looked at her lap.

Think of it this way, she said. Your da's out there in the country somewhere getting on like he's landed gentry with his guns and his clay pigeons, and he's shitting himself. He's looking over his shoulder every single day, waiting for us to come after him. Telling you, he was paranoid out of his mind when I was with him. He thought people were coming to kill him, and to be fair, they probably were. The things he's done. That's why he moved away. He knew the Ra were gonna execute him. Now he's got his wife and daughter and his big house in the country. He's got too much to lose, and he knows it's coming. He knows he's gonna get a knock on the door some day and it'll all come crashing down.

You don't know that for sure, I said.

I do. I know it more than I know anything, son. He'll get his come-uppance. Long runs the fox, that's all I'm saying. Long runs the fox.

24

That Kundera book Conor ordered for me was ready to collect. I got the text while I was sitting on the 81 bus heading up to Holy Trinity. He invited me to a book launch, and I appreciated him making the effort, but I was tired. Work had been hectic that day. Nobody got a proper break; five minutes to maul a ham and cheese panini and that was us, straight back on the tills. It was dead warm too, on the bus. The glass trapped the heat, and there was no shade, no air even with the windows open. I closed my eyes for a second, and when I opened them again we were at the top of the Grosvenor. Across the road, a woman stopped outside McPeakes and bought a bunch of flowers. She was wearing a navy nurse's uniform, and I watched her carry those flowers across the road to Dunville Park, where a crowd of wee girls from St Louise's had taken their shoes off and were lying with their bare feet on the grass.

The lights turned green, and as the bus moved along the Springfield Road, past the mural for the Springhill Massacre, the one on the side of the house facing the peeler station, with the portraits of the five people who were murdered by the Brits that day, I wondered if I should message Daniel Jackson and tell him I was sorry. It seemed like the right thing to do, but when I searched his name on Facebook nothing came up. Then I messaged Mairéad to see if she could find him and she sent me a screenshot of his profile page. He had blocked me, and I thought that was fair enough.

I locked my phone and stared out the window as the mountain came into view. Written across it in massive white letters were the words:

ÉRIU IS OUR QUEEN

The bus dropped me off as it always did, at the top of Norglen. The sun was out and everybody was in their gardens. Instead of cooking, they sent their kids across the road for fish suppers they ate straight from the papers, in the middle of the street. They threw chips at each other, and they picked those chips up off the ground and blessed them. One woman came right out on to the road. She slapped the dirty chip out of her wee boy's hand and dragged him by the scruff into the house. He came out a couple of minutes later with a plate he wasn't allowed to take out of the garden, his face shiny with tears.

I went into the chapel to find Paddy and the rest of them, but there was nobody there. I stood for a while in the middle of the empty gallery, staring around, watching the light come through the stained-glass windows. Then I followed the Stations of the Cross from one side of the chapel to the other. I don't know what I was expecting. I hadn't been to Mass since I was a kid, and the last time I said a prayer was at Bronagh McCardle's funeral. I took Communion that day, and I kneeled down and said, Please, God. Don't let any more of my mates die. Three weeks later, John Paul Burns overdosed on pregabalin. I never went up for Communion again.

Look at this chancer, Paddy said, glaring at his watch. Twenty minutes late.

Sure it's his last shift, Róisín said. He's allowed.

Who said that?

I did. I'm the new supervisor.

Is that right? Paddy said, crossing his arms. When did this happen?

We took a vote when you were upstairs. It's been decided.

Happy days. I'll go home and leave you to it sure, will I?

No, Paddy. You've to stay here until we've all finished our hours. That's your punishment.

I sat down at the far side of the table and reached for the Hobnobs. No work tonight then? I said, and everyone looked at me.

You serious? Róisín said.

Right enough, we've a job to do, don't we? Paddy said, pushing his chair back as if to stand up.

Awk, tell us more about The Troubles, Paddy. Go on.

Do you not wanna do a wee bit of hoovering?

No, please. I've been whitening teeth all day.

But Sean's looking to do a bit of work. It's his last shift.

Send him up then.

I was up there and all, the place is spick and span, I said.

What were you doing, lighting a candle?

Aye, one for Paddy. For being so good to us.

Paddy's always good to us, aren't you, Paddy? That's why he's gonna let us take it easy tonight, isn't that right?

Paddy grumbled. Get the milk out of the fridge, he said.

Róisín opened the carton and gave it a sniff, made a face, but handed it to Paddy anyway, and then lingered with her hand on the back of his chair. No offence, Paddy, I love you to bits, but I can't wait to see the back of this place, she said.

Sure you've a while to go yet, Paddy said.

Do I fuck. Five hours after tonight and that's me done.

Five? I'm near sure you've fifteen.

Paddy, don't even. Swear to God.

Paddy took his wee book out. He flattened it on the table in front of him, put his glasses on, and used his index finger.

Let's see. Róisín O'Hara, fifteen hours.

Go away.

Seriously. Look.

Róisín snatched the book off him, saw that he was winding her up, and threw it back across the table. Don't even joke, she said. Seriously. I've too much to do.

She had been talking for weeks about going back to these night classes she was doing. She had started up her own business online, selling hair extensions. Now she was working towards opening up a premises. All she needed was a few qualifications to get her head around the finer details and she was good to go. Paddy had a soft spot for her. He liked that she had goals. There's a woman with a plan, he liked to say. She's got her eye on the bigger picture. He leaned with his elbows on the table and surveyed the room. What's your plans, Seany-bo? What're you gonna do when you've put all this behind you?

I'm gonna move out of my ma's, I said.

Good lad, aim high, Paddy said, rolling his eyes. While you're at it, away and take the bins out there, will you? Since it's your last night.

On my own?

Sure look at the arms on you. Away you go.

The bins were out the back of the chapel. There were brakes on the wheels you had to kick upwards to unlock. It was all downhill to the front gate; I let the first bin roll most of the way and used the momentum to guide it across the car park. When I was going back for the second one, I saw the priest. He was in his front garden, pulling weeds. He had ginger hair and a round face. He wore glasses too, and his cheeks were flushed in the sun. I wanted to ask him what he thought about that priest up in Banbridge, the one who had been caught taking gear. I wanted to say something like, You haven't got any swastikas hanging up on your wall now, do you, Father? But he had turned his back to me and was dead-heading the flowers in his window box. I dragged the bin out on to the tarmac. He didn't turn round.

When I got back to the room, Paddy was teaching Róisín how to dance. It was hard to believe, what with the way Paddy was built, but he was an Irish dancer back in the day. He had won competitions all over the world. He showed Róisín how to point her toe and use her back foot to push forward – and a one, two, three, four. See? The lads watched from their places around the table, bemused. Then Cricky jumped out of his seat. I'll show you how it's done, he said, and started flying about the place with his hand in the air like Michael Flatley. We clapped and cheered and took videos on our phones. Róisín glared at him. Then she saw him coming towards her with his arm held out and had a change of heart. She slipped her arm through his arm and circle-danced with him around the room.

It was my last night at my ma's and there was no packing left to do, just the few things I had to grab from the room above the barbers next door. It was mostly stuff from university: my assignments, my note-books, and those Moleskine journals I used to carry around with me in Liverpool. I opened one and read an entry from March 2010. I was sitting in a coffee shop on Bold Street. It was sunny outside, and I tried to describe how the pigeons moved back and forth across the pavement. That's what I thought you had to do back then: describe everything. Then I said I was reading *Being and Nothingness*, which made me laugh. I didn't know what Sartre was on about half the time back then, but I thought existentialism was brilliant. All that stuff about despair being a universal human condition. I talked about it with anybody who would listen, but I learned pretty quickly that there's a time and a place, and that wasn't while sitting on somebody's living-room floor at five o'clock in the morning, blasting lines of M-Cat.

Next to the university stuff was a big box of books from when I was a kid. All those fantasy novels I was mad about back then, with the elves and the magic and the big wars against foreign invaders, where the odds are always stacked. I decided to just leave it there in the storeroom. I said to myself, When I get to a point that I know where I'm at, I'll come back for them. I'll take them with me. Then I saw the corner of a wooden frame poking out of a black bin bag and recognized it straightaway. It was the dog my ma had painted when I was a kid. I pulled it out of the bag and brought it in to show her.

God, it's terrible looking, isn't it? she said.

I think it's brilliant.

Really?

Aye, I love it. Can I take it with me?

My ma looked sceptical. You sure you don't want me to paint you something else? she said. I could do a portrait of your man you used to love, what's his name? Tupac?

No, I want this one.

Right, okay.

She went to the cupboard under the sink where she kept all her painting stuff and got some string. She tied it to the hooks at the back of the frame and checked to make sure they were secure.

Looks good, she said.

I told Anthony not to worry, he didn't have to help me carry everything into the house. But he wanted to see what the place was like. I noticed how dark the hallway was, and the state of the carpet as we walked up the stairs. The bedroom was nice and bright though, there was plenty of space. Then I realized that the windows looked out on to the alley and the alley was lined with bins. There was a smell. Anthony dropped a box of books and surveyed the room.

The wallpaper's been painted over, he said. See how it's bubbling? He went around the room, knocking the walls. That's solid concrete, he said, chuckling. No insulation.

Serious? I said, as if I knew what that meant.

You're lucky it's the summer, that's all I'm saying.

On the way downstairs, he asked if he could have a look out the back. I just wanna see what we're working with here, he said. I opened the gate and had to pull my top up over my nose. There was rubbish everywhere, and all along the entry, seagulls swooped down from the rooftops and tore bin bags apart.

They've done some job on it, Anthony said, about the extension. Is it dodgy?

Nah, they've just done it on the cheap. You'll feel the cold at night though.

When we went back into the house, Tung was standing at his bedroom door. Anthony shook his hand.

Make sure he does his share of cleaning now, he said, about me.

Tung smiled. It was hard to know how much he understood.

I walked Anthony out the door. He stopped on the front step and looked up and down the street. You're gonna love it down here, he said. All the students and all, you'll have some craic.

I'm not a student any more though, am I?

Sure you may as well be, all those books you read.

He jabbed me on the arm. Then he leaned with his back against the wall. I know I've been melting your head about that script, but –

Anthony.

Wha?

Do you know a fella called Fra McCullough?

I know a Fra McCullough from down the road, he said, scratching the paint from his hand. Why?

I know who Terry Brennan is. Ma told me.

Did she, aye?

You brought him back to her gaff.

Anthony smirked. She talks too much, that woman, he said.

He looked at the paint on his arm, picking it, and then twisted his arm round so he could get at the specks on his elbow.

What do you wanna know? he said.

I wanna know if Fra McCullough was the other fella.

What other fella?

The other fella who came with Terry to shoot my da.

Nah, it wasn't him. It was another Fra.

Fra who?

Cosgrove, I think. Can't remember. He was from down the road as well.

There was no reason for him to lie to me, as far as I could see. But at the same time, nothing he said made me feel any better. He was too calm, and he kept looking at me out the corner of his eye, as if he was trying to suss me out.

Your man Fra McCullough asked me about my da one day I was cutting grass in Milltown, I said. I don't know, I thought —

You thought what?

I thought he was trying to get to me.

Anthony leaned with his hand on my shoulder. Nobody's trying to get to you, he said. You think I'd let anybody touch you?

It's not that, it's just . . . I don't want you to do anything stupid.

Anthony laughed. Me? What would I do? Shoot the cunt?

Probably, I said, and he went quiet. For a while, neither of us said anything, and then he looked at me.

You know where he is, don't you? he said.

I admitted it, I did. His shoulders slumped.

You raging at me? I said.

Raging at you? He repeated this phrase again, and then he grinned. Do me a favour, he said. Stay down here, you hear me? I said I'd try to, and he said, You won't try anything, you'll do what I tell you.

He held his hand out for me to shake. I shook it and he pulled me into a hug.

What're you doing? I said.

I fucking love you, that's what I'm doing.

I tried to get away from him, but he was stronger than me and he wasn't for letting go. Get off, I said, and he giggled and kissed me on the ear and on the side of the head, my face and neck and anywhere he could reach with his arm around me. And while he did this he told me he loved me. I love you to death, he said, and he kissed me and kissed me.

*

I put bedsheets on the bed, the same ones I had in the flat with Ryan. Then I unpacked my clothes and put them away. The plan was to make the office into a study, but then I thought it would be nice to keep my books in the bedroom, there was plenty of space, and it was brighter with the windows. I dragged the bookcase in and organized the books in alphabetical order. When I finished doing that, I dragged the desk in too and hung the painting of the dog on the wall above it. Then I sat on the bed and took it all in. It felt like somewhere I could live.

At four o'clock, I went up to No Alibis and picked up that book. Conor wasn't there. The fella who served me was sound though. He told me they were in Bookfinders.

That's where they usually are anyway, he said.

I walked round to the red door, but I couldn't bring myself to go in. I was too nervous. Instead, I dandered up to Queen's and had a mooch around the campus. There were people sitting on benches around the university buildings, smoking, reading books. At Botanic Gardens, there was music. Crowds of students lay on the grass drinking wine from plastic cups. They didn't try to be sneaky about it either. The peelers were right there, at the gates, and people were swigging away, without a care in the world. Walking through it was nerve-wrecking. I was just waiting for one of those rugby balls the big lads in Ireland tops kicked back and forth across the grass to smack me up the back of the head. Worrying about that made me pay less attention to where I was going; I tripped over someone's bag and nearly went on my hole. People laughed. I hurried on scundered to the far side of the field. There were trees over there, and shade. I sat with my back against a trunk and watched a beautiful girl with curly hair play the guitar. She sang with her eyes closed, but I couldn't hear her voice. There was too much noise, and for a while I just sat there, watching everybody have a good time. Then I opened my book and read:

So here I was, home again after all those years.

ACKNOWLEDGEMENTS

Firstly, I would like to thank my agent, Eleanor Birne, for being a calm and reassuring presence throughout this process, and a spectacular agent, the very best in the game. I would also like to thank my editor, Hermione Thompson, whose friendship and solidarity has meant the world to me. This book wouldn't be what it is without her. Milo Walls too, for everything they've done to make the book as good as it can be. Hannah Chukwu, Simon Prosser, and everybody at Hamish Hamilton and FSG, for their work and dedication. Everybody at PEW: John Ashe, Patrick Walsh and Margaret Halton, and my supervisors: Darran McCann, Sinead Sturgeon, Michael Pierse, Ian Sansom and Glenn Patterson, for their guidance and generosity. And Ciaran Carson, of course, for all the things he taught me.

Shout-out to my mates: Padraig Regan, Dane Holt, Sacha White, Manuela Moser, Stephen Connolly, Scott McKendry, Stephen O'Neill, Matthew Rice and Stephen Sexton, for the swalls and conversations, the shite talk, and the smokes. I'd also like to thank Mary Denvir, for the best days in Bookfinders, the business meetings and the toasties. My God, the toasties. Thanks also to Damian Smyth, for the support. Susannah Dickey too, whose early reading of the book went a long way towards helping me figure out what I was trying to say. Louise Kennedy (Auntie Louise), for bringing me to Sligo and filling me with wine, and John Patrick McHugh, for reading the things I was too embarrassed to show anybody else – where would we be without Frank O'Connor?

I'd also like to take this opportunity to thank the headcases I grew up with: Decky, Desie, Dowdzy, Mooney, Quinn, Aydzo and Dermey. Gareth, Keven and Charlie. Conor and Ciaran. Big Bird, Wee Bird and Bronagh Massey. Marty Berry. Kevy Mullan. Ciara McAree. All the Poleglassers. All the Twinbrookers. Everybody from Areema, and all the wingnuts I went to school with. You know yourselves.

I can't go any further without thanking Thomas Morris, whose friendship has become invaluable to me. Thank you for making me write that letter, and for the title, and for everything you've done for me, both as a person and a writer. There wouldn't be a book without you. Thanks also to Kevin Breathnach, my friend. For the time we spent together on South Parade – I'll never forget it. Also, Tara McEvoy, for always being there for me, as a friend, as a reader, and as somebody who will always see a night through, until the Centra opens. Finally, I'd like to thank Ellen, for going to *The Tangerine* launch in the American Bar and buying a copy of the magazine off me. I couldn't have got through the last three years without you. You're my gorgeous love and I love you. Agnes too. Our wee girl.

Thank you to my mother, for everything.

Granny and Granda.

Mark and Ciarnan.

Ciarnan, Rhys and Chloe.

Tim.

Jim, who used to take me to see the swans.

Mary McAree (Auntie Mary), for teaching me how to type my name.

Alicia Stubbersfield, for showing me the ropes.

And Gerry Sullivan, who taught me English in school.